Ann Barker was born and brought up in Bedfordshire, but currently lives in Norfolk. For more information about Ann Barker and her books, go to www.AnnBarker.com

THE OTHER MISS FROBISHER

Elfrida Frobisher leaves her country backwater and her suitor to chaperon Prudence, her eighteen-year-old niece, in London. Unfortunately, Prudence has apparently developed an attachment for an unsuitable man, which she fosters behind her aunt's back. Attempting to foil her niece's schemes and prevent a scandal, Elfrida only succeeds in finding herself involved with the eligible Rufus Tyler in a scandal of her own! Fleeing London seems the only solution — but Prudence has another plan ... Elfrida yearns for her quiet rural existence, but it takes a mad dash in pursuit of her niece before she realises where her heart truly lies.

Books by Ann Barker
Published by The House of Ulverscroft:

HIS LORDSHIP'S GARDENER
THE GRAND TOUR
DERBYSHIRE DECEPTION
THE SQUIRE AND THE
SCHOOLMISTRESS
THE ADVENTURESS

ANN BARKER

THE OTHER MISS FROBISHER

Complete and Unabridged

ULVERSCROFT
Leicester

First published in Great Britain in 2006 by
Robert Hale Limited
London

First Large Print Edition
published 2007
by arrangement with
Robert Hale Limited
London

British Library CIP Data

Barker, Ann
    The other Miss Frobisher.—Large print ed.—
Ulverscroft large print series: historical romance
1. Love stories
2. Large type books
I. Title
823.9'14 [F]

ISBN 978–1–84617–665–4

Published by
F. A. Thorpe (Publishing)
Anstey, Leicestershire

Set by Words & Graphics Ltd.
Anstey, Leicestershire
Printed and bound in Great Britain by
T. J. International Ltd., Padstow, Cornwall

This book is printed on acid-free paper

For those sporting persons who threw themselves into the Regency spirit for my daughter's benefit

1

'Elfrida, my dear, come in, come in! Oh, how good of you to come! But then, I knew that you would, my dearest and best of sisters!'

Elfrida Frobisher disentangled herself from her sister's plump, scented embrace, and smiled as she recalled that Anthea had always spoken as if her conversation was littered with exclamation marks. 'Well I'm glad I'm the best,' she replied, 'but by the same token I must also be the worst, since we only have each other.'

'Oh, you know what I mean,' replied Anthea. 'Let me conduct you to your room! How tired you must be!'

'No, not at all,' Elfrida demurred. 'The Mail was very comfortable, not at all crowded, and only took sixteen hours.'

'You should have allowed me to send our post-chaise for you,' answered Mrs Winch-comb, as she walked beside her sister up the stairs in order to conduct her to the room that had been prepared for her. 'It would not have been any trouble.'

'Yes it would have been,' said Elfrida matter-of-factly. 'You and Clive want to set out yourselves, very soon. Your coachman will have preparations to make, no doubt.'

'Well, there is that,' agreed Anthea running her hand over her stomach. 'Clive does so much want me to go to the country as soon as possible.'

'Is that what the doctor advises?' Elfrida asked, as they got to the door and Anthea put her hand on the handle.

Her sister smiled. 'We are so fortunate to be having another child, especially after such a long period, and several . . . ' she paused, 'several disappointments. So Dr Deakin insists that I go to the country so that I can be quiet and get some fresh air before my confinement.'

Elfrida nodded seriously. Her sister had presented her husband with one daughter, Prudence, eighteen years before and since then, she had suffered a number of distressing miscarriages but no second child. Anthea's younger sister could well understand why she did not want to take any chances.

They stepped over the threshold and Elfrida looked around the room with genuine delight. 'This is charming!' she exclaimed.

'I know you would much rather be in the country, but I've tried to make it as . . . as . . . rustic as possible.'

With its bed hangings in an exquisite shade

of green silk, its newly hung wallpaper decorated with flowers and its thick carpet, in a design to tone with the walls, it was not exactly typical of most rustic dwellings that Elfrida had visited recently. But taking the thought for the deed, and especially appreciative of the flowers arranged on the tall cupboard near to the window, she smiled warmly and said, 'I shall feel very much at home. And just because I prefer the country does not mean that I cannot enjoy a few days in London from time to time.'

'I will leave you to settle in,' said Anthea. 'Come downstairs when you are ready and we will have a cup of tea.'

Elfrida smiled. Her sister had always been the vivacious, colourful one. It sometimes seemed to her, in fanciful moments, as if there had only been a certain amount of liveliness to be shared between them, and Anthea had inherited the major part. In appearance and in character, Anthea took after their mother, whereas Elfrida was very much her father's child.

The two sisters had grown up in a small village, slightly to the south of Dunstable, where Mr Frobisher had inherited a property that had belonged to his uncle. Along with the property had come a modest competence. In these circumstances, some men might have made their money work for them and transformed a small fortune into a large one. Yet others might have lived beyond their means and lost what they had through gambling and other forms of high living. Mr Frobisher did neither, being quite content to live comfortably and provide for his wife and daughters, without questioning where the money came from. Essentially a countryman, he took no interest in London life, and was quite happy for his wife to travel to London each year for the season, escorting her there after Christmas, and collecting her when the fashionable round was over. Mrs Frobisher was not an extravagant woman by London standards, but she knew how to spend. The consequence was that by the time Anthea was due to appear on the social scene, it had become apparent that neither daughter could be provided with more than a few hundred pounds by way of a dowry.

As far as Anthea was concerned, this was not too much of a drawback. She was fashionably dark, lusciously curved, and she knew to a nicety how to goad perfectly intelligent men to the very edge of madness. Even in and around the village where they resided, she was much sought after and was nicknamed 'the divine Miss Frobisher' by her attendant swains.

It had always been clear that Elfrida would not rival Anthea for beauty. Where Anthea's hair was dark, Elfrida's was light brown, very fine and defiant of any attempts to tame it into a fashionable style. Where Anthea's eyes were sparkling blue, Elfrida's were a dreamy grey; and whereas Anthea's form was full and rounded, Elfrida's was slender, almost boyish. By the time that Anthea was twenty, Elfrida, at sixteen, was already known as 'the other Miss Frobisher'.

Anthea's season was a modest success. She did not exactly take the town by storm, her fortune not being sufficient for that, but she attracted a number of admirers, and from their number eventually chose Clive Winchcomb to be her husband. Although untitled, Mr Winchcomb came from an old and distinguished family, and was, in addition, exceedingly handsome. His fortune, like that of Mr Frobisher, was comfortable rather than ample, but since he was also remarkably indolent, he made no objection when his wife, who had always hankered after a fashionable life, made sure that their finances were stretched to the limit.

Mrs Frobisher died when Anthea had been married for two years, and her husband followed her within a matter of months. This had the effect of rendering Elfrida homeless, for the Frobisher estate was subject to entail, and was inherited by a distant relative, who barely knew the family. Elfrida went to London to live with her sister and husband, but the arrangement, although a very natural one, did not prove to be successful. Anthea and Elfrida had never been alike either in temperament or in tastes. Anthea's new status as a fashionable matron only accentuated the differences. After one disastrous season, during which Elfrida failed to attract a single offer of marriage despite her sister's best efforts, she resolved to retire to the country if at all possible.

She was still trying to work out how, given the family's limited means, this might be managed without offending Anthea, of whom despite everything she was very fond, when a letter arrived at the Winchcombs' town house. It was from their grandmother's sister, Great-Aunt Hilda. Miss Filey, who had never married, lived in a neat country house in a small village not far from Grantham, with a friend of her own age who acted as her companion. This friend had recently died, and Miss Filey, stricken in years and very lonely, had decided that she would benefit from having some young company. She had come to the conclusion that Elfrida, being the daughter of her dear niece, would do very nicely.

To Anthea, the request seemed like an intolerable imposition. To Elfrida, it seemed more like a chance of escape. The only problem lay in convincing Anthea that she would truly like to go, and in making sure that her older sister did not feel slighted. Fortunately, Anthea had been feeling the tension between the two of them just as much, and although she had protested at the idea of Elfrida's burying herself away in the country, she had had to admit that the solution really was a very practical one.

Happily, all the tension between the two sisters evaporated once they were apart, and they soon got into the habit of writing very affectionate letters to one another. Indeed, Elfrida quickly came to the rueful conclusion that they got on much better when they were separated by more than a day's journey.

Great-Aunt Hilda died six years later, when Elfrida was twenty-five, and left her the house and the bulk of her comfortable independence, with a small bequest for Anthea.

Anthea, for all her faults, had never been a jealous person, and she did not begrudge her sister her good fortune, telling her husband frankly that if Elfrida had been prepared to put up with living in the country with Great-Aunt Hilda for all that time, then she deserved every penny she got.

Elfrida had been delighted with the bequest. She had always known that the old lady intended to leave her something, but she had not dared to hope that it would be sufficient to make her independent. She and Miss Filey had got on well from the very first, and she was soon fulfilling her companion's duties as much from pleasure as out of obligation. She had mourned her elderly relative's death sincerely, and had settled down very happily to remain in the country, as she had always intended. Anthea had accepted her decision, and apart from occasionally marvelling how Elfrida could stand the quiet, and at other times wondering why her sister did not sell the house and come to London, she generally gave Elfrida the credit of knowing her own mind.

Quickly, Elfrida finished tidying her hair and made haste to go downstairs. She had never visited this house before, for Mr Winchcomb had inherited it very recently from his godfather. It was a modest but well-proportioned house in Brook Street, and Elfrida could well imagine how pleased Anthea must be to have her own property in London, rather than having to hire something for the season each year.

Elfrida was conducted to the drawing-room

where Anthea was waiting for her, with her feet up on a small stool. 'I won't get up,' she said smiling. 'You see, I am obeying doctor's orders. Winchcomb insists upon it.'

'Insists?' murmured Elvira, with a smile. She could not remember her indolent brother-in-law ever insisting upon anything.

Anthea smiled back. 'I know, it sounds improbable, but it is quite true. We never thought that we would have any more children, you see, and he is hoping for a son, so he is being very protective. I do declare, Elfrida, I am rather intrigued by this new side of him. I think I am falling in love with him all over again. Will you ring for tea while you are on your feet, dearest?'

Elfrida complied, and turned back to see that her sister was looking at her admiringly.

'Upon my soul, Effie, you are looking very smart,' she declared.

'Did you expect me to appear with a straw at the corner of my mouth, then?' Elfrida asked, amused.

'Well no; but I wouldn't have been surprised to see that you were ten years behind the times,' Anthea admitted frankly.

Elfrida stroked the folds of her new gown with some satisfaction. It had been made for her by Madame Patrice, the Grantham dressmaker who was entrusted with the task of making all her clothes. This particular craftswoman maintained links with a cousin whose business was in a little thoroughfare just off Bond Street, and her creations were far from being provincial. Elfrida had left the London scene behind her with very few regrets, but she had never wanted to appear dowdy. Having little understanding of her own concerning what might suit her, she had put herself unreservedly in the hands of Madame Patrice, with the consequence that in her own social circle, she was spoken of as being if not the prettiest, certainly one of the best-dressed ladies in the area.

'I had thought,' Anthea went on, pouring the tea that had just been brought, 'that we would need to send you immediately to a London modiste, but I see that I was mistaken.'

'No doubt that was why you wanted me to come as soon as possible,' murmured Elfrida.

'By no means!' exclaimed Anthea, but she flushed at the same time. 'Oh well, perhaps that was part of my reason,' she admitted, knowing that she had given herself away. 'But my chief purpose was so that I might have the chance to take you about a little before I have to leave London. It will be much more comfortable for you if you have made a few friends before you are left to look after

Prudence on your own.'

It was Elfrida's turn to flush. 'That was kind of you,' she said warmly.

'And perhaps we might fit in a little shopping, too,' suggested Anthea. 'The style of your gown cannot be faulted, I'll admit, but perhaps a little more colour?'

Elfrida shook her head. 'You are the one who wears colours,' she said. 'Madame Patrice has convinced me that I appear to the best advantage in greys and light blues and fawns. Everything else I leave to you — or to the flowers in my garden.'

Anthea, although essentially a town dweller, took a keen interest in her own small garden in London, and in the plants which were to be found in the gardens near the house on her husband's country estate. For the next little while, therefore, the ladies were happily absorbed in discussing what was in bloom at that season. 'I do declare, you are quite making me look forward to seeing the gardens again,' Anthea said at last. She paused briefly, then went on, 'No doubt you are wondering why Prudence does not come with us at once.'

'I must admit that the thought did cross my mind,' Elfrida agreed. 'She is after all a grown girl of eighteen. It would not do her any harm to miss a ball or two at the end of the season, surely?'

'No,' agreed Anthea doubtfully. 'But there are other factors to be considered. I know! We'll have another cup of tea while we talk about them.'

'Oh dear,' murmured Elfrida. 'As many other factors as that?'

Miss Frobisher would have been the first to admit that she did not know her niece well. It was probably her own fault, she acknowledged. She was, after all, very contented in her country retreat, and so although she and Anthea wrote regularly and met occasionally for high days and holidays, her contact with Prudence had been somewhat limited. She only hoped that the young woman who was shortly to become her responsibility, if only for a brief time, would not prove to be difficult to handle. She was not at all sure that she would know what to do with a recalcitrant eighteen-year-old.

'Come on then,' she said as soon as the fresh tea had arrived. 'Tell me about these other factors.'

Anthea preened a little. 'As I expect you may be able to guess, Prudence has had a successful season,' she said, unable to keep the pride out of her voice. 'Really, I know that as she is my daughter I should not boast, but it is not boasting to tell the simple truth, is it? Of course, as you know, her fortune is not large, but as she is our only child — '

'At present,' Elfrida put in with a smile.

'At present, as you say,' Anthea replied, returning the smile, her hand going automatically to her stomach. 'She has been the target of some who are more interested in her fortune than her other attributes.'

'In that case, I would have thought that removal from the London scene would be advantageous rather than otherwise,' Elfrida remarked.

'So it would be, if none of these needy gentlemen were neighbours,' answered Anthea frankly. 'Unfortunately one of them is Digby Collett, and the Colletts have run tame in the neighbourhood for years.'

'In the neighbourhood of Mr Winchcomb's estate, you mean?'

Anthea nodded. 'The Colletts are an old-established family, distantly related to the Earl of Clare, but the family is large, the house as well as all its inhabitants has a slightly grimy air, and they are always on the edge of being in debt. And Digby is not even the eldest son!'

'Do I take it that Prudence has shown an interest in this young man?' Elfrida asked.

'They have always been close,' answered Anthea. 'Once we are away in the country and I am distracted with the new baby and there is no one else around, I'm afraid that something may happen between them.'

'Yes, I understand,' replied Elfrida. 'Is Digby Collett in town at present?'

'Yes, he is on leave from his regiment,' answered Anthea, sighing.

'Oh dear,' murmured Elfrida. 'A man in regimentals.'

'Precisely. But in my opinion, Rufus Tyler cuts a finer figure, and I did have such hopes of him.'

Elfrida wrinkled her brow. 'Rufus Tyler? Is he also a soldier?'

'Not any more, although I believe he was at one time. He is a son of the Earl of Clare, the family that I was telling you was related to the Colletts,' Anthea explained. 'He is older than Prudence by quite a few years, and although a younger son, he has a fortune in his own right. He has been on the social scene for ever and has resisted all lures, but he is bound to succumb some time, and he certainly seems very taken with Prudence.'

'But not yet sufficiently taken to commit himself,' Elfrida hazarded.

'Well no, not yet, which is precisely why I want her to remain in London.'

'And does she like him?' Elfrida asked.

'Like him?' exclaimed Anthea incredulously. 'Of course she likes him. Who would not like him? He is attractive, he is pleasant, he is easy . . . Depend upon it, if he proposes, she will accept him.'

'Presumably, though, he will need to come and speak to Mr Winchcomb.'

Anthea shook her head. 'No, there is no need,' she answered positively. 'If Mr Tyler asks for permission to address Prudence, then you may grant it, in our name.'

'And if any other gentleman approaches me?' ventured Elfrida.

'Then you must send him packing,' declared Anthea. 'These penniless soldiers seem to congregate together, so keep her well away from every man in a scarlet coat.'

'What, every single one?' exclaimed Elfrida, half amused, half puzzled.

'Every one,' Anthea reiterated firmly, 'and most especially if his name is Digby Collett!'

2

At exactly the same time as Elfrida and her sister were having their conversation, a young man in a scarlet coat was eyeing Miss Prudence Winchcomb with a very anxious expression on his face. Even when he was in his uniform, he could not appear to be anything other than a rather callow youth.

'No Pru, honestly, I can't do this, and I don't know how you can expect it,' he complained. They were part of a group visiting Richmond on a party of pleasure. It gave Prudence the perfect opportunity to take Digby on one side and explain her plan.

Miss Winchcomb, a young woman of commanding presence, looked at him measuringly in the manner of one who had been offered a piece of cloth for sale which, although quite inadequate for her purpose, was nevertheless all that was available.

'Digby, for goodness sake, don't be so unhelpful,' she replied unsympathetically. 'You know perfectly well that I would do the same for you, given the necessity.'

This was undoubtedly true, Digby acknowledged inwardly. In all the years that they had been growing up together, she had always been the instigator of any scheme in which they had taken part, strong-mindedly directing him, his numerous brothers and sisters, and any other children who came into her orbit. He could not guess from where she had gained her capacity for leadership. Mrs Winchcomb, although as firm as a mama should be, never seemed to be particularly dictatorial; as for Mr Winchcomb, his languor was so pronounced that on occasions he appeared to be about to expire from sheer boredom. Nevertheless, Prudence had inherited habits of command from someone. In very disloyal moments, it sometimes occurred to Digby that she bore more than a passing resemblance to his senior commanding officer.

Even taking this into account, however, there was much that bound them together. Their shared history was no small thing, the connection of his family to that of the exalted Earl of Clare making their friendship acceptable to Mrs Winchcomb. They had got into many childhood scrapes together, Prudence often gallantly shouldering more than her share of the blame in order to save her childhood playmate from a beating.

In their early teens they had made a pact to marry, but this agreement had not outlasted their childhood, and the incident during

17

which they had cut their wrists in order to mix the blood was now as much a cause for amusement as embarrassment for them both. But although they no longer had the slightest desire to marry one another, Mrs Winchcomb had never rid herself of the idea that such a match was a possibility. Union with one of the impoverished Colletts was not part of her plan for her daughter's future, so in her anxiety, she tended to see danger where there was none.

Prudence's season had been a moderate success. As her mother was currently expressing to her sister, she did not have a large fortune, and her appearance could have been described as handsome rather than pretty. She had inherited her father's height, together with his plentiful dark-brown hair, and often found herself looking any potential suitors directly in the eye, rather than peeping up at them, which most gentlemen preferred. This, coupled with the determined set of her chin, and the intelligent look in her brown eyes did not tend to arouse the male protective instinct. But although determined, she was not a bullying kind of girl, and her essential good humour, combined with her pleasing looks, acceptable portion and good family, had ensured that she never lacked partners.

She was, in addition, a practical kind of person, and she knew that marriage and motherhood was essentially the only path open to someone of her standing. Bearing this in mind, she had come to London quite prepared to find a husband among the ranks of the ton. It was only when Digby Collett had come to town that her attitude had changed, for Digby's advent had also meant the arrival of other young men from his regiment, most notably Captain Daniel Black.

Captain Black was tall, dark and handsome, with deep-blue eyes, a tanned complexion, a firm, determined chin, and an excellent seat on a horse. In sum, he looked every inch a hero. Sometimes, of course, appearances can deceive, but in this case, Captain Black was as splendid as he looked. Mentioned more than once in despatches by Wellington for actions of outstanding gallantry, he was highly regarded by fellow officers and by the rank and file alike. His visit to town had been to enjoy some much needed recreation after a distinguished campaign, and he had had no thoughts of marriage in his mind.

The captain, although very unlike Digby Collett in that he came from a family in which the army had always figured strongly, had this in common with his friend: they were both as poor as church mice, and with no rich aunts or uncles in the offing who might be counted upon to remedy the situation.

It had been when they had been attending a ball together one evening towards the beginning of the season that Digby had introduced his brother officer to his childhood playmate. Each had been attracted to the other from the very first, and since that meeting, the attraction between Prudence and the handsome captain had only grown, until on a night that Prudence would never forget, Daniel had escorted her out on to the balcony at a ball that they were both attending and confessed his love.

He had been all for approaching Mr Winchcomb immediately to ask for his consent, but Prudence had pleaded with him to wait. 'Mama will never agree so close to the beginning of the season,' she had insisted. 'She will say that I have not had time to look about me or some such thing.'

'She will say that you are throwing yourself away, and with good reason,' the captain had replied, looking nobly into the middle distance.

'If she says that then she will be telling a lie,' Prudence had insisted. 'She will surely come to see your worth eventually. But for my sake, do not put matters to the test just yet.'

So the captain had agreed to keep their mutual attachment secret, although it went very much against the grain with him.

'I really cannot understand Mama at times,' Prudence had said to him some little time after their ballroom tryst. On this occasion, they had met in Hatchard's bookshop, and were holding their conversation whilst pretending to examine some of the volumes in front of them. 'It seems as if almost any man will do, so long as he is wealthy.'

'You do your mama an injustice,' the captain had replied. 'I am sure that she would never consider offers from men of bad reputation. But she quite rightly wants to see you well provided for. And what am I? The penniless son of a country vicar, with nothing but his officer's pay! I cannot blame her, for I see the justice of her sentiments.'

'It is just as this author writes at the beginning of her book,' she had observed with a sigh, showing him the very volume which was on the shelf in front of them. 'A single man in possession of a good fortune must be in want of a wife.' That is what Mama wants for me; and all the more so, now that she is expecting another child. Oh, do not think that

21

I am not pleased for them, but it does mean that I will no longer be my parents' sole heir.'

'I understand,' the captain had said. 'But surely there must be a way to win them round?'

'I do have a plan,' Prudence had assured him. 'It is my fixed intention to make quite sure that none of the men of my acquaintance makes me an offer. That should be quite easy to do. After all,' she had continued resolutely, 'I am not exactly pretty.'

'You are not merely pretty,' the captain had asserted, covering her hand with his manly one in a masterful way which had sent tingles up and down her spine, 'you are without parallel!'

'In your eyes,' Prudence had answered, smiling up at him. 'But I am not to every man's taste, you must agree. I shall simply paralyse them all with repulsive coldness, so that by the end of the season, I will not have received a single offer. Then, when the season is over and I return home ignominiously, Mama will be much more inclined to accept you as a son-in-law.'

To begin with, their plan had appeared to go well. To her mother, Prudence had given the distinct impression that she was ready and willing to receive the addresses of suitable men, but to the men themselves, she had contrived to be cold, indifferent, or even downright rude, and none of them had come up to scratch.

Then, quite unexpectedly, when Anthea was beginning to despair, and Prudence was starting to think that her plan had succeeded to perfection, the Honourable Rufus Tyler had appeared to enter the lists. Excessively eligible, being in possession of a handsome personal fortune, besides being a younger son of the Earl of Clare, Mr Tyler was, in addition, very well-looking, although not conventionally handsome. His relationship to Lord Clare meant that Prudence already knew him slightly.

As Anthea had expressed to her sister, Tyler had been on the town for some considerable time, and despite the encouragement that he had consistently received from numerous match-making mamas, he had never committed himself to matrimony. His acquaintance with the Winchcomb family was of very long standing, and it would have been strange if he had not paid them some attention whilst they were all in Town. But this year, with Prudence making her come-out, his visits had become more frequent.

Suddenly, Mrs Winchcomb's hopes had soared, and without being vulgarly thrusting, she had done her best to put her daughter into Mr Tyler's way. Prudence had tried very hard to put him off, but since he was related to Digby, of whom she was very fond, she did not wish to do anything to destroy the goodwill of one who had it in his power to make a difference to her friend's well-being. She was consequently not as repulsive towards him as she had been towards any other gentleman, and he had continued to show an interest in her. In any case, he was also a little older than any other possible suitors, and would probably have been too mature to be put off by her tactics.

To be truthful, she could not be sure how great his interest might be, for rumour had it that he was in the throes of an affair with one Mrs Fossey. But in order to avert the possibility of his pursuing her in earnest, and by way of carrying out more drastic action, Prudence had decided that Digby must appear to be romantically smitten with her.

'I shall induce Digby to make a play for me,' Prudence had told Captain Black, her eyes sparkling. 'Mama hates the idea of my marrying him worse than poison. Any other man will be acceptable to her, and as for Mr Tyler, he will soon become disgusted by the idea that I seem to prefer Digby to him.'

Captain Black had been very much against

this idea, chiefly because he loathed subterfuge of any kind. Prudence had eventually persuaded him to agree, however. 'It is not subterfuge, it is strategy,' she told him. 'In any case, none of us will be obliged to lie at all. Digby is my childhood friend. What could be more natural than that he would want to spend some time with me? All the romance will be in Mama's mind.'

Captain Black was not the only one to dislike Prudence's plan. Digby had not been at all impressed with this notion from the start, and had said so in no uncertain terms. His will was not proof against Prudence's however, and in obedience to her commands, he had appeared at her side with what her mother considered to be quite exasperating regularity. Digby had always been welcome in the Winchcomb household, for Mrs Winchcomb had no wish to alienate her neighbours by being uncivil to him. To have him as an occasional visitor was one thing, however; to to have him running tame in her home whilst other more eligible gentlemen kept their distance was quite another.

But although Mrs Winchcomb had become quite as alarmed as Prudence could have wished, other parts of her scheme had not gone as planned. Far from appearing to be disgusted, Mr Tyler had seemed more amused than anything at Digby's presence, and he refused to treat him as a serious rival. Now the time for leaving the capital was drawing near. The degree of Mr Tyler's interest was, as ever, impossible to calculate, but popular rumour seemed to say that being now in his late thirties, and with his brother being the father of a fine family of healthy girls, but having as yet no son, marriage must surely be in his mind. Soon they would all be back home, Mr Tyler would be within easy reach of her, and Captain Black would have no excuse for calling. Matters were becoming urgent. This was the reason for her meeting with Digby on the day of her aunt's arrival.

'I do not see that it is a complicated request,' Prudence replied, in reasonable tones. 'All I want you to do is compromise me.'

'But I don't want to,' Digby replied desperately. 'I don't want to compromise anyone. Not the deed of a gentleman, you know.'

'If the lady requests you to do it, then it is the deed of a gentleman,' Prudence replied calmly.

'But if I compromise you then your mama will insist that I marry you,' Digby protested. 'And I really don't want to.'

'Well, of course, you don't, and I don't

want to marry *you*,' she agreed. 'But it is of no use asking Daniel to compromise me because he will say it is ungentlemanly.'

'Aha!' Digby exclaimed triumphantly. 'Didn't I say so myself?'

'But the cases are not the same,' Prudence said, in the kind of patient tone that is used when speaking to a small child. 'If Daniel compromised me, he would be benefiting directly from the consequences of his actions, whereas for you, the deed would be purely altruistic. In any case, the time is perfect.'

'Why?' Digby asked her.

'Because my parents are to go into the country very soon — for Mama's health, you know. Mama does not want me to miss a single minute of the season, so she has asked her sister — my Aunt Elfrida — to chaperon me for the rest of the season. Mama will warn her all about you, but Aunt Elfrida is a spinster and has been out of society for years and years, so she will be very easy to fool. Once you have compromised me, she will want to hustle me out of London as quickly as possible: I shall be in disgrace. Mr Tyler will want nothing more to do with me; Mama will still not want me to marry you, but will see no alternative; then Daniel will appear and offer for me, and she will receive him with a thankful heart.'

'Do you really think so?' Digby asked doubtfully.

'Yes I do,' she replied; then, seeing that he still looked anxious, she added, 'Just think about it as a military campaign.'

'Something like the 'forlorn hope'?' he suggested under his breath; but fortunately, she did not hear him.

3

It was a very thoughtful Elfrida who sat up in bed that night after the rest of the household had retired, turning over the events of the day. In honour of her visit, Mr Winchcomb had dined at home and then remained with his family for the evening, rather than retiring to his club as was his usual custom.

He had greeted his sister-in-law in much his usual careless fashion, and had thrown himself down in his chair in the indolent way that had always seemed to be so much a part of him. The only anxiety that he betrayed during the course of the entire evening was centred upon Anthea's plans. Even then, his concern seemed to be about his own comfort rather than his wife's well-being.

When Anthea declared her intention of taking Elfrida shopping, he said, 'Make sure you take the carriage, my dear, and sit down whenever you can.' When she referred to the few social occasions that she was to attend before leaving town, he remarked carelessly, 'You may very well excuse yourself if it seems too much for you.' When the topic of travelling to his country estate was discussed, he drawled, 'We shall go by easy stages. I cannot abide being made to rush.' Elfrida thought about her sister's words with regard to her husband's care for her. She was bound to acknowledge that Anthea must surely know Mr Winchcomb better than she did herself; in her opinion, though, it seemed that in this matter of going to his country estate, the gentleman was thinking chiefly of himself.

Prudence had appeared shortly before dinner with apologies for having missed her aunt's arrival. She had already accepted an invitation to go out with friends that day. She hoped that her aunt would excuse her. At least, that was what she had said. The impression that Elfrida had received, however, had been that Prudence had done what she had wanted to do, and had no intention of curtailing her activities on her aunt's account.

Naturally, Elfrida had excused her as requested. It would have been more courteous of her to have been at home when her aunt arrived, especially since that lady was to have sole charge of her for the last part of the season. Had such a visitor been expected when she and Anthea were children, Elfrida reflected, then going off on an expedition of pleasure which meant that the arrival would have been missed would have been out of the question. Still, Elfrida sighed, that was about twenty years ago. No doubt times had changed. Not for the better, she found herself saying, then frowned in disgust. Why, she was thinking just like some middle-aged spinster! Angrily, she pounded the pillows, and settled down to try to go to sleep.

She allowed her mind to drift around the pleasant evening that they had had, gathered around the table. It was a novel experience for her, and one that she had enjoyed. She was much more accustomed to sitting down to a solitary repast. True, not many days ever went by without a dinner invitation, and she could have dined out more than she did, but it was not the same as having the company of one's own family at home, a thing which, because she lived alone, was a very rare pleasure for her.

Of course, even at the advanced age of 34, she was conscious that there were those who would like to ensure that her table was no longer a solitary one. The rector for example, Revd Stanley Erskine, was very attentive. He was a handsome, tall and well-built man with dark-brown wavy hair, and a fine pair of grey eyes, which sometimes sparkled with friendliness, but could, when he was strongly moved in the pulpit, pierce uncomfortably into the souls of hitherto unrepentant sinners. They were also known to pierce the hearts of less religiously minded damsels, several of whom attended worship in order to experience the thrill of the rector's flashing eyes. Fortunately, he remained unaware of the fact, and was simply grateful for the increase in his congregation.

Mr Erskine had been the rector in the village of Fernleigh for five years. He had arrived already an engaged man; but his bride-to-be had succumbed to an illness shortly after his arrival. It had been a struggle for him to fulfil his duties at the time, but he had received able assistance from his curate. The rector had recovered from his loss, and if, in some opinions, his expression still sometimes held a faraway look, as if he were thinking of past griefs, this was thought to add to the romantic nature of his appearance.

Elfrida was not unaware of his charms, nor was she oblivious to what was being said, namely, that the rector was now looking about him for a helpmeet, and that she was one of the more likely candidates. True, she was his elder by three years, but when two people had reached more mature years, that hardly mattered.

No self-deceiver, she had a fair notion as to what her attractions for the clergyman might be. First of all, she had an independent income and property. It was known locally that the rector had a private income, but it was respectable rather than large, and a little extra would always come in handy. Secondly, the rector would certainly expect his wife to be fully involved in the affairs of the parish, and Elfrida attended church regularly, come rain, come shine. She always took her turn at arranging flowers in the church, and was ready to help whenever there was any extra effort to be organized. The third reason why she suspected the rector might be attracted to her was that, unlike a number of the ladies in the neighbourhood, she had never set out to thrust herself under his nose. Gentlemen, or so she was told, liked a challenge, and even gentlemen of the cloth liked to do their own chasing.

Of course, some men, including the reverend gentleman, would have been able to tell her that there was something about her slight figure and dreamy eyes that aroused the male protective instinct, but since no one had ever said this to her face, she remained unaware of the fact.

It had been the rector who had escorted her to Grantham so that she might catch the Mail. She had ample means to hire a conveyance to take her to the Mail Hotel in the High Street, but he had insisted that he would do what little he could to ensure her comfort.

'Would that I could convey you all the way to London,' he had said regretfully, 'but there are parish matters which demand my attention that cannot be left to anyone else.'

'I shall be perfectly all right on the Mail coach,' Elfrida had replied. 'My seat is booked, and the journey only takes sixteen hours. Just think of that! I shall be in London at noon tomorrow.'

'It seems amazing,' he had exclaimed, shaking his head. 'No doubt our grandparents would have been horrified at the idea of such speed. But there is this to be said for it: the sooner you arrive, the sooner you will return.'

'I shall be glad to get home again, I must admit. I'm quite a stay-at-home body, I'm afraid.'

'You cannot think how happy it makes me to hear you say that,' Mr Erskine had replied earnestly. 'I, too, shall be counting the hours.'

This was the nearest that he had come to a declaration, but Elfrida was not sorry that he went no further. For one thing, she had her mind on the coming journey, and this was neither the time nor the place. For another, although she undoubtedly liked and respected the rector, she did not think that *she* would be counting the hours until she saw *him* again.

'Let me know when you intend to return,' he had said after he had organized the removal of her luggage from his gig to the Mail coach. 'I will come here and collect you.'

'Thank you,' Elfrida had replied, giving him her hand. He had looked for a moment as if he might have kissed it, but he had contented himself with giving it a little squeeze, bowing decorously the while.

'I hope that you will have an enjoyable time,' he had said dutifully, looking as though he hoped no such thing. Elfrida had climbed into her corner seat and waved goodbye.

It was probably a good thing that she was to be away if only briefly, she reflected as she eventually began to drift off to sleep on her first night in her sister's house. It would help her to make up her mind about the rector. Her earlier thoughts about family life had slightly tilted the balance in his favour. No doubt he would make an admirable husband and father.

★ ★ ★

The following morning, she was up in good time and when she had dressed, with the assistance of a maid who had been assigned to her for that very purpose, she went downstairs to the breakfast parlour. 'Mrs Winchcomb takes breakfast in her room, ma'am,' said Kimble the butler, when he had helped her to a place. 'The master will no doubt be down in due course.'

'And what of Miss Prudence?' asked Elfrida.

'Miss Prudence's plans vary,' replied Kimble. 'Shall I procure tea or coffee for you, ma'am?'

She opted for coffee, and as he left the room, she smiled to herself, remembering the thoughts that she had had the night before about the congeniality of being amongst a family. That did not apply at breakfast, evidently. She recalled that when she and Anthea had been young women at home, they had both been expected to make an appearance at the breakfast-table. No breakfast in bed for them! Either they joined the family at the appropriate time or they did not eat. Evidently such formality did not reign in the Winchcomb household. Clearly it would be impossible for anyone to insist that Prudence should be at the table when her mama did not appear at it. She was very pleased, however, to approve one agreeable luxury, when Kimble appeared with the coffee pot, and also carrying the papers.

The bacon, she decided, was not as good as the home-cured bacon that she generally purchased from Mr Sampson's farm, but it was tasty enough, and having consumed two rashers, with an egg and some toast, she settled down with her coffee and the paper. She had never troubled to have a newspaper sent up from London, but she could well afford to take such a measure, and she resolved that on returning home, she would make sure that the news was delivered regularly to her door.

It was as she was perusing the columns concerning the doings of the upper 10,000 that she read the following lines:

It is widely rumoured that the Honourable R — s T — r, expected in some quarters to make an offer for the lovely Miss W — , has concluded that bachelordom is best, and resumed his intimate connection with the obliging Mrs F — . Although disappointed in terms of worldly advancement, Miss W's relations must take comfort in the fact that their charming relative will not be united with one who shows an alarming tendency to fling himself into the arms of the *demi-monde*.

Elfrida stared at this paragraph for a long time, her brow furrowed. 'The Honourable R — s T — r.' Could that be the Rufus Tyler whose suit Anthea wanted to encourage? Could the 'Miss W' mentioned be Prudence? Elfrida's first instinct was to take this article immediately to her sister, but something inside made her hesitate. Such news would only make her sister anxious when it was of the first importance that she should be calm and happy as she left London and her only daughter. A greater worry in Elfrida's mind, however, was the idea that despite Mr Tyler's evidently doubtful reputation, Anthea might be prepared to accept any offer for the sake of worldly advantage. Elfrida was determined that her niece would not be sacrificed on that particular altar. Mr Tyler might petition all he liked, but *she* would not accept an offer from one whose entanglements with lightskirts were the subject of scurrilous newspaper reports.

She had just laid down the newspaper, having gleaned from it anything that was of interest to her, when Mr Winchcomb came in, bidding her a rather lazy 'good morning'. 'Never find it easy to stir myself first thing,' he acknowledged.

Tactfully refraining from commenting that 10.00 a.m. was hardly first thing, Elfrida merely greeted him in turn, saying, 'Do you wish for company, sir, or shall I leave you to your breakfast and your paper?'

'Of course, you are very welcome to stay,' he replied courteously.

Elfrida could see his eyes straying longingly to his paper, so she said cheerfully, 'I think you would rather be left in peace, so I shall go and find something to do.'

It was as she was leaving the breakfast parlour that the front door opened to admit Prudence in her outdoor clothing, followed by her maid.

'You've been out early,' remarked Elfrida.

'Yes, it's such a lovely morning that I couldn't resist,' replied her niece carelessly.

'Where have you been?' asked her aunt.

'Just out. I'm going to take off my outdoor things, so I'll see you later.' With that, Prudence walked up the stairs, her maid following meekly behind her. Elfrida tried to imagine what would have happened had she addressed her papa or mama in such a way. Certainly she would have been called severely to task. It also occurred to her that during her disastrous season in London, when her sister had been her chaperon, Anthea would never have tolerated such an off-hand reply from her younger sister. The impression that Elfrida got was that Prudence was rather spoiled, and far too accustomed to having her own way. It was a thought that filled her with foreboding.

After a little hesitation, she went up to her own room thoughtfully, her mind turning once again to the article that she had read earlier. What if Prudence herself saw the article in the paper? How would she feel about being allied to such a man? She did not yet feel that she knew her niece well enough to predict what her reaction might be. Furthermore, from what her sister had said the previous day — or rather, surmising from what her sister had left out — it seemed possible that Mr Tyler might have lost interest in Prudence anyway. If he had indeed done so, then the whole matter would be merely academic. Of one thing she was quite certain: she would make sure that she kept that article from the newspaper so that she would have it available to show in time of need.

★　★　★

Anthea finally made her appearance downstairs at about half past eleven, and came into the library where Elfrida was reading a copy of Richardson's novel *Clarissa*. 'My dear, I hope you have not been dreadfully bored,' exclaimed Anthea.

'Not at all,' replied Elfrida. 'It is seldom that I have a chance to enjoy a library as fine as this.'

Anthea looked around as if seeing the room for the first time. 'Oh. Yes, I suppose it is rather fine,' she remarked. 'But now to more important things — shopping!'

Much though Elfrida protested that she did not really need anything, Anthea insisted on bearing her sister off in her carriage to sample all the various goods that were to be found in the busy streets of the capital city. Prudence also went with them, and proved herself to be such a congenial companion, and so ready to offer helpful suggestions, that Elfrida began to wonder whether she had imagined that there might be difficulties between her and her niece.

Although Elfrida had arrived in London convinced that she had everything she needed, she found the extensive array of goods on display too tempting to resist completely, and by the time they returned to the Winchcombs' town house was the possessor of several pairs of silk stockings, two bonnets, a shawl, a pair of sandals, and some perfume. She also ordered a new gown from Mme Lisette, the cousin of Mme Patrice who had her business in Grantham. The most astonishing thing to Elfrida was how alike the two cousins were; indeed, in their slight figures, their dark hair with greying temples, their slender hands with long fingers, and their penetrating grey eyes, they might have been twins and not cousins.

Mme Lisette was pleased to approve the gown of Mme Patrice's making, but in the most tactful way possible, and without uttering any criticism of her country cousin, she suggested that a little more colour might be beneficial. 'My cousin is very right in saying that strong colours are not for you,' said Mme Lisette, 'but probably she does not have such extensive an array of fabrics on which she may draw. If you will put your trust in me, *mademoiselle*, I can guarantee that you will look as stylish as my cousin could wish, but perhaps a little more vibrant, *hein*?' Elfrida smiled and gave her consent. Anthea's expression seemed to convey 'I told you so', but she said nothing.

That afternoon, after they had taken their purchases home and rested for a while, they went out to call on one or two of Anthea's acquaintances. Again, Prudence went with them obediently and Elfrida, watching her carefully, was pleased to note that there was no fault to be found with her company manners. She answered her elders politely when spoken to, and showed herself to be very willing to sit and chatter with other girls of her own age. Her manner when in company with young men was also all that it should be, neither over-familiar nor over-shy. Elfrida began to relax. Looking after Prudence was not going to be very taxing after all.

Another discovery made that day also pleased Elfrida. As they sat talking with other visitors at Mrs Hickox's house, she heard the name of Mr Tyler mentioned, and pricked up her ears. 'Is Mr Tyler not to return to London this season, then?' said one lady, whom Elfrida remembered was called Mrs Cliffe.

'I don't believe so,' answered another. 'I heard someone saying that his father had sent for him, and he will now probably stay on the family estate for the summer.'

'That will put a spoke in someone's wheel,' replied Mrs Cliffe, lowering her voice a trifle. 'I'm told that Augusta Fossey was observed looking at rings the other day.'

'For all the good it will do her,' put in the other. 'She will not have been the first to count her chickens as far as that gentleman is concerned.'

Then the lady with whom Elfrida was sitting made some remark that required an answer, and the next time that Elfrida heard the two ladies speaking, they were discussing some other matter.

Later, Elfrida ventured to tell her sister about what she had heard — missing out the bit about Mrs Fossey — and Anthea wrinkled her brow. 'That is exceedingly vexatious,' she said. 'I really did think that he might be interested in Pru.'

'Do you want to change your plans and take her home with you after all?' Elfrida asked.

Anthea narrowed her eyes. 'No, I don't, so you needn't think to wriggle out of this London visit so soon,' she said. 'There are still plenty of other eligible men about, and I do not despair of Mr Tyler's returning to London. He might be back yet.'

Elfrida said nothing, but privately, she hoped that Anthea would prove to be mistaken. No Mr Tyler meant no dilemma as to whether to show Prudence the newspaper article which she had carefully saved.

That night, they went to the opera, and again Anthea took pains to introduce her sister to her acquaintances. Elfrida was grateful for her consideration. She had begun to realize that she would have been lonely indeed after Anthea had gone without a few friends to mingle with. Elfrida remembered a few of the people that they met from her last visit to London, but most of them were strangers, and all were very fashionably dressed. She was all the more thankful that she had taken the trouble to ensure that she did not look dowdy.

Mr Winchcomb went to the opera with them, and Anthea rounded off the party with two gentlemen, Sir Peter Wilson, a gentleman of about forty, and Mr Colin Fraye, a young man in his twenties.

'We have met before, Miss Frobisher,' said Sir Peter, as they sat at dinner. He was a kindly-looking man, not handsome, but with a healthy complexion, and a fine head of light-brown hair.

'Are you sure, sir?' asked Elfrida, wrinkling her brow.

'I am certain of it,' he answered with a twinkle, 'but obviously it was not a memorable encounter, since you do not recall me at all.'

'You must forgive me, sir,' smiled Elfrida. 'I have been out of society for some years. You, on the other hand, are more used to London, and probably more accustomed to seeing and remembering a variety of different faces.'

'Perhaps,' he conceded. 'Tell me about what you do when you are not in London, ma'am. Are there assemblies that you attend in Grantham?'

'Very seldom,' she admitted. 'I'm very

much a stay-at-home body, content to enjoy my garden and my painting.'

'Very unlike your sister, then.'

'As you say. So you must tell me all about what I have been missing in the London scene.'

'With the greatest of pleasure,' he declared. Elfrida allowed much of what he was saying to wash over her, for she had now remembered that Sir Peter had been one of the court that had surrounded her sister during her successful season. Anthea had told her that he had now been a widower for some years, and she had obviously invited him for her younger sister's benefit. It was a kind thought, Elfrida decided, but as she listened to Sir Peter talk about town life, she could tell that their interests lay in very different spheres. She would do much better to settle for the Revd Stanley Erskine, and she smiled as she found herself wondering what her sister would think if she announced that she was marrying the local rector. Sir Peter, who had at that very moment concluded an amusing anecdote, decided that the other Miss Frobisher, though not as pretty as her sister, had a decidedly winsome expression, and might be well worth pursuing.

The opera was well attended and Elfrida, who had not attended Covent Garden for some years, had to stop herself from looking overwhelmed like some country yokel at the brilliant spectacle of the ton gathered for the evening performance.

'It must be some years since you have attended the opera,' Sir Peter remarked, as they took their seats.

'Yes, I think it must be,' agreed Elfrida as casually as she could. 'No doubt the audience will give its usual undivided attention to the music.'

Sir Peter laughed. 'No doubt,' he agreed.

As always, the incessant chatter continued whilst the singers were giving their all. It seemed to Elfrida that the performance on the stage took second place to that which was happening in the auditorium as the spectators took careful note of who was flirting with whom.

Of course, the whole business became more intense when the interval arrived and there was no further distraction from the 'caterwauling on the stage', as Mr Winch-comb put it. He had ordered wine to be brought for them, and Elfrida was pleased to accept one glass, firmly refusing when her brother-in-law offered to fill it again.

'I'm afraid that wine and I really do not mix,' she said ruefully.

'Oh, do you still suffer from that little

problem?' asked Clive. 'I thought that it was a childhood affliction that you had long since outgrown.'

'I fear not,' his sister-in-law replied.

Anthea laughed. 'I well remember that evening when we went to a ball held locally — at Clare Hall, wasn't it?' She paused in thought.

'I really don't recall,' answered Elfrida untruthfully, in the most discouraging tone that she could manage. Then, to take her sister's mind off past history, she said, 'Who is that lady in the box over there — in green, with a gold turban?'

Anthea glanced obligingly at the woman in question. 'That's Honoria Lethbridge,' she replied, but if Elfrida had hoped that the subject of her little lapse would be dropped, then she was doomed to disappointment. 'Yes, that's right, it was after Clive and I had been married for a short time and you came to us for a visit with Mama and Papa,' Anthea went on. 'Poor Clive didn't realize that you cannot drink more than two glasses of wine without becoming very silly, and of course you, being young, didn't really know either.'

Elfrida could see Prudence's intrigued expression, and she was not surprised when her niece prompted, 'Do go on, Mama, it sounds so very diverting.'

Before Anthea could finish her tale, however, Elfrida broke in saying, 'Anthea, you surely aren't going to drag me down completely in my niece's eyes by telling all about my youthful mistakes, are you?'

Anthea, remembering the impropriety of doing such a thing, smiled and shook her head. She did add, looking in Prudence's direction, however, 'There's nothing more to tell. But it is a warning to you, miss, not to allow anyone to overfill your glass. More reputations have been ruined through over-indulgence than I could care to name.'

Prudence did not say any more, but she looked speculatively at her aunt, possibly wondering whether there were more reasons to Elfrida's departure from the social scene than met the eye.

To take her mind off the recent conversation — which did indeed give rise to embarrassing memories — Elfrida tried to concentrate on what was going on in the auditorium. She looked round at all the well-dressed ladies and gentlemen and wondered whether Mr Tyler might be in the audience. Then she remembered hearing at Mrs Hickox's house that he was out of town. That did not mean, of course, that Mrs Fossey was not somewhere in the auditorium, but Elfrida did not know whom she could ask. If Mrs Fossey were indeed a woman of easy virtue, then it might not be wise to be heard to be making enquiries about her.

'Would you like to walk about a little during the interval?' Sir Peter asked her, when they had all finished their wine. 'I might be able to point out one or two notables to you.'

'Thank you, I should like that,' she replied. Once outside the box, it seemed as if walking about might not be very easy, since half the rest of the audience had had the same idea, but Sir Peter managed to steer a way through the press of persons, and was soon introducing her to some of his acquaintance.

It was while they were exchanging remarks about the performance with Mr and Mrs Clements that Elfrida's eye was caught by the bright colour of scarlet regimentals and, turning her head, she saw that Prudence, still escorted by Mr Fraye, was talking animatedly with a soldier in his dress uniform. Her heart sank, but she gave no indication of this. She simply waited until Mrs Clements had finished speaking about an art exhibition that she had attended, then excused herself, saying, 'Your words have put me in mind of something that I need to say to Prudence, if you will excuse me.'

Elfrida and her escort wandered over to her niece's side.

'Oh, hello, Aunt Elfrida,' said Prudence, as her aunt approached. 'Hello, Sir Peter. Aunt, I don't suppose you have met Captain Black yet, so may I introduce him to you? He is one of our heroes, home from the Peninsular. Captain Black, this is my aunt, Miss Frobisher.'

Elfrida, politely acknowledging the introduction, decided that the wearing of regimental dress ought to be abolished, for the sake of everyone's peace of mind. Seldom had she ever seen a more handsome man. He was tall with broad shoulders which filled his coat admirably, and his dark hair and eyes were well set off by the scarlet of his uniform.

'A pleasure, Miss Frobisher,' he said, in a pleasantly musical voice. 'Miss Winchcomb exaggerates I'm afraid, reluctant though I am to contradict a lady. I was by no means a hero.'

'But you were, Captain,' Prudence protested.

'Only if it is heroic to do one's duty, in which case the army is peopled by heroes,' he replied lightly.

'That may be true,' replied Elfrida. 'Are you to leave the army now?'

'I have not yet decided,' he replied. 'The army has been my life, part of my family, even. I will have to think hard about what to do next.'

Sir Peter touched her on the shoulder. He and Black, who were slightly acquainted, had nodded to one another. 'I think it is time we resumed our places.'

'Yes; thank you, Sir Peter,' she acknowledged. 'It was a pleasure to meet you, Captain Black.'

'The pleasure was mutual, ma'am,' he replied, his eyes sparkling.

4

It had been some time since Elfrida had given very much thought to the events that had taken place at Castle Clare. That night, after she had gone to bed, Elfrida searched her memory and for the first time in quite a while, she allowed herself to remember what had happened that evening seventeen years ago.

She had been only seventeen, and Anthea had been married for just a few months. Although the two sisters had always been very different from one another, Elfrida had felt the loss of company very keenly, so she had been quite excited when a letter had arrived from Anthea inviting them all to go to Winchcomb Hall for a short visit. The new bride had gained dignity with her marriage, and a London stylishness that had made Elfrida feel dowdier than ever, but Anthea had been delighted to see her little sister again, and very willing to take her about a little. It was while the three Frobishers were staying with the Winchcombs that the invitation had arrived from Castle Clare. It was not often that the Earl of Clare held a ball, but his own son had just become engaged to be married and the occasion was to be marked with a grand ball at Castle Clare, with sumptuous food, the gardens to be illuminated, and fireworks to close the proceedings.

Clive and Anthea were invited to the dinner beforehand and Elfrida and her parents were included in the invitation. It was one of the first such events that Elfrida had ever attended. Anthea lent her sister one of her gowns for the occasion. It was of a shade of lemon, a colour that she had never cared for, and with her hair powdered and dressed high, she felt quite unlike herself.

Then, the very afternoon before they were due to go to Castle Clare, her father had been taken ill, and her mother had declared that she would remain behind to look after him. 'Anthea will take good care of you, you may be sure,' Mrs Frobisher had said. Anthea had enthusiastically agreed that she would do so, revelling in her new status as a married lady, and Elfrida, who did not really care for these big occasions, found herself travelling to Castle Clare with just her sister and brother-in-law for company.

She was certainly one of the youngest at the table and, as such, did not find herself anywhere near either the earl or the countess.

Being self-conscious, however, she felt that this was all to the good, and in such undemanding company as Mr Steele, a man of her father's age, on one side, and a distant relative of the countess on the other, she was able to enjoy the dinner without any anxiety.

She remembered glancing further up the table and noting a group of people more highly placed than herself with whom she was very glad that she did not have to mingle. Two gentlemen, dressed in a very elaborate and artificial way, were entertaining the ladies seated with them in such a manner as to make their part of the table stand out from the rest. These gentlemen had high, elaborate hair arrangements, and complexions enhanced with paint and patches.

'Damned macaronis,' grumbled Mr Steele. 'Popinjays, the pair of them.'

Elfrida had never seen anything like them, but she decided to keep well away. They appeared to her to be so strangely attired that they could almost have been from an alien race.

She had been very careful at the table not to have more than one glass of wine, for she knew very well the effect that it had upon her. Sometimes, she resented the fact that whereas her mama and papa and even Anthea could each enjoy several glasses, she could barely touch more than one before collapsing into a giggling heap. It was no use bemoaning the fact, however, and fortunately, on this particular evening, Lord Clare had ordered lemonade to be available for the younger guests. After only one glass of wine, she had asked for this harmless beverage to be served to her; looking at those around the table, it seemed to her that some of them would have been well-advised to do the same!

After dinner was over, the rest of the guests had begun to arrive, and soon Anthea was happily greeting those of the neighbourhood who had become her friends since her marriage. Some of the time, she had wanted to talk secrets and on one of those occasions, she had instructed Clive to look after her little sister. 'Find her a drink, my love,' she had said. 'In truth it is very warm in here.'

Mr Winchcomb had obediently wandered off to fetch a drink for his sister-in-law, and it was while she was sitting in a small recess that the two macaronis had wandered over, and stood looking down at her with their quizzing-glasses, their eyes magnified horribly through the lenses.

'Well here's a nice little wench,' one of them declared.

'And detherted, by Gad,' drawled the other, his carefully cultivated lisp at variance with his rather deep tones. 'Can't have that, can we, Fletcher?'

'By no means,' answered the one called Fletcher. 'Come, my dear, we'll promenade.'

'I am waiting for . . . for — ' she managed to say.

' — For a damned laggard,' laughed the other man. 'Come, thweetheart, let'th show him he'th not the only fellow to apprethiate you.'

They were clearly favoured guests of the earl, they were older than she by about half-a-dozen years, Clive was nowhere in sight, and she did not know how to persist in her refusal without giving offence. Reluctantly she stood up, and said bravely, 'Just one turn, gentlemen, but then you must return me to this place or I shall be missed.'

'Upon my honour,' replied the one with the lisp, bowing. They insisted on walking either side of her, taking an arm each, and Elfrida felt very conspicuous. Other men were dressed elaborately but none like these, with their painted faces, highcut, tightly fitting coats, with rather large nosegays fastened to them, pantaloons fastened with ribbons at the knee and striped stockings. She wondered whether anyone she knew could see her walking with these strange beings, and if they could, what they would think.

Whilst they were strolling along, the two men talking to one another for the most part, but throwing her the occasional remark, sometimes couched in fashionable slang which she could barely follow, a footman came past with a tray, and the man called Fletcher relieved him of three glasses, one of which he handed to Elfrida.

'Oh no, but I . . . ' she began to protest.

'It'th all right,' the other man reassured her. 'It'th champagne. Champagne won't do you any harm.'

'No harm at all,' agreed the other. 'Nothing but bubbles.'

Elfrida had never had champagne before, but she could see that it was very fizzy. It could surely not be harmful. She had known that she must be careful about wine at the table, but no one had warned her about champagne. Cautiously, she took a sip, and the bubbles made her sneeze. The two men laughed. 'Drink some more,' said Fletcher. 'That'll soon put a stop to the sneezing.'

Obediently, she finished the glass, and found that he was right. Only now she felt a little strange. She was glad when she caught sight of her brother-in-law looking about him, a glass in his hand, and while the two men had turned aside as one pointed out something to the other, she slipped away, and reached Clive's side. 'Oh there you are,' he said. 'Have you been keeping yourself amused? I've brought you some champagne.' A newcomer to the family, he was unaware of Elfrida's affliction and had simply thought to bring a drink in keeping with the occasion.

'Oh thank you,' she said, taking the glass, and drinking from it. 'Do you know, I feel much braver now?' So saying, she slumped down on to the seat behind them and began to giggle.

Mr Winchcomb eyed her in consternation. As far as he was aware, his sister-in-law had had very little to drink, but she bore all the signs of someone in the throes of inebriety. He had visited Castle Clare before, but not frequently, so had no idea whether there might be some quiet room to which he could take her so that she might sleep the worst of it off. He looked around for Anthea, and eventually thought that he could spot her on the other side of the room.

He turned to Elfrida. 'Stay there,' he said, 'and don't move. I'm going to find your sister.'

As he walked away, Elfrida stared after him for a moment, then got to her feet with the dignity that only the inebriated can achieve. 'I don't need anyone to help me to find my own sister,' she said carefully. 'Anybody who needs

59

me to tell them to tell me that I need them to tell me how to find my own sister needs me to tell them to tell me that I don't need them to help me to find them; *or* their sister.' Suddenly conscious that what she had said made no sense at all, she started to giggle. Then she saw a lady wearing a gown of exactly the colour that her sister was wearing; she was walking towards the conservatory. Some ladies walked across Elfrida's line of vision, and when she looked again, the lady had gone, but the door to the conservatory was just closing.

'She shouldn't be going in there,' Elfrida said. 'There will be a scandal. I shall go and save her.' She decided to negotiate the room by the edge, so that she could keep touching things just in case. 'I must speak to the earl,' she said to herself. 'He has very wobbly furniture, *and* wobbly walls.' At last she reached the door of the conservatory and walked inside. It was markedly cooler in the green darkness, and for a moment she reeled at the change in temperature. Then she realized that it was not completely dark, for the countess, whose pride and joy the conservatory was, had caused lamps to be placed here and there so that fine plants, tiny pools and exquisite beds could be shown to advantage. Briefly, Elfrida was diverted by the beauty of the scene, but soon her attention was caught by the sounds of low laughter and, following her ear, she came upon a couple cosily ensconced upon one of the wooden seats that had been placed in there for the comfort of visitors.

Briefly, Elfrida paused in outrage. The lady, whom she had already identified as her sister, was on the gentleman's knee. The gentleman, who, by his dress and his wig, was one of the two macaronis, was clearly delighted to have her there. Taking a deep breath, Elfrida stepped forward and pulled her sister's arm so that she slid off the gentleman's lap and on to the floor. 'How could you, you . . . you snuttergipe!' she exclaimed. The lady squealed and looked up at her from her position on the floor. Now, seeing her full face, Elfrida discovered that it wasn't her sister after all; it was a lady of the same shape and size and with the same coloured gown. 'Oh! Oh dear,' she murmured. 'Let me help.'

'Get away, get away,' the lady retorted, struggling to her feet unaided. Elfrida was amazed to see that the gentleman had succumbed to mirth, and was roaring with laughter.

'Come back here, Amy,' he said, when he was able to speak again.

'I'm going back to the ballroom,' she

replied, brushing down her gown. 'This little chit is doubtless a tattle tale and will spread the news of these events far and wide if she can. If Graham gets to hear then I *shall* be in the suds.'

'Amy,' he called again, standing up, but Amy hurried off to the ballroom without a backward glance. He looked down at Elfrida, one eyebrow raised. 'Well you've thpoiled my fun and no mithtake.'

'You shouldn't be having fun with a married woman,' she retorted; then reflected that since the lady had not been Anthea, she did not know whether she was married or not.

'Thinthe when did you become the guardian of other people'th moralth, wench?' he asked her, catching hold of her by both arms. Really, he had more strength than one would have expected of one who chose to dress so effeminately and adopt such an affected mode of speech. He dragged her into the light. 'Why, it'th the little chit from the ballroom,' he declared. 'Gad, but you're a tooththome wench when one conthiderth the matter. And theeing ath you've thpoiled my fun, you might ath well provide me with thome yourthelf.' So saying, he sat down again, pulled her on to his lap and, holding her still with one hand whilst lifting her chin with his other proceeded to kiss her very thoroughly on her mouth.

For a few moments, the feeling of his lips moving on hers simply added to the intoxication to which she was already a prey. Then she woke up to her situation and began to struggle. 'Calm down, thweetheart,' he murmured in caressing tones. 'What could be more pleathant than thith?'

'This!' she declared, and dealt him a ringing slap across the face.

'What?' he exclaimed, slackening his hold. She slipped off his knee, and he got to his feet. 'Look here, wench,' he began.

'No, *you* look here,' she responded, pulling off his wig, thus exposing his bald pate, and throwing it into the pond that glistened next to them.

'You little fiend!' he ground out, and reached for her. She eluded his grasp, and hurried to the entrance to the ballroom, but before she could open the door, it flew open in front of her and her furiously angry sister stood in front of her.

'Elfrida!' she exclaimed in outraged accents. 'What are you doing in this secluded place? Come with me at once.'

Anthea had been furious with her sister, first for drinking champagne, and secondly for going off into the conservatory unescorted.

Elfrida had apologized remorsefully, but unfortunately, the effect had been ruined somewhat by a rather drunken hiccough that she had been obliged to release part way through. At least Anthea had been sporting enough not to mention the matter to their parents, Elfrida recalled. With hindsight, she realized that probably Anthea had felt a little guilty for neglecting her. Possibly that was why she was so anxious now that Prudence should be properly chaperoned.

What had happened to the gentleman called Fletcher and the other man whose name she had never discovered? No doubt by now they were both fathers of hopeful families, she reflected, as she closed her eyes and drifted away.

5

The following morning, Prudence suggested a ride in the park, and Elfrida gladly agreed.

'Mama will not come,' Prudence told her. 'She has been advised not to do so by her physician.'

When Mr and Mrs Winchcomb finally appeared, however, Anthea declared her intention of going with them after all. 'I do feel extremely well today, and the doctor only advised, he did not precisely order me not to ride.' They were gathered together in the saloon, waiting for Prudence to fetch her crop.

'You must do as you think fit, my dear,' Mr Winchcomb replied, his lazy voice just a fraction short of a yawn. 'Pray do not be ill and make it necessary for me to call the doctor, though. I should find it much too fatiguing.'

At this, Anthea smiled, and walked gracefully over to where he was sitting, putting her hand on his shoulder. 'There, you see,' she remarked to her sister. 'Clive is quite determined, and I must not go against him.'

Elfrida smiled, thinking that Anthea was

creating a man of her own imagining from her husband's very placid remarks. As she and Prudence were about to leave the house, it suddenly occurred to her that her sister might want some errand run while she was out. She went back to the saloon and was about to enter it when she saw that Anthea was still standing beside her husband's chair, but that now Mr Winchcomb's arm was firmly about his wife's waist. To her astonishment, she heard him say in tones of unmistakeable sincerity, 'I don't want to curtail your enjoyment, my darling, but if anything happened to you, I don't know what I should do.'

'No doubt you would find the funeral too fatiguing to arrange as well,' Anthea suggested. In response, Mr Winchcomb laughed and pulled his wife on to his knee. As much astonished as pleased at this evidence of affection between them, Elfrida left without interrupting them. This rather intriguing scene caused her to revise her opinion concerning Mr Winchcomb and his supposed everlasting indolence. She resolved that before her sister left London, she would suggest that they should all go out in the carriage in preference to riding, so that Anthea might go too.

The season was drawing to its climax on

that fine June day, and the park was full of people taking the air on foot, in carriages or, like themselves, on horseback. Elfrida was mounted upon Penny, a placid, mature mare, who took the noise and bustle in her stride. Prudence was mounted upon a rather more mettlesome creature, but she seemed to be well in control, responding to her horse's antics with a calm demeanour and light hands. As before, they were accompanied by Manners, a sensible, middle-aged groom, and Prudence accepted his presence without the slightest demur. As they entered the park, Elfrida breathed a happy sigh of relief that all her anxieties about this visit and all the responsibilities attached to it appeared to be without foundation.

As they rode sedately through the park and acknowledged various acquaintances, she had to admit now that she was glad that Anthea had insisted that she should come for a slightly longer visit. It was certainly a relief to discover, for example, that as three young men in uniform came galloping towards them, one of them, Captain Black, was already known to her.

'Good day!' he exclaimed cheerfully. He had, as might be expected of one of His Majesty's dragoons, an excellent seat on a horse. 'Miss Frobisher; Miss Winchcomb. A

67

fine day for our ride, is it not?'

'Good day, Captain,' Elfrida replied. 'Yes indeed, very fine.'

'Allow me to introduce two of my brother officers to you,' he went on. 'This is Captain Graves, and this is Lieutenant Collett. Gentlemen, Miss Frobisher. Miss Winchcomb I think you have met.'

Elfrida acknowledged the introduction politely, but inside, her mind was seething as she realized that one of the young men to whom she had just been introduced must be Digby Collett, the childhood sweetheart from whom she was supposed to keep Prudence separated.

Lieutenant Collett was probably the least impressive looking of the three, being slender and fair, with a rather thin face and prominent nose. Of the two, Elfrida would have judged that Captain Graves was the more likely to be in love with Prudence. He had dark-brown hair and eyes, and a tanned complexion; his expression was rather serious, and his gaze was often concentrated upon the younger woman, whom Elfrida observed casting him the occasional saucy glance.

'Are you to attend the ball at Lord and Lady Bayley's house at the end of the week?' Captain Black asked eventually.

'Yes, we are,' replied Elfrida. 'It will be one of the last events of the season, will it not?'

'Then, ma'am, may I hope that I may be permitted to ask Miss Winchcomb to dance with me?'

Elfrida glanced at Prudence and saw that she was looking very demure, quite unlike herself, and she felt suddenly suspicious. Anthea had given her no reason to repulse Captain Black in particular and it seemed quite unreasonable to refuse this perfectly natural request simply because he was acquainted with Digby Collett. Despite Anthea's strictures with regard to penniless soldiers, she could not, after all, wage a campaign against the whole of the British Army. Nor would Prudence be at all impressed if she suddenly started to become heavy handed. In fact, a stern line from her now might well have the effect of making these soldiers seem much more glamorous than they really were.

Taking this into account, therefore, she simply replied, 'You have my permission to ask her, Captain. But perhaps her hand is already spoken for?'

This was clearly the right approach, for Prudence laughed and said, 'My aunt flatters me. Yes, of course, I will spare you a dance, sir.'

Almost inevitably, Captain Graves and

Lieutenant Collett also asked for permission to dance with Prudence, and having given permission to one, Elfrida could not very well refuse one of the others. With a sinking heart, she resolved to be particularly on the watch for when her niece danced with Digby Collett, and very alert as to where they might go when their dance was finished!

She would have liked to have chatted to Prudence a little more about Digby, in order to discover whether she showed any signs of extraordinary interest in him, but as soon as the three soldiers had left them, they were hailed, this time by a woman of Elfrida's own age, driving herself with commendable skill.

'It must be Elfrida Frobisher,' she declared. 'I protest, I haven't seen you for an age.'

Elfrida eyed the other woman thoughtfully, then her brow cleared. 'Rosemary Feltwell! Yes, it must be at least ten years since we met. Only you aren't Rosemary Feltwell any more, of course.'

'No, I married Dunstone at the end of my first season. Is this your niece?'

Elfrida confirmed that it was, and introduced the two ladies. 'I am only here to enable Prudence to finish her first season,' she explained. 'Her mama and papa are to travel into the country very shortly.'

'And I am just steering my stepdaughter Julia through the final stages of hers,' said Lady Dunstone. 'She has just become engaged to Robin Wednesbury, so I shall have a wedding to arrange before long. What are your plans for the summer? Surely you are not staying in London?'

'No, indeed,' agreed Elfrida. 'We shall travel together to Prudence's home at the end of the season so that she can join her parents.'

'And then, no doubt, you will return to your sleepy rural backwater,' teased Rosemary.

'Yes I shall,' Elfrida replied, wondering why the prospect seemed less alluring. It must be because she was getting used to London life, she decided, as they rode back towards the entrance of the park after bidding Rosemary farewell. She realized with some surprise that she might even find it agreeable to come for the season again another year. Now that Anthea had stopped matchmaking on her behalf, she was much more comfortable to live with.

★　★　★

Captain Black was sharing lodgings with Captain Graves, and after bidding Digby Collett farewell — since he needed to return to his own lodging in order to get changed for the evening — they both rode back to Half Moon Street in order to make their own preparations. They were not due to see Prudence that evening — to Black's great regret — since the Winchcomb family were to have a private family dinner at home, but he comforted himself with the thought that at the Bayleys he would be able to dance and talk with her and with any luck take her down to dinner.

'Some letters for you, Cap'n,' said his batman, as he and Graves entered the cosy first-floor room which served them as a living area. Unlike most bachelor accommodation, it was meticulously tidy, neither man caring to live in a muddle.

'Thank you, Crew,' replied Black, taking the letters from him. 'None for you, Edmund. No one like you again?'

Captain Graves grinned. His family was a large and affectionate one, but none of them was a good correspondent. 'I'm glad of it,' he replied, allowing Crew to help him out of his coat, so that he could lounge in his shirt sleeves. 'The last three communications I have received have been bills, every one.'

Black laughed. He picked up the first of his letters. 'This is Mama's hand,' he said, surprised. 'I wonder why she should write to me now? She knows that I will be home before long.'

'Perhaps to tell you not to come because she's let your room to a lodger.'

Daniel laughed perfunctorily, opened his letter and read in silence, a frown beginning to wrinkle his brow as he did so. 'Mama's brother is expected to arrive at Dover within the next few days,' he said, when he had finished. 'He has been on the Continent, acting as bear-leader to some sprig of the nobility. But the young man has sadly died of some fever and Uncle, who has also been taken ill, is returning.'

'Can he not remain in France until he is better?' asked Graves. 'Travelling with a fever must be unwise, surely.'

'Presumably he cannot afford to remain in a hotel any longer,' replied his friend. 'My family is not noted for its ability to amass wealth. I shall have to set off for Dover in the morning. I cannot risk his arriving with no one to meet him.'

'What of Miss Winchcomb and the ball?' Edmund Graves was privy to his friend's hopes.

Daniel's face fell. 'It cannot be helped,' he answered. 'My duty is quite clear. I shall inform her of my errand, then leave. You will have to deputize for me at the ball, old man.'

'With the greatest of pleasure,' his friend replied gallantly. 'Although I suspect that all the pleasure will be on one side.'

★ ★ ★

When they met the following morning in Hatchard's, Prudence was understandably very disappointed at the news that Captain Black was obliged to leave London, and said so. 'Surely, you could wait until after the ball at the Bayleys?' she asked him.

He shook his head. 'I fear not,' he replied. 'My uncle will almost certainly arrive at Dover before then. I must be there to give him every assistance. Family affection and plain duty demand it.'

Prudence looked up at him and sighed. 'I suppose that this is the kind of thing that must happen when one gives one's heart to a hero,' she said resignedly.

'What a soldier's wife you would make, my love,' the captain uttered in low but vibrant tones. Then, after a short pause, he spoke again, his face set. 'This has decided me. There can be no more delay. I must go to your father and ask for your hand.'

'No!' exclaimed Prudence loudly. Then, because everyone looked round, she had to go on, 'My dear sir, you really must not buy that book. You would not enjoy it at all.' All the customers within earshot resolved to seek out the offending book as soon as possible. Pulling him to another part of the shop, she dropped her voice and went on, 'It is still too soon. Mama must be convinced that I intend to marry Digby. I will send you word from my home when I have convinced her that she cannot hope for me to marry Mr Tyler, or any other man.'

The captain shook his head. 'I cannot like it,' he said.

'Believe me, it is the only way,' she answered. At that moment, they were joined by some acquaintances, and no further conversation was possible. Prudence left the shop disappointed at the captain's news, but not entirely dissatisfied at the notion of his absence.

Captain Black had given reluctant assent to her plans to deter other gentlemen by her cold behaviour. He had protested so vociferously about her plans to pretend to encourage Digby that they had very nearly quarrelled for the first time. He had begged her pardon in the end, but with that memory in mind, she had said nothing to him about her decision that Digby must compromise her. That, she decided, could be best explained after the event. She now realized that if the captain

75

were absent from London whilst she carried out this final most daring scheme, then he might never need to find out about it at all.

For all her careful calculations, however, Prudence had reckoned without the determination of her gallant lover. 'There are certain matters of duty and honour that must be attended to before I go,' he had managed to say to Prudence whilst the acquaintances they had met in the bookshop were still present. Prudence did not think too deeply about the meaning of his words. She simply assumed that he was referring to military tasks that must be carried out.

This was not what the captain had in mind. He had intended to wait until the very end of the season in order to ask for Prudence's hand, as she had wished. He had hated the idea of clandestine meetings and subterfuge, but he had met her in secret because she had insisted that it was the only way. The present situation changed matters, however. He would no longer be in London for the end of the season, and he dared not risk her being snatched up by another simply because he had not had the courage to put his fate to the test.

Courage was not something that Daniel lacked. Shortly before he was due to depart, and at a time when he knew that Prudence would be absent, he presented himself at the Winchcombs' town house, his uniform spotless and beautifully pressed, his silver gleaming, and his boots polished so highly that one might have combed one's hair by the reflection. He asked for Mr Winchcomb but, as luck would have it, that gentleman had escorted his sister-in-law to his bank in order to make sure that she would have enough funds to draw upon in case of need. Had Clive Winchcomb been within that day, events might have taken a very different turn. As it happened, he was shown into the saloon where Mrs Winchcomb was sitting.

Her first impression was a favourable one. She was no more immune to the attractions of a handsome face, a splendid physique and a scarlet uniform than the next woman. 'This is an unexpected pleasure, Captain Black,' said Anthea. 'May I offer you some refreshment?'

'Thank you, ma'am,' the captain replied. A man of courage he undoubtedly was, but in this situation, remembering how his very life's happiness hung in the balance, he suddenly found himself feeling nervous. 'I am shortly to leave London, and wanted to pay my respects before I left,' he explained by way of introduction.

'Are you recalled to your military duties,

sir?' Anthea asked him, thinking what pleasing manners he had.

'No, I am to go down to Dover without delay,' he answered, going on to explain his mother's request. 'I can do no other than go,' he concluded, accepting the glass of wine with which Kimble had presented him during his explanation.

'No indeed,' agreed Anthea warmly. 'Do I take it that your uncle is a clergyman?'

Daniel nodded. 'It is always the church or the army on both sides of my family,' he smiled. 'My father is a clergyman in Lincolnshire, and my mother, as well as being a clergyman's sister, is a clergyman's daughter.'

'And are you intending to go into the church as well?' Anthea asked.

He shook his head. 'I don't have a vocation,' he answered. 'But you are right, I must find some occupation. I cannot . . . ' He was about to observe that to be a peace-time officer on half pay was not an attractive prospect, when he suddenly realized that with every sentence, he was telling Mrs Winchcomb what an unsuitable husband he would be, and he fell silent.

Anthea looked at him through narrowed eyes. It had suddenly occurred to her that this handsome young man might have come in order to attempt to plead his friend's cause. If he were leaving town, then that would explain why he had come today. Clearly, it behoved her to disabuse him of any idea that a marriage between Prudence and Digby could be permitted.

'There must be many officers about who find themselves in difficult circumstances, now that the war is over,' Mrs Winchcomb said gently.

'I know this to be true,' the captain replied steadily.

'All of them will no doubt be in pursuit of gainful occupations. Will there be enough of them to go round, do you think?'

'Some will have to continue on half pay, no doubt,' Daniel said reluctantly. He could feel his hopes shrivelling even before he had given voice to them.

'It must be very hard, say, for a young officer who is desirous of marrying, yet feels he has nothing to offer,' said Anthea thoughtfully. 'If a young officer were to come to you for advice in such a circumstance, Captain, what would you tell him?'

Daniel looked at her, his face set. 'I would advise him to wait, ma'am,' he answered. 'No man of honour could possibly ask the woman he loved to live in poverty.'

'Your sentiments do you honour,' Anthea

replied; then, with only a tiny qualm of conscience, she added, 'it is always a relief for a mother when she finds that a loving child is going to contract an advantageous union. In confidence, I must tell you that we are in expectation of receiving a declaration from Mr Tyler, as soon as he returns from consulting with his family. I know that Prudence, bearing our changing circumstances in mind, will make a wise choice.'

'I am sure she will,' Captain Black answered, feeling as if his voice were coming from a very long way away. He drained his glass, and stood up. 'I will take my leave now,' he said. 'Pray give my compliments to your husband and to Miss Winchcomb, my . . . my best wishes for her future happiness.'

As he walked down the steps outside the house, his heart felt like a stone in his breast. Mrs Winchcomb, in the kindest way possible, had told him that his suit was not welcome. He longed to prove her wrong, to exert himself in some profession and show himself to be worthy of Prudence's hand, but he could not see his way forward. He was a soldier, and that was all he knew how to be; soldiering was not profitable in peace time. Even if he did find a lucrative career, establishing himself would take time. By then, no doubt, his love would have married someone else, and from what Mrs Winch-comb had said, that someone would very likely be Rufus Tyler. Prudence herself had said that she would not do so, but Mr Tyler was personable, available, clearly willing, and already acceptable to the family. Gallant soldier though he was, at that moment Captain Black could quite easily have wept.

★　★　★

It was before Elfrida and Mr Winchcomb had finished their errand and not long after Captain Black's departure, that Prudence came back to the house accompanied by her maid; she had been visiting one of her friends. Before going upstairs, she stepped briefly into the saloon to let her mother know that she had returned.

'Did you have an agreeable visit, my love?' Anthea asked her, her fingers busy with the tiny garment that she was fashioning in preparation for her baby's arrival.

'Yes, very agreeable, thank you,' Prudence replied. 'Agnes's wedding dress is lovely. Has all your packing been done, now?'

'Very nearly, I think.' Prudence had just turned to go, when her mother went on, 'I had an unexpected visitor this afternoon — Captain Black.'

Prudence's figure stiffened, but as Anthea was looking down at her sewing she did not notice this. 'Did he have any special reason for calling, Mama?' she asked, her voice casual.

Anthea was not deceived. 'I believe he did,' she answered. 'Pray do not suppose, Prudence, that Digby Collett's suit will prosper any more because his friends plead for him, because it will not.'

Prudence did turn then. 'Why are you so against him?' she asked, trying to keep the relief out of her voice. When Daniel's name had first been mentioned, she had been convinced at once that he had come to ask for her hand. Clearly, whatever might have been his intentions, he had not actually done so.

Anthea put down her sewing. 'My dear, need you ask?' she said. 'You are fond of Digby, I know, but I truly believe that it is a fondness that stems from a childhood relationship. It really will not do, my love, and your father and I would never permit it. Think of him as a brother, rather than a suitor, and find some worthier man.' She paused, then stood up, walking towards her daughter. 'He is poor, with only his officer's pay — half pay, now that the war is over. He has no prospects and no title. His immediate family is not distinguished enough to secure

82

his advancement, and his connection with the Clares is too distant for him to be able to expect anything from them. Your fortune is not large, and you will now have to accustom yourself to expect less because you will have a baby brother or sister to be provided for. It would be quite impossible, believe me.'

Prudence briefly took and squeezed the hand that her mother held out to her, before leaving the room without another word. It was only later that she thought about whether she would have behaved in such a way had she really been committed to Digby. The fact of the matter was that her mind had been too full of the implications of all that her mother had said with regard to Daniel. Every criticism that she had uttered concerning Digby could equally well have been levelled at Daniel. The only exception was in Digby's favour, for Digby was at least connected to the Clares, whereas Daniel was not connected to any high-ranking family as far as she knew. Their situation was as hopeless as it could be.

6

When the time came for Anthea and her husband to leave for the country, Elfrida did not know whether to be glad or sorry. On the one hand, every day that passed meant that she was one day closer to going back to her much loved home. On the other, she was finding that to be in London as a woman of over thirty, with no interest in catching a husband, was far more enjoyable than to be there as a debutante overshadowed by her glamorous older sister. It could, of course, be something to do with the fact that Anthea's attention was now concentrated upon her marriageable daughter rather than upon her spinster sister, which meant that Elfrida could thankfully step into the background. Anthea's departure would mean that Prudence would be entirely in her aunt's care, and Elfrida was feeling much more sanguine about this responsibility than she had when she first arrived in London. Then, she had feared that Prudence would prove to be strong-minded and difficult. Now, she had seen that her niece could be polite, obedient, and full of fun. Her remaining time in London would be very enjoyable, she decided, and she might even leave the capital with some regret.

The house seemed very quiet after Mr and Mrs Winchcomb had gone, and Elfrida was about to suggest that they should go for a ride in the park, when a messenger came to the door with a letter for Miss Winchcomb. Both ladies were still standing in the hall, and Elfrida knew a moment's consternation. What should she do about this? No letters had come for Prudence whilst her parents were still at home, so Elfrida did not know whether they would permit their daughter to receive letters that they had not first perused themselves. She herself had never been permitted to receive private correspondence, but that had been fifteen years ago, and times had changed. She decided to be guided by Kimble's actions. If he presented it to Prudence straight away, then she would not interfere, but if he gave it to her as the senior member of the household, then she would open it first.

She reckoned without Prudence's determination. Giving the butler no chance to bring it to either of them, she stepped forward and picked it up, glancing at the writing. 'Ah, a letter from my friend Millie, who is just married. I will take it upstairs to read if you don't mind, Aunt. Then shall we go for a ride?'

Elfrida took a deep breath. 'By all means,' she answered. 'You must tell me what your letter says later.'

'You may be sure I shall,' Prudence answered, an expression in her eyes that Elfrida found hard to read.

★   ★   ★

Prudence forced herself to walk up the stairs in a leisurely manner. She had recognized the writing as Captain Black's immediately, and was horrified that he had taken such a risk. Naturally, she was relieved that Elfrida had not insisted on looking at the letter, as she suspected her mother might have done, but along with the relief went a sensation of foreboding as she contemplated what might have prompted him to write, an action which was out of keeping for a man of his character, who deplored clandestine behaviour, and anything that smacked of the dishonourable.

All her fears were confirmed when finally she opened the letter and devoured the lines written with care in the Captain's immaculate handwriting.

My dearest Pru
    By now you will have discovered that I have visited your home. I realize that in

doing so, I was going against your express wishes, but as you know duty to my family has called me out of town unexpectedly, and I could not go without attempting to ask for your hand in form. That at least, was my intention, but your mother's words have convinced me that you can never be mine.

Please do not think that she was in any way unkind. In the gentlest manner possible, she reminded me that you must marry a man who can support you as you deserve and, my darling, that is beyond my means. You must not blame her, either, for in very truth I already knew how unworthy I was before she said anything. Her words but confirmed my deepest fears. Your mama tells me that you are to receive an offer from Mr Tyler, and I beg that you will consider it carefully. He is well spoken of, and will at least be able to keep you in the manner which you deserve, which I, alas, am unable to do.

The day when you pledged your love to me and promised to be mine, must always be my most precious memory, but from now on, I release you from your promise, and must try to be content for it to be a memory alone. After I have attended to the matter for which I have been summoned, *and paid my respects to my family, I shall sell my commission, and go to seek my fortune in America. I have already set matters in train in order to do this. Much though I long to see your sweet face before I go, I must deny myself that joy, for fear that my resolve may be weakened.*

With all my heart I wish you happiness in the future. This letter comes to you from one who has been from the moment he first saw you, and will be for all time,

Your Daniel

Prudence sat looking at her letter for a very long time, the tears running unheeded down her face. She had always known that he hated the subterfuge involved in secret meetings, and had for some time been afraid that he would find a way of coming to the house and asking for her hand before the time was right.

He had not done that, but only because he had heard everything that her mother had said about Digby and applied it to himself. Her heart ached for him, and she wept again as she imagined what his feelings must have been as he left the house.

But as her tears subsided, she began to look more carefully at other parts of the letter and, as she did so, she could feel her temper rising. Quite clearly her mother had deliberately given the impression, not only that Mr Tyler was on the point of proposing — which was patently untrue, and looked more unlikely by the minute — but also that if he did so, she, Prudence would accept him. 'How dare Mama! How dare she be so . . . so deceitful!' she said out loud. She had always felt that there must be a way of bringing her parents round to her way of thinking. This mendacity on her mother's part only made her determined that this should not be the end of everything, whether they could be persuaded or not. There must be a way for them to be together, even if it meant her going to America with him. As she thought the matter over, she began to get the glimmering of an idea. Determinedly she wiped away the last of her tears. Crying would not help now: it was time for action. Laying her precious letter down, she found a clean sheet of paper and, dipping her pen in the ink standish, began to write.

★　★　★

Elfrida was pleased when Prudence came downstairs later and suggested that they might go for a ride in the park. 'I will tell you what Millie says in her letter as we go,' she promised.

'You don't have to,' Elfrida responded, as they went upstairs together. 'I have no desire to pry into your concerns.' Prudence felt a twinge of conscience but she suppressed it ruthlessly. She could not afford to have scruples when her affairs had reached such an urgent stage.

They met many acquaintances during their ride in the park, but although Prudence chatted merrily with her aunt, giving a wholly fictitious account of her imaginary friend's wedding, and greeted those around with the utmost friendliness, she was really only looking out for one person. She was conscious of a feeling of relief when she saw galloping towards her the familiar figures of Captain Graves and Lieutenant Collett. Very conveniently, Captain Graves engaged her aunt in conversation, which meant that Prudence was able to pass her note to Digby, who, after glancing at her with a startled expression, tucked the screw of paper into his glove. After this manoeuvre, Prudence directed a swift glance at her aunt, who although she did look in her direction, did not show by any sign that she had noticed anything untoward.

The rest of their ride proceeded without incident, and eventually they set off for home. They had almost reached the entrance to the park when a very sporting-looking curricle turned in and swept across their line of vision. It was driven by a fashionably dressed man accompanied by an equally stylish lady. Conscious of a degree of tension in the figure riding next to her, Elfrida said on impulse, 'Prudence, who was that?'

'That, my dear aunt, was Rufus Tyler,' she replied, a curious light in her eye. 'The lady in his company was Mrs Fossey.'

★ ★ ★

After Mr Tyler had taken Mrs Fossey home, he drove his curricle round to the stables where it was kept, then leaving it in the charge of his groom, he wandered around to his club, where he was hailed by various acquaintances, among them a rather stout man who put down his newspaper, exclaiming, 'Stap me, Tyler, but I thought you was fixed in the country.'

'Forgive me if I've disappointed you, Lightfoot,' Tyler replied, with a rueful smile. 'Shall I go away again?'

'By no means,' laughed Lightfoot, getting to his feet. 'Come and sit with me, and we'll share a bottle of claret.'

Another man wandered over. 'Back from the country, Rufus?' he said.

'So it would seem,' answered Rufus, taking the chair that Lightfoot had indicated. 'Join us, Wednesbury.'

'Thank you.' Lord Wednesbury took his seat. 'Not that I blame you, of course,' he went on. 'What man could remain in the country if he knew that Mrs Fossey and all her charms were awaiting him in London?'

'Oh Jack, Jack, I see you have been listening to gossip again,' murmured Rufus, watching appreciatively whilst Harry Lightfoot poured out the claret which had just been brought to them by a waiter.

'Is there no truth in it, then?' asked Harry, as he passed the glasses to his friends.

'Quite as much as there is in any tale that is going round London, I dare say,' remarked Wednesbury. 'Which reminds me, Rufus, are you still in pursuit of the Winchcomb chit?'

'Was I in pursuit?' asked Rufus in his blandest tone.

'Undoubtedly,' said Harry. 'Why, the rumours of your impending engagement have even given rise to an entry in the betting book.'

'And what is the nature of the bet?'

'That you'll be engaged to Prudence Winchcomb by the end of the season. Tell us straight: is it so?'

'And give you inside information? Gentlemen, you shock me,' Tyler returned. 'But come, what else has happened? I cannot be the only subject of discussion, surely?'

The conversation drifted on to other matters, but when eventually Tyler left his club, his mind went back to the rumours of his marriage, and to the recent conversation that he had had with his brother.

Tyler was the youngest of five children, his brother, Viscount Parry, being the eldest. There were ten years between the two brothers, the other three children all being girls who had been married for some years.

A message had reached Tyler that his father had been taken seriously ill, and this was why he had left London before the end of the season. On his arrival at Castle Clare, however, he had discovered that his father's condition had been greatly exaggerated, and after staying for a few days he had returned to town. But those few days had given him pause for thought. His father had always appeared to be very hale and hearty, but these events had reminded Tyler that the earl was not immortal. Because his brother was so much older than himself, and because he had been a little spoiled by his sisters, the possibility of his ever inheriting the title had always seemed remote in the extreme. Now, he realized that this was not so. Lord Parry had been married for sixteen years and he and his wife were happily content with a numerous family. This family consisted entirely of girls, however, and since Lady Parry had not now presented her husband with any pledge of her affection for some eight years, it seemed safe to assume that their family must be complete.

Whilst he had been staying at Castle Clare, Parry had questioned him almost too casually about the possibility of his marrying, and he had realized with a jolt that it was very likely that one day he would be the earl. This prospect did not attract him at all. He had inherited a snug estate in Berkshire from his godmother, together with a handsome fortune, and he had no desire to take on the many duties that would result from becoming the Earl of Clare.

One of these duties, of course, would be to marry. This did not attract him any more than becoming an earl. He was very fond of the company of women, both in and out of bed, but he had not yet found a female to whom he had wanted to link his life. As his father aged, and as the ton looked on and saw his brother producing only female children, match-making mamas, perceiving that he would be looking for a wife, began to parade their daughters in front of him again, and he had started to feel hunted.

In these circumstances, both Augusta Fossey and Prudence Winchcomb had proved to be very useful. Mrs Fossey, who had been left very comfortably off by her husband, had no more desire to marry than had he, and he therefore felt safe in pursuing her. Prudence Winchcomb, with whom he was already acquainted, was a sensible girl, not likely to be swept off her feet, or to fall in love with him simply because he had paid her a few compliments. Furthermore, he owed the family some attention because in the country they were neighbours.

There was no doubt, however, that he was now beginning to think of marriage as he never had done before, and he began to wonder idly whether Prudence would suit him. After all, she was intelligent and not ill-favoured, and she would certainly not be overawed at the idea of ruling over Castle Clare. As this point popped into his mind, he started to laugh out loud. Overawed! He would like to see it! Yes, Prudence was a splendid young woman, there was no doubt of that, but was she the girl for him?

★ ★ ★

After they had returned from their ride and put off their outdoor things, Elfrida and Prudence met together for a cup of tea, and Elfrida brought up the subject of Mr Tyler.

'I had thought that he was to remain at Castle Clare for the summer,' she observed. She wanted to find out whether Prudence would betray any kind of interest in the older man, but her niece showed by her reply that this was not the case.

'He never leaves before the end of the season, apparently,' Prudence answered carelessly. 'In any case, I doubt whether Mrs Fossey would permit him to do so.'

'Prudence!' Elfrida exclaimed.

'Well?' replied the other woman, returning Elfrida's shocked look with a bland expression. Then she smiled and went on, 'I do not see why I should pretend that I do not know about his mistress,' she said, shocking Elfrida even more. 'After all, everyone knows about her.'

Elfrida stared at her for a few moments. She was thinking of the cutting that she had kept out of the newspaper. 'Does your mama . . . ?' she began.

'Does Mama know about them? Oh yes, I should think so,' Prudence replied carelessly. 'It's all right, Aunt Elfrida, I know about Mama's plans to snare Mr Tyler for me, and they were never going to come to anything. Even if it hadn't been for . . . ' This time it was Prudence's turn to stop and colour.

'Even if it were not for Digby Collett?' Elfrida finished for her. 'Were you aware that he would approach us in the park today?'

'No, of course not,' answered Prudence a little too quickly. Then seeing that Elfrida was eyeing her suspiciously, she went on challengingly, 'Don't you believe me? I can assure you that I'm not in the habit of lying.' Then, in a moment of supreme daring, she added, 'You'll be saying that I was passing notes to him next.'

Elfrida eyed her in some dismay. It had, in fact been running through her mind to accuse Prudence of doing that very thing, but the effrontery of the girl's challenge completely threw her off balance, and she found herself asserting vigorously that the idea had never even occurred to her.

'I would never accuse you of lying either,' she assured her niece, keeping her voice as calm as she could.

Prudence stared at her for a moment, then said 'It's all right, Aunt Elfrida. You needn't pretend. I know that Mama has warned you about Digby. Well, it is of absolutely no avail. I have known him for years, so if she imagines that I am suddenly going to start ignoring him now, then she is very much mistaken. Furthermore, I have not agreed to marry him, in fact, I may never do so. When I *do* marry, though, it will be someone of my own choice, and not some old fogey, in order to satisfy my mother's machinations. And now, if you will excuse me, I have some letters to write.' Before Elfrida could make any response to this, the younger woman had left the room very much on her dignity.

After she had gone, her aunt got up to walk around the room, her expression one of consternation. No doubt those experienced in dealing with young people would say that she should not have allowed Prudence to speak to her in that way. Well, perhaps she should not have done, but, she reflected, it would be quite helpful if those experienced people could tell her how she could have prevented her from doing so. She was not a mother, nor had she had younger sisters to deal with. Her only experience of people of that age had been the visits that she had paid to those of her acquaintance in Grantham whose daughters were almost ready to come out. Without exception, these damsels had shown a demure front, speaking when spoken to, doing as their parents advised them and generally causing no difficulty whatsoever. Elfrida was beginning to realize that either these young women were the exception that proved the rule, or else they had simply been on their best behaviour in front of visitors, saving their tantrums and displays of wilfulness for private moments.

Clearly, she needed advice from a more experienced source, and she needed it quickly. On impulse, she scrawled a brief note to Rosemary Dunstone, and sent it round with a footman. A short time later, the footman returned with the information that Lady Dunstone was otherwise engaged, but would be glad to see Miss Frobisher on the following day. Elfrida bit her lip. What was she to do in the meantime? What would a mother do? Would she go upstairs and demand an abject apology and insist upon greater respect, or would she let this pass, and try to deal with matters in a more cunning way on the next occasion?

The question was answered for her when Prudence came downstairs looking very contrite. 'I have come to beg your pardon, Aunt Elfrida. I shouldn't have been so cross. But it seems rather strange — without Mama and Papa, you know.'

Elfrida's face softened. 'Yes, of course,' she replied. It had been foolish of her not to make allowances for the fact that Prudence was still just a young girl who had only recently been parted from her parents. She swallowed then went on, 'I am aware that I cannot replace your mama, nor do I wish to do so, but I hope that I might be a help to you in some way.' She thought of their conversation concerning Mr Tyler, and then, before she could consider whether such a disclosure might be wise, she said, 'You need not suppose that I would have any hand in compelling you to accept an offer that might be repulsive to you. Nor would your mama, you may be sure of that.'

Prudence darted a quick look at her. 'You may believe that, but I am convinced that Mama only thinks about worldly advance-ment for me.'

'No, no, that cannot be true,' Elfrida protested. 'She herself had several suitors and your papa was by no means the richest of them.'

'Well, perhaps she has forgotten what it was like to be young,' Prudence remarked. 'Certainly all she wants now is to marry me off to Rufus Tyler.'

'The old fogey?'

'Did I call him that?' Prudence asked grin-ning. 'Well perhaps that was a little unfair. But he is years and years older than me and I don't want to marry him in the least, and you have said that you won't let Mama make me.'

Elfrida stared at her in consternation. To decide in her own mind that she would not encourage her niece's marriage to a rake was one thing: to collude deliberately with Prudence against her mother's express wishes was quite another.

As she stared, Prudence's expression changed. 'You didn't really mean it at all, did you? You would be just as ready to force me into marriage with this ... this ageing libertine as she would!'

Elfrida's strong strain of common sense asserted itself. 'He can't be both an old fogey *and* an ageing libertine,' she declared.

At that most unfortunate moment, the butler came in. 'Mr Tyler is here, ma'am,' he said.

'Well, now you can make up your mind,' declared Prudence outrageously.

'Oh, good heavens,' exclaimed Elfrida, blushing furiously.

'Yes, here I am,' said Mr Tyler. 'Which of the two do you think I am, ma'am?'

7

He did not look like either. As he had driven past in the curricle, Elfrida had gained no very clear impression of his appearance. Now, she could see that he was of medium height, with a good pair of shoulders. His face was lean with a strong jaw and a rather prominent nose, and his hazel eyes glittered below black brows, whether with anger or amusement it was hard to tell. The lines on his face were not pronounced, but revealed that as Anthea had said, he was not a young man; Elfrida judged him to be about forty. The most startling feature about him was his hair, for it was a strong dark red and very plentiful. He was dressed fashionably but without affectation in a dark-blue coat with buckskin breeches and highly polished boots. As he waited for a reply, his eyebrows raised, Elfrida had a sudden quite inexplicable feeling that she had met him before.

'How do you do, sir,' she said, pulling herself together with some difficulty and going forward to greet him. 'I am Prudence's aunt.'

'So I surmised,' he answered, bowing over

her hand. 'Rufus Tyler at your service, ma'am.' He turned to Prudence. 'Miss Winchcomb, you look as if you are enjoying your customary good health.'

Prudence curtsied, looking quite unabashed at the effect of her outrageous remark. 'Thank you Mr Tyler, I am quite well. My aunt and I were just discussing the character of Antony — in Shakespeare's play, you know. I was telling her that as she is now in London, she might get the chance to see how he is portrayed for herself.'

'How erudite conversation can be in the homes of the ton,' he murmured. 'I had no idea. And what conclusion did you come to?' he asked Elfrida.

'I think I must wait until I have had a chance to see the play for myself,' she replied, full of admiration for Prudence's quick thinking. After offering him wine, which he refused, she invited him to be seated, and went on, 'I thought that you were now fixed in the country.'

'I was obliged to leave town for family reasons, but always intended to be here for the end of the season.' Here Prudence glanced at her aunt as if to say, I told you so. 'I am sorry to have missed Mr and Mrs Winchcomb,' he went on. 'I understand they only left today.'

'Yes, that is so,' agreed Elfrida, wondering whether he had hoped to make his declaration. She could see by the expression on Prudence's face that her niece was thinking the same thing.

'I am, however, glad to make your acquaintance, Miss Frobisher, and in her parents' absence must ask for your permission to take Miss Winchcomb driving tomorrow afternoon.'

Elfrida remembered Mrs Fossey and felt a sudden revulsion of feeling at allowing her niece to go driving with a man who currently had a mistress in such public keeping that all of society knew about it. But she knew what her sister would say, were she here, and despite Prudence's protests, she could not go against Anthea's expressed wishes. 'By all means, Mr Tyler,' she said, not daring to look at Prudence. 'You do not have any other engagements for tomorrow, do you?'

Prudence did not speak, but she smiled, a brief, humourless smile, which only the most optimistic of gentlemen could have taken as enthusiastic consent.

Evidently Mr Tyler was one of those gentlemen, for after only a few more sentences of conversation, he got up to leave. 'I shall do myself the honour of calling upon you tomorrow at three,' he said to Prudence.

No sooner had the door closed upon him than Prudence rounded upon her aunt. 'Thank you very much indeed,' she said bitterly. 'Whose side are you on?'

'I'm not on any side,' Elfrida protested in exasperated tones. 'Remember that I am new to all this. I know that Mr Tyler is not your favourite person in the world, and from what you have told me about him, he is not mine either, but I cannot think of any reason why you should not go driving with him tomorrow.' She paused, then a sudden thought made her say craftily, 'After all he is clearly very fashionable: it cannot do you any harm to be seen with him, surely.'

Prudence's expression relaxed. 'Yes, of course you are right,' she said. 'And now, I've lost my temper with you again, and I didn't mean to.' To Elfrida's surprise, her niece came over to her and embraced her. She had not done such a thing before. The younger woman was taller than her by a head, and more generously built; oddly enough, it felt for a moment as if Elfrida were the younger one. 'I keep forgetting, all this is strange to you,' she went on, confirming that impression, and for a moment, this unexpected kindness felt more unsettling than all the rest.

* * *

Now that Prudence's afternoon had been arranged, Elfrida decided that she would use that opportunity to consult with Rosemary Dunstone. Her friend had managed to achieve a match for her daughter with one of the well-connected and influential Wednesburys. She should surely be able to give advice on some of the pitfalls to be avoided. And after all, Elfrida reflected, with only about a week of the season to go, how many pitfalls could there possibly be?

'Oh my dear, you would be surprised,' her friend answered frankly, when she voiced this same sentiment. 'A headstrong young woman can find pitfalls anywhere, believe you me. And Prudence Winchcomb, I would venture to guess, can be exceedingly headstrong.'

Elfrida sighed. 'I am afraid that she might be,' she agreed. 'There is nothing that I can precisely put my finger on, but I simply have the feeling that if I say or do the wrong thing, then she will be completely out of control and then how will I explain myself to Anthea?'

Rosemary looked at her through narrowed eyes, then said carefully, 'Don't you think that you might be getting this just a teeny bit out of proportion?'

'I know that I am over-reacting,' Elfrida

answered. 'But the fact of the matter is that Prudence is not my child and I don't feel that I know her very well. The last thing that I want to do at the moment is upset Anthea, for she might then feel obliged to come rushing back to London, and then I should have Clive Winchcomb to deal with.'

Again, Rosemary was quiet, a curious smile on her face. 'Strange that you should say that,' she remarked. 'Many people dismiss him as an idle park saunterer, but Dunstone acted as his second once when he fought a duel, years ago. I still remember Harold telling me that Winchcomb held his pistol in such a slack grip that he looked as if he were about to drop it out of sheer exhaustion, but for all that he winged his man quite neatly. More tea?'

Elfrida accepted gratefully. 'So if we have established that Anthea must not be distressed, and that Prudence is strongminded and likely to have her own way, what can I do to make sure that she does not destroy all my sister's plans for her?'

'What were the things that she was firm about?' Rosemary asked her.

'That I must accept any offer that Rufus Tyler might make — '

'Which he has not done — but you have made sure that she has gone driving with him which is as much as you can do on that score. Go on.'

'And that I must discourage every man in a scarlet coat, but most particularly that I must keep her away from Digby Collett.'

Rosemary stirred her tea thoughtfully. 'You cannot possibly keep every man in a scarlet coat away from her,' she said. 'As a matter of fact, I would have thought that to have a few more around might be a very good thing. Although young Collett is a pleasant enough fellow, he doesn't cut nearly so much of a dash as a good many others I could mention. Take Tyler himself, now.'

'He isn't in a scarlet coat,' protested Elfrida.

'No, but he used to be,' Rosemary replied. 'Before he came into money and an estate from his godmother, he was just another penniless redcoat, and my dear, he was gorgeous! But you see, that proves my case. There's many a soldier living only on his pay who nevertheless has excellent prospects. No, my instinct, if I were you, would be to make sure that Digby Collett kept away from her, and never mind the rest; if there are a good many of them, well, all the better. There's safety in numbers, I say.'

'So you think that I have been worrying unnecessarily?' suggested Elfrida.

'I think so, but then, worrying is one of the inevitable elements of parenthood. To Prudence you do stand in the place of a mother, at least for the time being.' Rosemary looked at her friend curiously. 'It is still not too late, you know — should there be anyone in your eye.'

Elfrida hesitated briefly, then found herself telling Rosemary about the Revd Stanley Erskine. It was the first time that she had spoken to anyone about her clerical suitor, and she suddenly realized that she lacked a really close friend in whom she could confide concerning things of this nature. She had enjoyed the company of Miss Filey; her death had left her alone, and she had accepted her solitude as a matter of course. It was only since coming to London this time that it had occurred to her that she might be not just very much alone but also lonely.

'He sounds charming,' said Rosemary, after Elfrida had finished speaking. 'Why do you hesitate?'

Elfrida paused. 'I do not think I could have told you before I left Fernleigh,' she confessed. 'But it has now occurred to me that perhaps I have been lonely, and Mr Erskine provided sympathetic company.'

Rosemary shrugged. 'There are worse reasons for marrying a man,' she remarked.

'There isn't anyone you like better, is there?'

'No,' agreed Elfrida thoughtfully. 'But . . . '

'But?'

'He isn't very exciting,' Elfrida blurted out, feeling very disloyal.

'My dear, men are only exciting when they don't belong to you,' Rosemary replied cynically. Seeing Elfrida looking shocked, she went on, 'Please don't misunderstand me. Of course I love Dunstone, you know I do. Believe me, there was a time when I found him very exciting indeed. But one cannot live on excitement for ever. It has to mellow into something more lasting. But if you don't find your clerical suitor exciting now, before you've caught him, well . . . ' Her voice tailed off.

'What do I do, then?' Elfrida asked her.

'You may find that when you see him again, after a short absence, you will be convinced one way or the other,' suggested Rosemary. 'You say that he is going to meet you at Grantham when you return home. Why not write informing him of when you are to leave London, and invite him to escort you to your sister's home and then stay for a few days? Your sister would, I know, be delighted to meet him — I presume she hasn't met him yet? — and there, amongst your own family, you might be able to get a better idea of whether he really is the man for you.'

Elfrida smiled. 'That sounds like an excellent scheme. Then if I decide I don't like him after all, I can always persuade my brother-in-law to challenge him to a duel.'

She left Lady Dunstone's house in a much more settled frame of mind. She told herself that the unfamiliarity of her chaperon's role had allowed her to become too anxious about Prudence. Needless to say, she would have to be alert about the girl's involvement with Digby Collett; it would, though, be quite absurd to suspect every man in London. She must try to stand back and take a more detached view.

She set off to walk back down Albemarle Street, intending to go back to Brook Street by way of New Bond Street. She had hardly taken more than a dozen steps, however, when a carriage pulled up beside her, and she found herself looking up at Mr Tyler. His groom went to take the horses' heads, and he himself sprang down and inclined his head politely.

Acknowledging his courtesy, she said, 'Your drive with my niece is finished then.'

'As you say; so, you see, I am at liberty to drive you home.'

'There is no need,' she replied. 'You forget

that I am a countrywoman, and therefore used to walking.'

'No doubt, but not along such busy streets as these. Give me the pleasure of your company, I pray.' He looked around and before she could answer, said, 'Where is your maid?'

'I did not bring one,' she replied calmly.

'Your footman — or your friends, then.'

'I am unaccompanied.'

His brows drew together. 'In that case, ma'am, you have no choice: I must insist that you accept my escort.'

'I repeat, there is no need,' she said, a touch of indignation in her voice. 'No doubt if I were a young girl of Prudence's age — '

'If you were a young girl of Prudence's age, such folly might be excusable,' he interrupted. 'Someone of your years ought to know better. Were you never told that you should not walk about London on your own?'

'Well, of course I was,' she answered indignantly. 'But that was fifteen years ago.'

'The same thing applies,' he answered. 'Your reputation will be just as much at risk as it was then. Now get up into my curricle before I throw you into it.'

She opened her mouth to protest, but as she did so, he took a step closer to her and she saw that he meant exactly what he said.

'Thank you,' she said instead, through gritted teeth. 'Your gallantry is much appreciated.'

He handed her up with a chuckle, then got up himself. 'I'm not just throwing my weight about, you know, so you don't need to look as if you would like to hit me,' he remarked as the horses began to move off. 'Your sister, were she here, would tell you the same. Walking alone in London isn't the same as walking alone in the country.'

His mention of Anthea gave her pause. She had supposed that she could easily ignore this small regulation because of her age, but she must not do anything to endanger Prudence's reputation. It would be ironic indeed if whilst in London to keep an eye on Prudence, she were to commit some solecism herself.

'You are very right,' she said eventually. 'I had forgotten how circumspect one must be in the town.'

'Well that's taken the wind out of my sails,' he remarked. 'I'll have to abandon all attempts to give you a thorough reprimand now, won't I?' She laughed. He glanced at her briefly, his eyes narrowed. 'I can't rid myself of the notion that we've met before. Where could it have been?'

'I can't imagine,' she replied. She had been conscious of the same sensation, but she

113

didn't say so. 'Perhaps during my first season in London?'

'Possibly. You aren't at all like your sister, are you?'

'No, I'm the other Miss Frobisher,' she replied.

'The other Miss Frobisher? Explain.'

'It's just that Anthea was always the pretty one who attracted attention, whilst I was in the background. More than once, I overheard myself referred to as 'the other Miss Frobisher'. It is how I have thought of myself ever since.'

'Mistakenly, as it happens,' he replied, unerringly steering his curricle through a gap that most people would have thought was not wide enough.

'I beg your pardon?' she asked him, not sure that she had heard him correctly.

'Your notion is a mistaken one,' he explained calmly. 'Your sister must have been married for at least eighteen years. It follows, therefore, that for that length of time you have been 'the only Miss Frobisher'. Indeed, you might more appropriately be called 'the unique Miss Frobisher'.'

'Good heavens,' Elfrida replied. 'That is something that I had never considered.'

'Then I am glad that I have prompted you to do so. Far too many people live their lives under the judgement someone made of them years ago. It's quite absurd, in my opinion. And here we are at your door.'

'Thank you,' she said to him as he handed her down. Really, that hair of his was an extraordinary shade of red.

'We *have* met before,' he said thoughtfully. 'Before long I shall remember where and when.'

'I don't think we can have done,' she said shaking her head. 'I would have remembered your hair.'

He laughed. 'Your servant, Miss Frobisher,' he said. He watched her as she walked to the door. She was a dainty little thing, he decided, and her figure was excellent. Her manner displayed an intriguing blend of maturity and innocence. No doubt that was due to her prolonged sojourn in the country. Before she entered the house, she turned and smiled at him. In any other woman, he would have put down such a glance to flirtatiousness. Briefly he wondered what it would be like to kiss those smiling lips, then deliberately he adjusted his grip on the reins and drove away.

It was only as Elfrida was closing the door that she gave any thought to Mrs Fossey. No doubt Mr Tyler's mistress was used to his squiring debutantes about during the season, but a lady of her age? Heaven forbid that Mrs Fossey should suppose that she was seeking to supplant her! This was such a shocking thought that she hurried inside as quickly as she could, determined to find something useful to do.

★ ★ ★

After setting Miss Frobisher down outside her front door, Mr Tyler turned his curricle round and made his way directly back to New Bond Street. In truth, that had been his destination all along. 'Make yer mind up, guv,' muttered Jerry Alban, his groom, a man of his own age with whom he had climbed trees, fished streams and swum in the lake at Castle Clare thirty years before.

'Stow it,' replied Tyler amiably. 'There was a lady in the case.'

'Ain't there always?' Alban replied.

On arrival back in Bond Street, they drew up outside Gentleman Jackson's Boxing Saloon at number 13 and Tyler sprang down, handing the reins to Alban. 'Take this round to the stables. I'll walk home.'

'Right you are, guv.'

Once inside, Rufus was greeted by a number of men, some of them preparing to leave, having taken exercise, whilst others, like himself, were hoping for a bout or two.

'Well met, Tyler,' exclaimed Dunstone. 'Are you coming or going?'

'Just arrived,' Tyler answered him, nodding a greeting to another man who clapped him on the shoulder in passing. 'And you?' He did not really need to ask, for Lord Dunstone was looking flushed from his exercise.

'On my way, covered with shame,' replied his lordship ruefully. 'I must come here more — or less!'

Tyler laughed, and walked on into the inner room, where several pairs of gentlemen were sparring, guided by some of Jackson's assistants. Others were standing around the outside, watching. Only the favoured few, of course, would receive Jackson's personal attention, and in the past Tyler had been one of those. Just now, the former champion was sharing his expertise with a man whom Tyler thought he recognized. He watched more carefully until, his impression confirmed, he stood observing the bout, before permitting one of the attendants to help him off with his coat, waistcoat and shirt. As he came back into the sparring room again, Jackson's favoured pupil was just leaving the floor, but when he saw Tyler, he stood still, observing his approach. He was much the same height and build as Tyler, but with fair hair, and scars on his shoulder and chest that proclaimed the soldier.

'Worn out already?' Tyler asked provocatively.

'Damned if I am,' replied the other, pulling his gloves back on.

'Now, gentlemen, you know the rules,' said Gentleman Jackson, 'and you abide by them — if you want to come again.'

'Of course I know them,' answered Tyler, never taking his eyes off the fair man's face. 'The question is, does this damned redcoat?'

'Put 'em up,' responded the fair-haired man. 'Just put 'em up — fribble.'

If those who were watching had been hoping for the two men to throw themselves at one another in a frenzy then they were to be disappointed. If, however, they were hoping for a display of good science, then they were to have a treat. Both men had been coached in this very boxing school over several years, and took time, carefully circling one another in order to gain the other man's measure. The fair-haired man was the first to make a move, jabbing with his left hand, a blow which Tyler dodged, moving out of reach before popping in a hit of his own over the other man's guard.

'Fluke!' said his opponent, moving in again, and retaliating with a blow of his own.

They continued to spar for a little while longer, before Jackson stopped them.

'That's enough, gentlemen,' he said, smiling. 'You're just as equal as ever you were.'

The two men stopped, both breathing hard from their exercise. Rufus grinned, stripping off his gloves then putting out his hand. 'So we are,' he replied. 'My God, it's good to see you back, Douglas.'

For reply, his opponent grasped the hand held out to him, and returned Tyler's grin with an engaging one of his own. 'It's good to be here,' he said. 'Come, let's get dressed and repair to White's, then you can tell me all the news.'

A short time later, the two men left Jackson's, Tyler once more immaculate in his dark-blue coat, his companion looking impressive in the uniform of a major of dragoon guards. 'When did you get back?' Tyler asked, as they walked.

'Just a few days ago,' the major replied. 'Just my luck! I would have been back before, but Nosey found other things for me to do.'

'Serve you right for catching his eye,' Tyler retorted unsympathetically, identifying Wellington without difficulty.

'You're only jealous,' the other man retorted. Then, seeing the look in Tyler's eyes, he added in quick sympathy, 'I'm sorry. I know you'd have liked to have been in on it.'

'Wouldn't I just?' Tyler replied feelingly. 'But what with the land I inherited, and the concerns about my father's health, I didn't feel that I could leave.'

'Never mind, I can bore you all evening with stories of soldiering,' replied the major.

'You can try,' Tyler answered, inclining his head to an acquaintance who passed him in the street.

'Or, alternatively, you can tell me about the young lady you're going to marry — unless, of course, rumour lies.'

Tyler directed a sharp look at his companion. 'Where had you this?' he asked.

'A paragraph in the paper — and a conversation I overheard between a couple of tabbies at a dinner I was obliged to go to. It does lie, then?'

'Most assuredly,' Tyler agreed.

'And there was I, hoping to stand up with you at the church,' complained the major. 'I look so splendid in my full regimentals, as well.'

'It's my belief that that's half the reason you joined the army in the first place,' Tyler replied. 'You always did enjoy dressing up.'

'So did you,' the major retorted. 'Do you remember when we both took a fancy to be macaronis? Lord, what a dust we caused!'

'We certainly did,' Tyler agreed. 'I thought my father would burst a blood vessel when he first saw me.'

The major laughed. 'Thank God we realized how absurd we looked before we really made fools of ourselves.'

'Yes, thank God,' Tyler agreed, his voice fading away as he struggled to get hold of a memory that was slipping just out of reach. Then they were walking up the steps of White's and, as other acquaintances hurried to greet Major Douglas Fletcher, the moment was lost.

★   ★   ★

Before going upstairs after Tyler had left her at the front door in Brook Street, Elfrida wandered into the saloon and found Prudence in there standing by the window, reading what appeared to be a note. Knowing her duty, she walked over to her niece, saying, 'What is that?'

'Just a list of things for me to do before we go into the country,' replied Prudence a little too quickly, as she screwed up the paper that she was holding. Elfrida looked at her doubtfully. What would Anthea do at this point? Would she insist upon reading it? As if knowing her thoughts, Prudence smiled rather contemptuously. 'Would you like to make sure that I am telling the truth?' she asked. 'I'll straighten it out for you, if you like.' So saying, she began to smooth out the tight ball of paper.

'There is no need,' answered Elfrida with dignity, her colour a little higher. 'I was only going to say that perhaps it would be a good idea to make such a list together.'

'Then I will throw this one away and we can start again,' returned Prudence. She walked to the door. 'I'm going to lie down now, to make sure I'm not tired for the evening,' she said. 'I suggest you do the same.' She smiled again at Elfrida, then threw the ball of paper up into the air, caught it, and left the room.

Swallowing an urge to follow the girl and tell her that she knew perfectly well what she needed to do to prepare herself for an evening's entertainment, thank you very much, Elfrida stood looking at the closed door, wondering what had really been written on the piece of paper that Prudence had screwed up. Was she being too suspicious, and had it been exactly what Prudence had said? Or was it, as she suspected, a note from Digby Collett? She sighed with relief at the idea that soon they would be returning to the country, and she would be able to put the worry about young Collett behind her, together with the responsibility for Prudence. Let her indolent father deal with her!

She looked at the clock. Prudence was right, in that she ought to go upstairs soon for a rest. But before she did so, she decided to write to Mr Erskine as Rosemary had suggested. Her conversation with her friend had been good for her, she decided. Then, as she sat down and began to prepare a pen for use, she realized that the talk that she had had with Mr Tyler had done her good as well. It had made her think about herself in a more positive way, as if she were not simply a shadowy version of her sister, one who had never quite succeeded, but a person in her own right whose tastes and interests were equally as valid. Straightening her shoulders, she set a piece of paper before her and took up her pen.

Upstairs, Prudence straightened the piece of paper and frowned down at the message it contained.

Dear Pru
  Why the deuce do you have to embroil me in your schemes? You know I'm no hand at them. I'll be at the ball, right

enough, and I'll do what I can, but I'll be thankful when this is all over.

Digby

Poor Digby, she thought to herself. She could almost find it in her heart to feel sorry for him, were her own situation not quite so urgent. But now was not the time for her to weaken. Her mama had made it quite plain that she would not countenance her daughter marrying a man in Daniel's situation, and now Daniel, in the most irritatingly gallant way, had decided to give her up, without even consulting her to discover whether she was prepared to be given up or not.

Prudence's chief anxiety was that Daniel would leave England before she had a chance to join him, and in order to prevent that undesirable contingency, she determined to get away from London as soon as possible. The best way that she could think of doing this was to create such a scandal that Aunt Elfrida would be obliged to take her away. Daniel was far too honourable to resort to unscrupulous methods, but thankfully she, Prudence, was not hampered by such concerns. It was a good thing that Aunt Elfrida had not insisted on reading the letter.

124

The true extent to which she and everyone else had been fooled would then have been revealed, and that would never do — especially when the time of the most daring plan of all was fast approaching.

8

During the few days which passed before the final ball that they were to attend, Prudence's mood of defiance seemed to dissipate. She even apologized for screwing up the note and making it difficult for Elfrida to ask to see it without looking unpardonably intrusive. Elfrida, having written her letter to Mr Erskine, was in a mood to be gracious, and she made nothing of it.

They rode in the park on several occasions, and often met with Captain Graves and Lieutenant Collett. At no other time apart from that one occasion did Elfrida ever observe Digby attempting to pass notes to Prudence or to have secret conversations with her. To give Prudence credit, she gave no sign that she was anything other than perfectly satisfied to ride in company with the whole group.

They often encountered Mr Tyler as well. He did not appear again in the company with Mrs Fossey, but was frequently on horseback, mounted on a thoroughbred chestnut, whose pedigree was clearly the envy of the military gentlemen. 'You were in the army yourself at one time, I believe,' Elfrida said to him on one occasion.

He inclined his head. 'That is so,' he agreed. 'It's often the fate of younger sons. In my case, however, there were other reasons.' He paused. 'You don't ask me what they were.'

'No doubt you will tell me if you think I should know,' Elfrida replied.

'To be honest, I made rather a fool of myself, and wanted to get right away,' he confessed. 'The army suited me very well; in fact I rather enjoyed it.'

'You don't wish you were one of them now?' Elfrida asked, watching the young people. On this occasion, they had also been joined by Miss Clyde, a friend of Prudence, and the two young ladies and two military gentlemen were conversing happily together.

He grinned ruefully. 'Other responsibilities meant that I could not join up again as I would have liked,' he said. 'Of course, there are advantages to being in uniform. There's no denying that there's something about a scarlet coat — to attract the ladies, you know.'

'Oh, I know,' she sighed, forgetting for a moment to whom she was speaking. 'It's enough to make the most unprepossessing man look dashing.'

'I'm obliged to you, ma'am,' he answered politely.

'I beg your pardon,' she exclaimed, colouring. 'That is not at all what I meant. I was thinking of their effect upon young girls, and especially upon Prudence. But I suppose there's safety in numbers.'

'I dare say you're right, ma'am,' he replied. It was only later that she recalled he was supposed to be a pretender to Prudence's hand. Thinking carefully over the matter, however, she decided that anyone would have been forgiven for not realizing this. True, he was a regular if not frequent visitor. He always made a point of approaching them at social functions, and usually danced with Prudence, but his approach towards the younger woman always held something of the avuncular, and he appeared to tease rather than to flatter. She wrote a letter to her sister, telling her that Mr Tyler was proving to be quite attentive, but she did not send it without a pang of guilt. She was well aware that she would be giving rise to hopes which she could not see being fulfilled.

Mr Erskine wrote in response to her letter to him, a courteous reply which could not conceal how pleased he was that she was to return. He declared himself delighted to accept her invitation to visit the family home. He was due for a holiday, and would put everything in place so that his curate would be able to manage without him. He was hers, etc.

Dear Stanley, she thought to herself. How lovely it would be to be safely at home without all this worry! Then she felt herself wanting to giggle at the very idea of addressing him as Stanley.

She was very thankful when the evening of the final ball of the season came round. Of course, it was not really the final ball; events of one kind or another would continue for the entertainment of those who chose to remain in London. But for those who were of the first consequence, London must be left behind in July, and seaside places and country estates must be repaired to. This struck Elfrida as being very amusing. For once in her life, she would actually be doing the fashionable thing.

The housemaid who had been assigned the task of helping her dress, put forward her best efforts, and soon she was examining her reflection with quite understandable satisfaction. The gown that she was wearing that evening was grey, and yet it was not of a shade of grey that Elfrida had ever seen before. Mme Lisette had encouraged her to choose a fabric which shimmered in the light, revealing a hint of violet. The daylight had not really done it justice; by candlelight, the movement of the gown made any observer want to stand and watch to try to discover what colour it really was. She found herself wondering what the rector would think of it, but then reflected that as the wife of a country priest, she would have very little opportunity to wear such gowns.

Prudence, who came in just as Daisy was brushing Elfrida's hair, pronounced herself to be very pleased with the result. She herself was completely ready, apart from putting on her gown. 'I didn't want to get bits of hair on it,' she explained, 'and I do want to help you with your hair tonight.' She pushed up the sleeves of her dressing-gown. 'Now let us see what we can do.'

She worked quickly and in no time had coaxed Elfrida's light-brown hair into a mass of curls on the top of her head.

'You are a marvel, my dear,' Elfrida exclaimed when her niece had finished. 'No one else has ever made it look quite as well.'

'The secret is to allow it to do what it wants to do anyway,' Prudence replied. 'Then it will co-operate with you.' Their eyes met in the mirror and Elfrida was struck by the suspicion that Prudence was talking about more than hair. 'Why don't you wait for me downstairs?' the younger woman went on. 'I will join you as soon as I am ready.'

Elfrida readily agreed, and although Prudence had not as yet put on her gown, she must have had everything in readiness in her room, for in a surprisingly short space of time she had joined her aunt at the foot of the stairs, a light cloak around her shoulders. 'We shall be the belles of the ball,' she said gaily. Elfrida smiled. Prudence was proving to be quite charming after all. Now that the end of the season was well and truly in sight, she could feel all her worries beginning to melt away. True, Mr Tyler had not proposed and as far as she could see was not likely to, but all major pitfalls had been avoided, redcoats kept at arm's length, and Prudence's reputation preserved intact ready for the next season. Really, she could not see that any diligent aunt could have done more, given her woeful lack of experience with young people.

The journey itself to Lord and Lady Bayley's house did not take long, situated as it was in Berkeley Square. By far the greatest part of the journey was spent in waiting for other carriages to set down their passengers so that they could alight outside the door.

'I do declare, this is the most tiresome part of going out,' said Prudence wearily.

'Yes, I well remember during my own season, it was exactly the same,' replied Elfrida. 'Will they ever discover a swift and easy way of setting people down, do you think?'

Prudence looked a little surprised then said, 'Oh yes, of course, you had a London season, didn't you?'

'Not a very successful one, I'm afraid,' Elfrida admitted ruefully.

'Perhaps you weren't wearing the right sort of clothes,' suggested Prudence.

Elfrida agreed that there might be something in that, but privately reflected that her shyness and lack of self-esteem might have been more to blame. It was only since she had come to realize that most people were far more concerned with the impression that they themselves were making than with what others might be doing, that she had become more comfortable on social occasions. And the knowledge that she was an independent woman, no longer on the catch for a husband, gave her an ease of manner that she had previously lacked.

Of course she did not need to look for a husband; there was one ready and waiting at home. It was of Stanley that she was thinking as she got down from the chaise. What would it be like, she wondered, to be the mother of Stanley's daughter, bringing her to an occasion such as this? She looked at Prudence, still half caught up in her fantasy;

then her dreams, together with all her newly found assurance disappeared as Prudence took off her cloak and Elfrida had her first clear view of the gown that her niece had chosen to wear that evening.

To begin with, it was of a rather stronger shade of pink than would have been considered appropriate for a young girl in her first season. In addition, the neckline, though flattering to its wearer's generous bosom, was certainly cut far too low for a single lady of eighteen, and clung far too closely to her form. Furthermore, the diamonds clasped around her neck were much too ostentatious for a girl of her years. All of this would have been bad enough, but what was worse, to Elfrida's way of thinking, was the look of smug triumph on the girl's face. She had succeeded in bamboozling her aunt completely, and Elfrida knew that there was nothing that she could do about it. A parent would insist that she should go home and change. But a sensible parent, she decided angrily, would certainly have insisted on inspecting what lay beneath Prudence's cloak before they had left the house.

To her disgust, she found herself murmuring in ineffectual tones, 'I was just wondering; that gown, my dear . . . '

'This one?' questioned Prudence as if

several gowns were the subject for discussion.

'Is it not a little . . . well . . . '

'Well?' Prudence echoed.

'Pink?' finished Elfrida rather lamely.

'Yes, perhaps, but then I adore pink,' laughed Prudence, starting off up the stairs.

'But . . . but surely you have a shawl,' Elfrida protested, following her and feeling very weak and feeble.

'Where?' asked Prudence, with an expansive gesture. Elfrida looked at her then looked away again. There was certainly nowhere on Prudence's person that a shawl might be hidden. 'Anyway,' Prudence went on, 'Mama herself chose it, and I thought I would wear it — in her honour, you know.'

'Your mama chose it?' Elfrida echoed doubtfully.

'Herself,' Prudence confirmed, her head held high. In other circumstances, had she been a man, it would have been possible to imagine her adding haughtily, 'Do you doubt my word?'

'But not for such an occasion as this,' Elfrida insisted.

'For just such an occasion,' answered Prudence, but her eyes flickered away from her aunt's and back again in a highly suspicious manner. Suddenly, Elfrida recalled that Anthea and her daughter were much the same size as one another, although Prudence was taller. Glancing down, she saw that the gown was finished with quite a deep frill.

'Yes, but for a different wearer,' countered Elfrida swiftly. 'That gown is one of your mama's is it not?'

Prudence's eyes widened. 'You're quicker than I thought,' she said admiringly. 'But it's too late to go back now, and besides, everyone has seen me.'

Nearly all of you, Elfrida said to herself, but reluctantly she was forced to acknowledge that Prudence was right. She had been a fool not to check the girl's apparel before they left the house. Now, thanks to her lack of foresight, her niece looked like a light skirt and would, no doubt, attract attention from the very worst type of man.

Feeling rather like a mouse called upon to watch over a playful and unpredictable cat, Elfrida followed her niece up the stairs to where Lord and Lady Bayley were standing, ready to receive their guests. Elfrida could see their eyes widen, her ladyship's in disapproval, her husband's for quite another reason.

'Miss Winchcomb,' she exclaimed, holding herself very erect and looking down her rather long thin nose. 'How delightful to see you.' Her tone implied the opposite.

'Ha, ha ha!' exclaimed his lordship. 'Hrmph! Jolly nice! Very welcome!' His normally florid complexion seemed, if anything, a little redder than usual.

Prudence curtsied prettily. At least her company manners were all that they should be, Elfrida reflected desperately.

'Thank you,' Prudence replied, her demure tone completely at variance with her gown. 'I am happy to be here and more than happy to be able to present to you my aunt, Miss Frobisher.'

'How do you do,' said Lady Bayley, her frosty expression thawing infinitesimally as she took in the understated elegance of Elfrida's gown. 'Mrs Winchcomb has arrived safely in the country, I trust?'

'Yes, we have had a letter from her,' replied Prudence.

'And you are chaperoning your niece, Miss Frobisher?' asked her ladyship.

'That is correct,' agreed Elfrida.

'I thought so,' remarked Lady Bayley, with a very measuring look.

The two ladies moved on and entered the principal rooms, which were already crowded. They were confronted by a mass of colour, movement and noise, and despite all her anxiety Elfrida felt her spirits lift.

'Aunt Elfrida, may I go and talk with Penny

and Christine Staples?' Prudence asked prettily.

Elfrida gave her assent and watched her niece as she began chattering with two young ladies dressed demurely in white muslin — as *she* should be, her conscience told her guiltily. Turning away, she walked to where some of the chaperons were sitting. There was nothing she could do about it now, she told herself, so there was no point in worrying about it.

Unfortunately, no sooner had she sat down than she became conscious of a conversation taking place between two ladies seated just behind her right shoulder.

'Good gracious, have you seen what the Winchcomb chit is wearing?' one of them was saying.

'It makes her look like an actress,' the other one replied. 'What can her mother be thinking of?'

'Her mother's out of town,' answered the first. 'Some aunt has the responsibility of her, I gather.'

'Well she ain't exercising it. How could she possibly allow the girl to come out like that? I'm glad she's no child of mine.'

'No indeed, your Marianne is undoubtedly in looks tonight. Is that young Higgins that she's talking to just now?'

Thankfully, the conversation drifted on to other topics, but Elfrida, her face aflame, could no longer be happy sitting there. She had done very wrong in allowing a situation to develop in which Prudence could appear dressed like this. She would take her home immediately, no matter what she said. She should have had enough resolve to do so as soon as she had seen the shocking neckline of that gown. But no sooner had she come to this decision than the Bayleys entered the room having left their post at the head of the stairs. The music struck up for the first dance and Prudence returned briefly to her side. She opened her mouth to announce her decision, but almost immediately a fair young man, whom Prudence introduced as Mr Grigson, came to solicit her hand for the first dance.

Elfrida's courage failed her. She nodded a feeble acquiescence, and as Prudence turned away, she was certain that the younger woman directed a look of triumph at her. Helpless to do anything, at least for the time being, Elfrida looked for a seat that was not anywhere near the two ladies whom she had heard discussing her niece. To her great delight, she saw Rosemary Dunstone sitting next to an empty chair and she went over to greet her friend.

'Good evening,' she said, as cheerfully as she could. 'Have you brought Julia with you this evening?'

'Yes, there she is, dancing with her fiancé — in white, with blue ribbons.'

'She looks lovely,' Elfrida replied honestly.

'She's a dear girl,' Rosemary declared. 'The same even, steady nature as her father, and very ready to be guided; which is a relief, I must say, when one sees how some girls have been allowed to trick themselves out. Look at the young woman over there, for example,' she went on, indicating Prudence with her fan. 'Whatever can her chaperon have been thinking of? She looks just like — ' She paused. 'Oh dear.'

'Is it so very bad?' Elfrida ventured. Rosemary looked at her without speaking, and Elfrida heaved a deep sigh. 'Rosemary, she came downstairs with her cloak on, and I had no idea what she had on under it until we were here and by then, it was too late.'

'If Julia played a trick like that I'd march her home faster than her feet could touch the ground,' Lady Dunstone said frankly. 'But then, I'm her stepmother, and furthermore, I know that her father would support me completely.'

'Being an aunt doesn't carry the same authority,' answered Elfrida wistfully. 'I was rather hoping that once the rooms filled up, there would be so many people here that no one would notice.'

Rosemary shook her head. 'People will always notice, especially if it's to one's detriment.' She put a hand on her friend's arm. 'I know Connie Bayley quite well, and she's more understanding than she looks. Would you like me to explain matters to her and see what she can do? She could loan Prudence a shawl, perhaps. That would at least help when she is not dancing.'

'Oh, thank you,' answered Elfrida gratefully. At that moment, the dance came to an end, and Prudence and Julia returned to their chaperons on the arms of their partners. Elfrida was pleased to be introduced to Julia's fiancé, Mr Wednesbury, a willowy young man with a cheerful face and pleasant, open manners. Why could not Prudence have accepted someone like that, she wondered? Then she would not have had to come to London at all.

Captain Graves approached at that point, politely greeted the company and claimed his dance with Prudence. He was accompanied by Digby Collett, who asked Miss Dunstone if he might have the pleasure etc. Julia cheerfully accepted and the couples went off to take to the floor, whilst Rosemary disappeared in search of Lady Bayley. Lieutenant Collett glanced at the other couple rather doubtfully, and Elfrida wondered whether he was resentful of the fact that Prudence was dancing with someone else. If so, then that must surely be a good thing. Even if the season did not end with Prudence's engagement to Mr Tyler, if would be very satisfying to inform Anthea that the romance with Digby Collett was over.

As if her thoughts had conjured him up, Mr Tyler suddenly appeared at her side. He was dressed immaculately in black evening clothes, the severity of his attire contrasting pleasingly with the flamboyant nature of the garments that some of the men present were wearing. He smiled as he bowed over her hand, then having murmured polite words of greeting he turned to look at the dancers. 'Good Lord,' he breathed. 'She's almost wearing that.'

It was too much. Had he been the first person who had made any comment on Prudence's attire, then she might have let it pass, but she was still feeling rather raw.

'How dare you!' she exclaimed, colouring.

'How dare I?' he replied, his brows soaring. 'I would not have thought that I was the one being daring in this instance.'

'No, but you are gloating,' Elfrida retorted.

'Gloating?' he responded, frankly puzzled.

'Gloating *and* slavering,' she insisted. 'Prudence might be dressed unsuitably, but she would never do such a thing if she did not have the encouragement of men-about-town such as yourself.'

'Now that really is most unfair,' he said roundly. 'I would very much like to know when I have ever encouraged Miss Winchcomb to dress in a revealing manner. In fact,' he went on, 'there is one person here who was surely in the perfect position to influence what she put on this evening, but did not choose to do so.' Suddenly reminded of her failure in doing her duty, Elfrida found herself without a response to this, and she simply stared at him helplessly. 'I shouldn't worry too much,' he added in a kinder tone. 'The season is nearly over, after all, and by the time the next one begins, some other bit of scandal will have taken over from what is, after all, a very minor misdemeanour.'

His dismissive tone did more to reassure her than anything that had been said so far. 'Do you really think so?' she asked him anxiously.

'Oh, certainly,' he answered carelessly. 'And as for gloating or slavering, let me tell you that I am one of those men who finds that the presence of a little more wrapping makes the appearance of a parcel far more tempting. Speaking of which, you look charming yourself this evening, ma'am.'

Elfrida pulled herself upright. 'Are you daring to compare me to a parcel?' she uttered.

'A very tempting one,' he replied, with a slight bow. 'Will you dance with me?'

The sudden change of subject took her completely aback, and she could only stare at him and utter, 'I beg your pardon?'

'I only asked you to dance,' he replied, his tone deceptively apologetic, for his eye held more than a hint of a twinkle. 'It is usual at these kinds of events you know.'

'Parcels don't dance,' she retorted.

'Oh dear, that did sting, didn't it?' he replied. 'What if I apologized — would you dance with me then?' The dance had just finished, and the dancers were leaving the floor, including Prudence and her partner.

By now, she had realized to her astonishment that she would very much like to take to the floor with Mr Tyler, but his bold comments about Prudence's appearance and even about her own could not quickly be forgotten. 'I suppose it has not occurred to you, in your conceit, that I might not want to dance with you?' she said, her head high. 'But here comes my niece. It would be more appropriate for you to dance with her.'

'I don't think it would be very wise,' he retorted, his colour a little higher than usual. 'I don't think I can trust my eyes not to stray to where they shouldn't, and if you caught me peering down her cleavage you would only give me another roasting.'

Elfrida looked at Mr Tyler's retreating back, satisfaction at having given him his own mingling with the uncomfortable sensation that she had been unforgivably rude. She had little time to think about their conversation straight away, however, for at that moment Prudence came back to her on Captain Graves's arm, and was immediately claimed by Digby Collett. Unable to do any other, Elfrida gave her consent, but she watched them warily as they took to the floor, berating herself inwardly for her lack of foresight. Had she not spoken so rudely to Mr Tyler, then he might have been the one to dance with her niece, and whilst she was not in favour of any man gazing down at Prudence's daringly displayed bosom, it would surely have been better for it to have been the desirable Mr Tyler than the undesirable Mr Collett. On the other hand, of course, had she, Elfrida, not been so prickly in her attitude, she herself might have been the one to dance with Mr Tyler. She told herself severely that she had no more desire for him to look down at her neckline than at that of Prudence.

When it was time for supper, Mr Tyler reappeared at Elfrida's side and requested the pleasure of taking her in. Looking round and seeing that Prudence was comfortably settled with Captain Graves, she gave her consent. Whilst Mr Tyler was escorting her, at least he was not charming any women of marriageable age, she reflected, which should surely please Anthea at any rate. Laying her hand on his arm, she recalled how rude she had been to him and glanced up at his face; his expression as he looked down at her was one of lazy amusement. For a moment, his eyes flickered to her neckline, then back again. 'Yes, much more tempting,' he murmured.

Before she could think of anything to say in response, he had taken her to a table at which Lady Dunstone and her husband were already seated, together with another couple of a similar age, and both the gentlemen rose as they arrived.

'Lord and Lady Dunstone, of course, you know, but I think you have not met Major Fletcher and his sister, Mrs Braybury,' said Tyler.

Elfrida acknowledged the introduction politely, and once the gentlemen had provided them with food from the buffet, they were soon chattering very happily together. Major Fletcher in particular had a very dry wit, and soon he and Mr Tyler were capping each other's witticisms and keeping the rest of the table well amused.

Mrs Braybury was a quietly spoken lady, fair-haired like her brother, about Elfrida's own age or a little younger, and looking charming in lavender. During a brief conversation with her, Elfrida discovered that her husband had been on Wellington's staff, but had lost his life at Salamanca. He had clearly been much admired both by the major and by Mr Tyler.

Elfrida was very careful to watch the amount of wine that she drank, only allowing Mr Tyler to refill her glass once, but the wine must have been quite potent, for when they had finished their meal and she stood up in order to go to the ladies' retiring-room, she could feel that she had drunk more than was customary for her. She was obliged to catch hold of the table for a moment until she regained her equilibrium.

'I can't rid myself of the notion that I have seen Miss Frobisher somewhere before,' Fletcher murmured to Tyler as she left.

'You too?' Tyler replied in an arrested tone, before Dunstone called to him to settle a difference of opinion about some other matter.

Some other ladies were already in the retiring-room when Elfrida arrived there. One was having her hair attended to by one of Lady Bayley's maids, two others were talking softly behind a screen, whilst one was pinning up a flounce for another. It was as Elfrida was walking past the screen that she heard Mr Tyler's name mentioned. She objected to eavesdropping as a matter of principle; later she would blame the amount of wine she had drunk for the fact that she quite deliberately listened to the conversation.

'He's not paying you very much attention tonight, is he Augusta?' one of the ladies said.

'Rufus and I don't live in each other's pockets, my dear,' the other replied in a husky, broken contralto voice. 'He will come round in the end, and if he doesn't, why, after all, there are plenty more fish in the sea.' That must be Mrs Fossey, Elfrida thought to herself.

'Like that, is it?' said Mrs Fossey's companion, if indeed Mrs Fossey it was. 'Just as well, perhaps. Rumour says he's thinking of offering for the Winchcomb chit.'

'Rumour misleads, in this instance,' replied Mrs Fossey. 'Mrs Winchcomb always read more into his attentions than was really there, in my opinion.' Elfrida found herself nodding.

The other woman laughed. 'There's match-making mamas for you. And Anthea Winchcomb is as ambitious as any of them.'

'Well, she's a fool if she thinks she'll get anywhere dressing the girl up like Covent Garden ware,' said Mrs Fossey. 'Have you seen the chit this evening? I'll hazard every rake in the room has stayed for an extra half-hour in the hope that she'll fall out of that gown. Are you ready now?'

There was the sound of rustling as the two ladies made ready to leave and Elfrida crouched down as if she were mending a broken shoe string. The two ladies dealing with the torn flounce also left and Elfrida sat up to think about what she had heard. Fond though she was of her sister Anthea, she had to admit that when Augusta Fossey had declared that she had probably exaggerated Mr Tyler's attentions, she was only stating what Elfrida herself had long been suspecting. Of course, it would be in Mrs Fossey's interest to think that, since she clearly believed that she only had to snap her fingers and Mr Tyler would run. Elfrida, remembering his attitude that evening, told herself savagely that she hoped he might.

But the conversation that she had over-heard had at least caused her to come to a decision. No matter what Prudence might say, she would take her home immediately. Mr Tyler might be right in saying that any scandal caused by the gown would blow over, but in the meantime, the longer that they remained at this ball, the more likely it became that someone would tell Anthea about the gown that Elfrida had permitted her niece to wear. At least if they left, every rake in the room would have to find something else to look at!

With this in mind, therefore, she attended to her toilet and went back to the ballroom to look for Prudence. Now that she had heard that conversation in the retiring room, the periphery of the dance floor seemed to be peopled chiefly by some of the most notorious rakes in town, all with quizzing glasses in hand. Yet, if they had been hoping to ogle Prudence Winchcomb, then they would be disappointed men, for, as Elfrida scanned the ballroom, she could not see her niece anywhere; worse still, nor could she see Digby Collett.

9

She would not panic straight away, she told herself. Just because Prudence was not in the ballroom did not necessarily mean that she was in a secluded corner somewhere, allowing Lieutenant Collett to take liberties with her person. She was certainly not in the ladies retiring-room, for Elfrida had only just left it. She went to the supper-room, but there was no sign of her niece there either. The card-room was inhabited only by gentlemen. She wandered back into the ballroom, hoping against hope that her charge would have returned, but it was not to be. Beginning to feel a little uneasy, she was pleased to see Rosemary standing alone, and hurrying over to her, she asked whether she had seen Prudence.

Rosemary shook her head. 'Not since we were all having supper,' she replied. She paused briefly. 'There need not be anything to worry about, you know.'

'Perhaps not,' Elfrida agreed doubtfully. 'But Lieutenant Collett is nowhere to be seen, either.'

'Do you want me to help you look?'

Rosemary asked. 'Lady Bayley has thrown open half her house this evening, it seems.'

'Oh, thank you,' said Elfrida gratefully. 'If you will start with some of the smaller rooms, I will begin with the conservatory.' A memory of the scene that had taken place at the Earl of Clare's house all those years ago flashed into her mind as she opened the door. Heaven grant that she would not discover Prudence sitting on Digby Collett's knee, as she had thought that she had discovered Anthea on the knee of that macaroni on that occasion!

* * *

Although Augusta Fossey had spoken to her friend in quite an airy tone, inside she was feeling a little concerned. The presence of Miss Winchcomb was not what was disturbing her. It certainly had seemed at one time that Rufus Tyler might have an interest in that young lady, and she had observed the situation with a degree of resignation. Of course, Rufus was bound to marry one day, and it might just as well be Prudence as any other. Augusta did not expect that he would marry her, nor did she want him to.

Stephen Fossey had been a man of noble birth with a remarkable head for business, and he had turned a comfortable independence into a handsome fortune. He had, however, been a very jealous man, and so afraid had he been that his wife would find consolation in the arms of another man, that he had stipulated in his will that if she married again, the bulk of the money was to go to charity, leaving her with only a small fraction of the whole. Augusta Fossey had long since decided that a man would have to be phenomenally wealthy for her to be tempted into a second marriage, and Rufus, though very well-to-do, was by no means rich enough for her to make such a sacrifice. The easy connection that they had enjoyed recently had been exactly to her liking, and she was by no means anxious to see it end.

Hard though it was for her to admit it, the concern that she felt was to do with the fact that she now sensed that he was tiring of her. It was some days since he had visited her in her charming little house in Albemarle Street and when he had last been to see her, he had not lingered.

He had been a very satisfactory lover, and she did not want to let him go by any means, but she was essentially a realist, and had no intention of demeaning herself by trying to fan the flames of something that had already died. For the sake of her pride, however, she was concerned that society should believe that she had tired of him first. Reluctant though she was to administer the *coup de grâce*, she might as well do it sooner than later. And where but at a ball such as this would she find a better place to begin to search for his replacement?

Having accompanied her friend back to the ballroom, she made an excuse to be rid of her, and went to the library where, most fortunately, paper and pens were set out in readiness. Hastily, she wrote a brief note which simply invited Rufus to come to the conservatory, and handed it to the first servant she met, telling him to take it to Mr Tyler. That done, she made her way there discreetly, and sat down to wait.

Mr Tyler opened the note and read it with a feeling of resignation. Mrs Fossey had been an agreeable companion for a time, but he had recently been conscious of a waning of interest in the kind of impermanent relationship that such as Mrs Fossey had to offer. His visit to his family home had given him a taste for a different kind of life. In the past, he had come back to London relieved to be free of the shackles of domesticity. This time, he had come back with some regret, and subsequent events had only confirmed this feeling. No doubt all the matchmaking mamas would be delighted if they were to learn that he was beginning to think seriously of marriage, he decided. They might be less delighted if they were to learn that none of the debutantes held any appeal for him.

If they did not, however, then neither did Mrs Fossey. As far as she was concerned, it was time for him to call a halt to things, and this interview in the conservatory might be the perfect opportunity. He screwed up the note, put it in his pocket, and in his turn also walked into the conservatory. He glanced round, smiling a little, then walked down one of the paths, and soon came upon Augusta. She was sitting on one of the stone seats, trailing her hand in the water. He noticed for the first time that she was dressed in exactly the same shade of pink as Prudence Winchcomb. On a more mature lady, of course, such a shade was perfectly acceptable.

'Isn't it lovely in here?' she murmured, standing up and swaying gracefully towards him. 'A perfect place for a conversation, wouldn't you say?'

'If you say so, Augusta,' he agreed. She really was very attractive, but as he looked into her eyes, he could see that she had come not for dalliance, but to give him his dismissal. He smiled ironically. He was, after all, a gentleman, so instead of calling an end to their affair, he took her hand, kissed it, and said, 'You are looking charming tonight, my dear.'

'I am glad to hear you say so,' she answered. 'But I am afraid that I have invited you here for quite another reason.'

'You have decided to move on,' he replied in subdued tones. 'I feared it.'

She smiled at him cynically. 'You don't fear it at all,' she replied forthrightly. 'Confess that you are relieved.'

'I would never dream of being so ungallant,' he answered. 'But you know, we always did think alike.'

She could not help laughing. 'Such a perfect place to end a romance, don't you think?' she said, looking around her. 'Why should one only ever think to begin relationships in romantic places? Surely something that is coming to an end deserves a charming setting.'

'I am sure you are right,' he agreed. 'Naturally, I shall take my *congé* like a gentleman. But I see no reason why we should not kiss goodbye.'

'Why not?' she replied, moving closer to him. When their lips met, Rufus felt nothing more than mild pleasure, and he knew that he had been wise in the decision that he had taken.

So it was that when Elfrida came upon them, she saw what she took at first glance to be her niece clasped in a gentleman's arms. 'Stop that immediately!' she exclaimed. 'What your mother would think — ' She broke off as Mrs Fossey turned round, and she realized that she had made a terrible mistake.

'Since my mother herself eloped with a married man, and is now living with him in Vienna, I doubt if she would have much room for criticism,' said Augusta, stepping back out of Mr Tyler's embrace. 'I will leave you to disentangle this one,' she added to Rufus, as she left them. If was only after she had gone that Elfrida realized she owed them both an apology.

'Oh, good God,' she said in mortified tones. 'I have made a dreadful mistake.'

'So you have,' replied Tyler, taking a step closer, 'and not for the first time, for I now recall where I have met you before. Only you are much prettier than you were then.'

She stared up into his face and, as if by magic, her mind added paint, powder, wig and extravagant clothes to his appearance. 'The macaroni,' she breathed.

'The very thame,' he replied wickedly. 'Large as life and definitely at least twice as natural.' He pulled her into his arms.

'Mr Tyler!' she exclaimed. 'You forget yourself!'

'You must forgive me,' he answered. 'The feeling of past blending with present is confusing me dreadfully. And I believe,' he went on, pulling her closer, 'I really do believe that your lips hold the only cure.' So saying, he covered her mouth with his, and kissed her. But now, something quite extraordinary happened, for whereas the kiss exchanged with the desirable Mrs Fossey had left him unmoved, the very first taste of Miss Frobisher's lips seemed to ignite a flame of passion within him, so that the kiss lasted far longer than he had intended.

As for Elfrida, Tyler's embrace took her completely by surprise. She had seen him kiss Mrs Fossey. She could not understand why, within moments, he could decide to kiss another woman. Pride told her that she could only be second best, and she began to struggle. Even whilst she was doing so, however, she was aware that her senses were being pulled in another direction. Her hands lost the will to struggle, they began to relax against the fabric of his coat, and for a few brief moments, she was in very real danger of surrendering to the mastery of his embrace.

Before she could so far forget herself as actually to wrap her arms around his neck, however, they were interrupted by a gasp and a shocked voice.

'Aunt Elfrida!' exclaimed Prudence.

Elfrida turned to see her niece looking at her with a horrified expression on her face. Standing with her were Lieutenant Collett, Captain Graves and a friend of Prudence's called Isobel Grainger. Immediately, Mr Tyler released her, but the damage was done. 'Oh my,' said Miss Grainger, somehow managing to look scandalized and delighted at the same time.

'Pray go to the ballroom, all of you,' said Prudence, taking command of the situation. 'My aunt is . . . unwell. And Isobel, if you breathe a word about this, I shall never speak to you again.'

'Of course I shall not,' answered Isobel, her eyes gleaming.

Tyler was the last to leave. He paused hesitantly, but receiving no encouragement from either lady to remain, he left, after bowing and saying, 'Your pardon, ladies, and especially yours, Miss Frobisher.'

'Well, that bit of behaviour certainly casts my gown into the shade, doesn't it?' said Prudence in a dispassionate tone after he had gone, but if Elfrida had been in the frame of mind to notice anything, she would have spotted that in her niece's eye there was a definite gleam of triumph.

'I wouldn't even have been in here if I had not been looking for you,' Elfrida answered crossly.

'You didn't seem to be looking very hard from what I could see,' Prudence commented. 'And as for *where* you were looking — '

'All right all right all right,' snapped Elfrida. 'Will that wretched girl keep quiet about what she saw?'

'I doubt it very much. She's not exactly known as the soul of discretion. And it is rather a tasty morsel.'

Elfrida sighed, annoyance lost in anxiety. 'What can we do?'

'To my way of thinking, there is only one thing we *can* do,' Prudence replied. 'Pretend to be ill, go home and then leave town as soon as possible.'

This was so much in accord with her own feelings that Elfrida willingly concurred with this suggestion. They had always intended to go to Prudence's home soon after the ball, so their travel plans needed little change. She made as if to leave the conservatory, but Prudence stopped her. 'One moment,' she said. 'Your hair is a little . . . ruffled.'

'You're enjoying this,' exclaimed Elfrida incredulously, as she allowed Prudence to

159

tuck in a stray curl or two.

'You must admit that it's an exquisitely humorous situation,' her niece replied. 'Oh, and by the way, you can be very sure that I won't be marrying Mr Tyler after that little episode. Clearly his tastes run to more . . . mature ladies, shall we say?' Elfrida's heart gave a little leap at these words, but she did not have time to ask herself why.

Luckily for them, Lady Bayley was talking with another lady quite close to the door into the conservatory. 'I am afraid that we shall have to ask to be excused,' Prudence declared, taking the initiative. 'Aunt Elfrida is not used to these big society occasions and she has been overcome by the heat.'

'Yes, so I understand,' answered her ladyship, with a disapproving look that spoke volumes. 'Is that why you took refuge in the conservatory?'

'That's right, is it not, Aunt Elfrida?' Prudence replied. 'But it did not help as much as she had hoped. She very nearly fainted, did you not?'

'Very nearly,' Elfrida echoed, feeling that she might yet do so.

'Fortunately, Mr Tyler was on hand and he caught her, but I think that she should now go home.'

Lady Bayley unbent a little. 'Really?' she

said. 'By all means go home and rest, Miss Frobisher. I trust that you will be feeling better soon.'

'That was very quick of you,' Elfrida said admiringly, as they travelled home in the carriage. 'That should kill all the gossip.'

'Oh, I doubt it very much,' Prudence answered dispassionately. 'After all, Isobel Grainger saw the whole thing with her own eyes, and he *was* actually kissing you.' She paused briefly, then went on curiously, 'By the way, what was it . . . ?'

'No!' Elfrida interrupted her in tones of horrified embarrassment. 'Not another word will I speak on the subject. It was all your fault, after all.'

'All my fault?' protested Prudence. 'How could it have been all my fault?'

'If you hadn't insisted on wearing that dreadfully improper gown, for a start,' Elfrida replied angrily. 'And if I were not having to keep a watch on you all the time, just in case — ' She stopped, horrified.

'Just in case I wanted to run off with Digby Collett, I suppose?' Prudence demanded. 'Oh, don't think I didn't know all about Mama's plans. You were to promote a marriage with Rufus Tyler, and make sure Digby came nowhere near me. That's it, isn't it? Was kissing Mr Tyler part of the plan? To make him seem more attractive to me by showing that he's desirable to other women?'

'Don't be so absurd,' Elfrida retorted, glad that the carriage was too dark inside for her blushes to be visible.

'No more absurd than this plan that you and Mama have cooked up between you.'

'I have not done any cooking,' Elfrida protested. 'What's more, I promise you that if I had known how things would have turned out, I would never have come.'

'Well never mind,' Prudence answered as they arrived at the house. 'You'll soon be able to get back to your garden and your cabbages, and forget all about us.'

'No, Prudence, wait,' Elfrida said, as they went inside.

Prudence turned to look at her. 'You are not well, Aunt Elfrida,' she said firmly. 'We'll talk in the morning.'

Mindful of the butler's presence, Elfrida simply murmured, 'Yes, we will,' before going up the stairs in her turn. In truth, she was very thankful to be able to go into her room and close the door. The task of chaperoning her niece for a short time had appeared to be so simple. How naïve she had been! How she wished with all her heart that she had refused her sister's request and remained in her own little village! Had she done so, she might have been engaged to Mr Erskine by now, and looking forward to a future that would have been, if not exciting, at least safe and protected from scandal. Now, thanks to this London visit, she had not only failed to check Prudence's wilfulness, she had also failed either to drive away the undesirable suitor, or to secure the man of Anthea's choice. She had permitted her niece to go to a major event of the social season in a gown that had only just fallen short of being indecent. Finally, to add to all her other failings, she herself had been caught by the very young woman whose morals she was supposed to be guarding in a compromising position with the aforementioned desirable suitor, a gentleman who, only a matter of moments before, had been in a close embrace with his mistress! She burned with shame.

The most ironic feature of the whole business, however, was that the incident in the conservatory this evening was not her first humiliating encounter with Mr Tyler. It was not surprising that she had not recognized him. The change from extravagant lisping macaroni to gentleman of understated elegance had been immense. It seemed much stranger that he had not recognized her, but then she had been dressed very differently too, in a gown of her mother's choosing, and with her hair powdered, and after all, they had not met since.

She could not believe that she would ever get to sleep, but she prepared for bed all the same, because she could not think of anything else to do. Whatever had transpired that evening, she would still have preparations to make for their departure from London, and a night without rest would not help her at all. Bother Tyler, and bother all military men!

Suddenly, she thought of the other military man that she had met that evening — Major Fletcher. Fletcher! That had been the name of the other macaroni! The alteration in him had been just as dramatic as in his friend. She had not recognized him, had not even thought about the name being the same until now. Had he recognized her as well? Were the two men sharing their memories of that ball at Castle Clare even now? Had Tyler ever told the major about how he had kissed her in the conservatory all those years ago? Had he even — shocking thought — told his military friend about the embrace that they had shared rather more recently? Blushing all over, she snuggled down under the covers, putting her fingers in her ears as if, by blocking out any outside noises, she could also banish the thoughts inside her head.

* ★ ★ ★

In her own room, Prudence smiled to herself. Really, she could not have planned the whole thing better if she had tried. She had decided to wear an unsuitable gown as part of a strategy designed to convince her aunt that they ought to leave London as soon as possible. She could never have imagined in her wildest dreams that Aunt Elfrida would somehow manage to compromise herself, thus completely drawing attention away from Prudence's own actions. Now, because of that minor scandal, Miss Frobisher would be doubly anxious to leave London, and that would give the opportunity that Prudence had been planning for.

Once her gown had been unfastened, she dismissed her maid, and finished undressing. Then clad in her nightgown and with a warm shawl around her shoulders, she opened her travelling writing desk, took out a sheet of paper, and, smiling, began to write.

10

Fortunately, there was so much to do in order to prepare for the journey that there was very little time to think about the events of the previous evening. Elfrida got up at her usual early hour, and was surprised when Prudence entered the breakfast parlour just as she was beginning her meal.

'I thought I would join you today,' she said, as she took her place at the table.

'How nice,' Elfrida replied, because she could not think of anything else to say. In the dark watches of the night she had wondered what would happen when they encountered one another again, since their last parting had been anything but cordial. She had imagined all kinds of acrimonious exchanges; she had not considered that their first words would be so commonplace.

No amount of turning over the whole matter in her mind could persuade her to come to any conclusion other than that she had been most culpably negligent. It was her fault that Prudence had gone to the ball so unsuitably dressed, and no one else could be blamed for the fact that she had mistaken

Mrs Fossey for Prudence. To her annoyance, she felt very much as if she were the naughty schoolgirl, and her niece the disapproving senior relative.

This impression was confirmed when, upon the exit of the butler, Prudence remarked, 'As for last night, I think that the less said the better, do not you, Aunt Elfrida?'

'You are probably right,' Elfrida replied. 'But,' she went on, determined not to be cowed by this young woman, 'at least my errors were the result of honest mistakes, whereas yours were quite deliberate.'

'Perhaps,' Prudence agreed coolly. 'But the result is essentially the same. Embarrassment, scandal, and the need for immediate departure. More coffee, Aunt Elfrida?'

This conversation so flustered Elfrida that she found herself quite unable to give her whole mind to the task of packing up their belongings and shutting up the house. After breakfast, Prudence announced that she would need to go to the library. 'I must return my books before we leave London,' she said. 'May I obtain anything for you whilst I am out?'

Elfrida responded in the negative. There might indeed be something that she might want to obtain, but she could not give her mind to the matter now. It would have to wait until she was feeling more clear-headed.

* * *

Obedient to Prudence's instructions, Digby was waiting morosely in Hatchard's to find out what her scheming would have in store for him next. As he waited, he allowed his thoughts to drift towards the kind of young lady that he would marry one day. She would have to have some money of her own, he knew that, but that would not be her most important attribute. She would be small, he decided; small enough to look up to him, and slender enough for him to feel strong and protective. He had no desire to marry a wife who could look him in the eye and boss him about. She would have fair hair and blue eyes, and she would be able to cry without losing her looks.

He picked up a book in front of him and absently began to turn the pages. She would not be very clever, and she would always think that he knew best, and would defer to him in everything. So lost was he in this delightful dream that Prudence had to say his name three times before he became aware of being addressed.

'Digby! Are you wool-gathering? Wake up,

for goodness' sake. We have vital matters to attend to.'

With great reluctance, Digby bade farewell to the dainty maiden of his dreams and prepared to deal with the Amazon in front of him. 'What vital matters?' he asked her. 'I have followed you about London like a puppy dog, fooled everyone into thinking that you and I are romantically attached to one another, and I have done my best to help you create a scandal so that you are obliged to leave London. As far as I am concerned, my part is played.'

'Oh no it isn't,' Prudence replied firmly. 'I have another task for you to perform.'

'No,' said Digby firmly, raising his hands defensively. 'No more. I refuse to pursue you any more.' He paused, then suddenly inspired, said, 'What if I should have missed my chance of fixing my interest in a girl that I am really attached to?'

'Is there one?' Prudence asked suspiciously.

Thinking of the maiden of his dreams, Digby said, 'Yes, there is. And before you ask, no, you wouldn't know her.'

'Oh,' Prudence responded. 'Well, never mind, I shall soon be leaving London and you will be free to pursue her to your heart's content. She does live in London, I take it?'

'Yes, but she does not go out in society,'

Digby replied, surprising himself at this sudden gift for invention and eager to exercise it to the full.

'I expect she is quite unsuitable,' remarked Prudence sweepingly, straightening her gloves. 'Well, you will soon be free to return to London.'

'But I don't need to return to London,' Digby protested. 'I haven't left it.'

'No, but you will have done,' Prudence told him. 'You are going to come to the house and offer us your escort for the journey north. Aunt Elfrida is only too anxious to get away after last night's embarrassment!' She chuckled. 'If I had guessed that she would end up compromising herself in the conservatory, I should never have bothered wearing that gown to the ball.'

'But why do you need my escort?' Digby asked.

'That isn't very gallant of you,' Prudence replied, putting on a simper. Then, returning to her normal manner, she went on, 'No one will think it strange if you offer to escort us. You are our neighbour after all. Then, at some point on the journey, I will give my aunt the slip and travel on to meet Daniel.'

A terrified look crossed Digby's face. 'Do you think I might give her the slip as well?' he asked.

Prudence eyed him in an exasperated way.

'Your task will be to lead her away from my trail, so that by the time she finds out where we are it will be too late. Really, you are so timid, I wonder why you ever joined the army,' she declared.

'Coping with you and your schemes is far more frightening,' he assured her. 'All right, I'll help you — but only if you give me your word that'll be the end of it.'

'It will be,' Prudence answered smiling warmly, 'for after that, I shall be married to Daniel. You are entirely at liberty to tell my aunt that I tricked you as well, if you like.'

'I don't suppose I shall,' he replied, a touch of indignation in his voice. 'I do have some sense of loyalty, you know.'

'Yes, I do know,' Prudence answered, giving his arm an affectionate little squeeze. 'Come after luncheon. That will just about give Aunt Elfrida enough time to realize that we have no escort. If she doesn't realize it by herself, I'll give her a little hint.' Digby, having had experience of Prudence's 'little hints' in the past, barely repressed a shudder.

* * *

After her niece had gone out, Elfrida went into the sitting-room, intending to send for the housekeeper. Instead, she sat down and

171

found herself going over the incidents that had taken place over recent days and, more particularly, the previous night. What a mercy it was that she was not obliged to earn her living as a chaperon, she decided. She would undoubtedly have found herself cast off without a reference after her appalling failure in that role. Not only had she been quite unable to exert authority over her niece's correspondence — and goodness only knew how many notes had been passed about which she knew nothing at all — she had failed to take even the most obvious measures to ensure Prudence's tasteful appearance. She had also allowed her to dance with the very man about whom Anthea had warned her, not to mention allowing the girl to slip out of her sight during the evening.

All these things were cast utterly into the shade, however, when set against her own appalling conduct. She had herself wandered off into the conservatory unchaperoned. She had interrupted a tryst which, even if improper in itself, was the business of the parties concerned and no one else. If that were not bad enough, she had allowed herself to be seized and kissed by a gentleman who, by his behaviour, was clearly a rake. No doubt he now supposed that she was in the habit of interrupting romantic interludes in order to steal one for herself! Worse than all this, not only was this the same man who had kissed her in a conservatory before, but also, ashamed though she was to admit the fact, she had actually enjoyed it.

So shocking was this reflection that she found herself blushing all over again. It was at this unfortunate moment that the door opened and the butler announced, 'Mrs Grainger, ma'am.'

It only took a few seconds for Elfrida to realize that this lady was the mother of Prudence's talkative friend Isobel who had witnessed her disgraceful behaviour in the conservatory the previous evening. Why, she looks positively avid, Elfrida thought to herself as she went forward to greet her guest, and offer her some refreshment.

'Thank you, I should be glad of something,' Mrs Grainger answered, as Elfrida rang for ratafia. 'We ladies are so full of stamina, are we not? Up betimes after our evening's exertions.'

'I expect plenty of people are still in bed,' Elfrida replied, trying to sound indifferent.

'I was a little surprised to find that *you* were up and about, my dear,' Mrs Grainger remarked. 'I had heard that you were taken ill during the evening, and went home early.'

Elfrida opened her mouth to assert that she

had been in perfect health all evening, when the butler came in with the drinks. Whilst he was pouring them out, she realized what an enormous gaffe such an assertion would be, for what excuse would she have for being discovered in Mr Tyler's arms if she had not been unwell?

'I was a little overcome by the heat,' she agreed, after Kimble had left the room, 'but a drink of warm milk when I got home made me feel much more the thing.'

'I am so pleased to hear it,' said Mrs Grainger. 'Dear Isobel told me that you seemed quite . . . overheated.'

'So kind of her to take such a keen interest in others,' Elfrida responded quickly, her chin going up a little.

Mrs Grainger's eyes snapped angrily. 'She could scarcely help it when the behaviour of those around her was so very absorbing,' she declared. 'Did Mr Tyler bring you home?'

At this most awkward of moments Kimble entered once more. 'Mr Tyler,' he said.

'Ladies, good morning,' said Mr Tyler, making his bow. He then turned to Elfrida. 'I am come to see if you have recovered from your faintness, ma'am,' he added politely. 'No doubt your daughter will have told you that Miss Frobisher was taken ill last night,' he went on, looking this time at

Mrs Grainger. 'I am very thankful that I was able to catch her as she fell.'

'Yes, Isobel told me everything that she saw,' replied Mrs Grainger, the malice disappearing from her face as she smiled in a welcoming manner at this eligible bachelor. 'I was quite shocked at her account.'

'I'm not surprised, ma'am,' replied Tyler, looking serious.

This response clearly startled Mrs Grainger, who opened her mouth to speak, then deciding that she could not think what to say, closed it again.

'Any mother would be concerned, I would imagine,' the gentleman added, after accepting the wine that Kimble brought in with a polite word of thanks. 'Would you not agree, Miss Frobisher?'

Quite unable to see what he might be driving at, but understanding at least that she must corroborate his words, Elfrida simply murmured, 'Exactly so.'

'I . . . I am glad that you appreciate my position,' Mrs Grainger uttered in mystified tones.

'Oh, we do,' replied Tyler in accents of sympathy, 'and feel for you extremely.'

'Extremely,' Elfrida added, then wished she had not done so, because it made her sound like a Greek chorus.

'Make no mistake, Mrs Grainger, you have done the right thing in coming here today,' Tyler went on reassuringly.

'I have?' Mrs Grainger murmured. Almost despite herself, Elfrida began to feel sorry for her. The woman looked completely lost. She was not surprised: she, too, did not have a clue where Mr Tyler might be taking them with this line of conversation.

'Absolutely,' the gentleman confirmed. 'These young girls can so easily develop a habit of gossiping, and it must be nipped in the bud from the very beginning. The best way of doing this is by warning those who might be a target of such gossip, as you have done today, most commendably. Some members of the ton can be exceedingly sensitive about these things, can they not, Miss Frobisher?'

'Undoubtedly,' Elfrida confirmed, determined not to echo him again.

'And, of course, the more distinguished they are, the more sensitive they will be.'

On hearing the first words of Mr Tyler's last two speeches Mrs Grainger had straightened and drawn a breath, her face indignant, but by the time he had finished speaking the second time she had begun to look thoughtful instead. 'Very true,' she acknowledged, looking at him with acute interest.

'Of course it was quite dark in the

conservatory,' Tyler remarked, pouring himself another glass of wine.

'Lady Bayley does not keep her conservatory well lit,' Mrs Grainger replied slowly. 'I have often remarked it.'

'A sad thing it would be if every gentleman who was bending over a lady who had fainted to check whether her breathing was regular, was suspected of nefarious activity,' the gentleman commented, lifting his glass as if to admire the rich red of the wine.

'It would indeed be sad,' Mrs Grainger added, rising. 'I shall warn Isobel not to make hasty judgements in future.' She paused and looked uncertainly at Rufus. 'What a mercy it is that you are not one of those sensitive souls.'

'A great mercy,' he agreed, bowing politely as she left.

'What are you doing here?' Elfrida asked, as soon as the door had closed. Relief at Mrs Grainger's departure made her speak more abruptly than she had intended and she blushed at her own rudeness.

'Merely making a courtesy call,' he replied blandly. 'After all, it is common knowledge that you were obliged to leave the ball last night because you were unwell, so — '

'How did you know that?' Elfrida asked, interrupting him.

'I should have thought that was quite obvious,' he replied, wandering over to an occasional table, picking up an exquisite china shepherdess, turning it over to look at the marking on the bottom and putting it down again. 'You did . . . ah . . . faint in my arms, after all. Isobel Grainger saw it and told her mother.'

Elfrida blushed. 'Oh yes,' she murmured. Then, pulling herself together she went on, 'Thanks to your intervention, she has perhaps been restrained from telling half of London as well.'

'Let us hope so,' he replied. 'There is no reason why we should not have been conversing together last night. After all, we are old acquaintances, are we not?' He glanced at her sideways. 'I cannot believe that it took us so long to recognize one another.'

'I think my failure is more understandable,' she said, taking the glass that he offered to her. 'Your transformation is quite remarkable.'

He grinned. 'Quite a sight, wasn't I? I remember my appearance drove my father mad at the time. Well, that was chiefly why I did it.'

The door opened to admit Prudence, her bonnet in her hand. 'Oh, I beg your pardon, I hope I am not interrupting anything,' she said, her eyes gleaming.

'Only a private conversation,' Tyler replied. There was something about his expression that caused Prudence to flush, and Elfrida, who had never seen this phenomenon before, looked on amazed. 'Don't you think you've exposed your aunt to enough humiliation already, without showing off your bad manners now?'

Prudence stared at him with an outraged expression on her face before stalking out of the room and slamming the door. 'What a brat,' Mr Tyler observed dispassionately. 'Is she completely spoiled?'

'No . . . no, I'm sure she is not,' said Elfrida doubtfully, disturbed by his words, but not able to think why at that moment. 'In any case, I do not think you were being entirely fair, just then. She was not the one who . . . who . . . ' Words failed her and she fell silent.

'Yes, but had she not appeared in an outrageous costume and disappeared from your side, you would not have been obliged to pursue her into the conservatory, would you?'

'No, I would not,' she replied, regaining her courage. 'And had I not gone into the conservatory, I would not have found you misbehaving with your . . . ' She stopped just in time.

'You are mistaken on two counts,' he told her, his eyes glittering in such a way that it was impossible to tell whether he was angry or amused. 'Trysting with a mistress is not misbehaviour; it is what one is supposed to do; otherwise, she would not be a mistress. But in any case, Mrs Fossey is no longer my mistress.'

'Oh,' she replied.

'Relieved?' he asked her, his brows raised.

'Certainly not,' she answered him indignantly. 'It is no concern of mine whether you keep a mistress or not. However . . . ' she began, then fell silent.

'However?' he prompted her.

'Another matter has occurred to me,' she said eventually. 'Will Major Fletcher keep quiet about what happened last night?'

There was a long silence. 'Why should he have anything to say upon the matter?' he asked her.

'Well, since he was there . . . on both occasions when you . . . ' she ventured.

'I beg your pardon, but he was not,' he said firmly, his face set. 'I repeat, why should he have anything to say about what had taken place?'

'I . . . ' she began, conscious that she had transgressed, but not sure how.

'Miss Frobisher, a gentleman does not

boast about his adventures,' he assured her, with the same stern expression. 'If anyone apart from ourselves knows about what took place in the conservatory at Castle Clare, then it is not because I told him; by the same token, no one, and I repeat, no one, will learn about what happened last night from my lips.'

'I beg your pardon,' she whispered, mortified.

There was a short silence. He put down his empty glass, walked across to where she was sitting and put out his hand. She stood up, whereupon he bowed over her hand, kissing it lightly. 'When do you leave London?'

'I . . . it is not decided definitely,' she answered, not wanting to give anyone, least of all this man, the impression that she was running away. 'Anthea has kindly invited me to visit them in the country when I take Prudence home.'

'Are you planning on staying with your sister for any length of time?' he asked her.

'I'm not sure,' she answered. Then, determined that he should not be the only person to be thought desirable, she went on, 'My close friend, the Reverend Stanley Erskine is to join us there, and he will take me home.'

'Will he?' Tyler replied smoothly, his expression unreadable. 'I am going north myself, and may perhaps call upon you. Naturally, I look forward to making the reverend gentleman's acquaintance as well.'

'If you dare — ' Elfrida began.

'Dare?' he queried. 'Personally, I have never found members of the clergy to be so intimidating, but I will take your opinion seriously concerning Mr Erskine, and be on my guard. Good day to you.'

He was gone before she could say anything to correct him. Perhaps it was just as well, she decided. She had only met him on a handful of occasions, and on two of those, she had, quite unintentionally, ended up in his arms. It would be far better not to see him again. It would also be much better if he and Mr Erskine were never to meet, but she was sure that she need not worry about that. Mr Tyler might speak about visiting her at Anthea's house, but he would never do it. Indeed, it was to be hoped that he would not, she told herself stoutly. She was guiltily aware that she had given him the impression that the relationship between herself and Mr Erskine was closer than it really was. If the two men were to meet, then Mr Tyler would discover the truth, and she would look more foolish in his eyes than she did already.

She also felt guilty about the way she had challenged him in her last remark. Of course he would not tell Stanley about the scrape that she had got into in London. Had he not defended her reputation from Mrs Grainger's probing enquiries just a short time ago? And had he not also defended her from Prudence's inquisitiveness? She recalled the feeling of uneasiness that she had experienced when she had heard him refer to Prudence as a spoiled brat. Surely if he had ever contemplated marriage with her, he could not still be doing so seriously if that was his opinion? Poor Anthea would be disappointed, but it could not be helped. Having had the opportunity of observing them both, Elfrida could not escape the conclusion that they would make a very bad match, and for all that Prudence had behaved badly, Mr Tyler had done so as well. He had defended her, however, albeit with the utmost effrontery.

All at once the recollection of Mr Tyler's effrontery on other occasions became so embarrassing that she rang the bell with far more vigour than she was wont to use and, in order to distract herself, instantly summoned the housekeeper so that together they could go through the house inventory.

11

It was while Prudence and Elfrida were sharing a light luncheon that the older lady suddenly exclaimed, 'Merciful heavens, we do not have a gentleman to escort us!'

'You did not have one coming down,' Prudence pointed out, trying very hard not to reveal the glee that she felt at having predicted so accurately the moment at which Elfrida would realize this deficiency.

'No, but we shall be making a longer journey, and besides . . . ' She was about to say that she did not relish the idea of having sole responsibility for such a strong-willed young woman on such a journey, but she realized just in time that this would scarcely be tactful. Instead, she went on, 'Besides, there will be more luggage to deal with and no doubt you will have jewellery with you. I should feel much easier in my mind if we had the escort of a gentleman.'

'Isn't Mr Erskine joining us at Grantham?' Prudence asked.

'Yes, but not immediately,' Elfrida replied. 'Recall that we are setting out a little earlier than we intended, so I have written to him to apprise him of our new arrangements.' She coloured at the recollection of the incidents that had made an early departure desirable. 'Mr Erskine will have his duties to perform on Sunday. We will be obliged to stay in Grantham for two nights. I would suggest that we go to my house, but my housekeeper is taking a holiday during my absence and the house will be shut up.'

'Well, it cannot be helped,' said Prudence carelessly. 'If you will excuse me, I will go and see how Scrivens is getting on with the packing.'

★　★　★

Digby Collett set off from his lodging and proceeded to walk unhappily along New Bond Street. He had always found himself obliged to be a party to Prudence's plans, he reflected. Obliged; now that was an interesting word. Thinking about it in the clear light of day, and without a commanding pair of feminine eyes to sway him, he could not think of a single thing that made it his duty to fall in with any of Prudence's schemes.

He had spoken to her of friendship and, of course, friendship meant that you were prepared to put yourself out for someone and they in their turn would put themselves out for you. But these days, there never seemed to be an end to her machinations in which he was involved. He was coming to dread those summonses to Hatchard's or to the park, because they always presaged some fresh complication in which he would become embroiled against his own better judgement. Would that he had realized in time what Black's departure signified. He would then have offered to accompany the captain on his journey and would have been well out of the way whilst Prudence hatched this fresh plot. Instead, he was now on his way to offer his services as escort to Miss Frobisher and her niece. That, at least, was how it would begin. Goodness only knew where or how it would end.

Suddenly aware that he was being addressed, he looked up from his contemplation of the ground to see Rufus Tyler emerging from Angelo's Fencing Academy. Digby smiled a little nervously. Although they were distantly related, Tyler never failed to inspire the younger man with a certain degree of awe.

'Miles away, Digby?' Rufus asked, smiling.

'Not yet,' Digby replied, thinking of the forthcoming journey. Then he blushed at the notion of how absurd and possibly suspicious this might sound and corrected himself, saying, 'I mean, that is to say, a little, sir. Are you . . . going anywhere?'

'Probably,' Tyler replied with a wry grin. 'What is preoccupying you? Can I help?'

'I don't suppose so,' Digby replied gloomily. 'Do women try to involve *you* in their schemes?'

'All the time,' Rufus answered sympathetically. 'The secret is to say no, and to say it consistently. You have to harden your heart, my dear fellow. In my experience, women's schemes and gunfire have this in common — one should try to stand well clear of both whenever possible.'

'Not so easy when you're a soldier,' Digby replied. 'It's all very well for you . . . ' Suddenly he stopped, colouring. He had remembered that Rufus had served with some distinction, and had probably seen more military action than he had.

'So what schemes have you become embroiled in now?' Rufus asked him, striving to remain patient. One of the younger Colletts, Digby had been a little spoiled by his older sisters and, at times, showed a distressing tendency to whine.

As they strolled along Bond Street which at this hour was full of people shopping or just out for a stroll, Digby eyed his companion moodily. The older man was dressed fashionably in buckskin breeches with very shiny boots and a dark-blue coat with silver buttons and he seemed to attract admiring glances and flirtatious acknowledgements from half the women in the street. Ladies were supposed to be attracted by a scarlet coat, Digby thought to himself resentfully. It was one of the reasons that he had chosen the army when it had become clear that he would have to earn his keep, the family estate not being wealthy enough to support him. But the magic of the uniform did not seem to work for him as it did for other men. Take Black, for example; or Graves! Girls buzzed around them like bees around a honey pot. As for Tyler, he wasn't even in uniform! He directed another resentful look at his kinsman, quite unaware that the very sulkiness of his demeanour tended to put women off, whereas the lazy good humour and charm exhibited by Tyler would always attract, no matter what he might be wearing.

'You really are miles away, aren't you?' commented Tyler in amused tones.

Digby flushed again as he realized that he had walked the length of Bond Street with his influential kinsman without addressing him once. 'I . . . I am thinking about my errand,' he answered rather lamely.

'Which is?'

'I am on my way to Brook Street, you

know; just to see the ladies.'

'Very commendable,' Rufus answered. 'I take it you mean Miss Frobisher and Miss Winchcomb in particular, and not just any ladies in general?'

'Of course I — ' Digby began impatiently, then he broke off, before saying in a more moderate tone, 'You are always funning, sir! Yes, I thought I would pay my respects to the ladies. They may be leaving any day now and I do not want to be backward in any attention.'

'You are very right to offer them that courtesy,' answered Rufus. 'But I must tell you that I was with Miss Frobisher this morning and she gave no indication of such an intention.'

'Oh,' said Digby, wondering how long it would be before Tyler would get to wherever it was he wanted to go and leave him alone. 'It is very good of you to bear me company, sir,' he said, a touch of desperation in his voice.

'Not at all,' replied Rufus politely. 'How are your mama and papa these days?'

Relieved to have been given a topic upon which he could at once speak with authority and enthusiasm and without guilt, Digby instantly began to talk at length, barely drawing breath until they arrived outside the

Winchcombs' residence in Brook Street. Once there, Digby turned to his kinsman. 'I must thank you for your company and say goodbye now, sir,' Digby said, putting out his hand.

It had not escaped Rufus's notice that Digby had seemed anxious to be rid of him from the moment that they had met, and so, as much from sheer devilment as from any suspicion that the younger man might be up to something, he said casually, 'D'you know, I rather think I'll go in.'

'But you can't,' Digby protested, appalled.

'Why not?' Tyler asked, as he stepped forward to lift the door knocker.

'Well . . . because . . . because you've already been once today,' Digby stammered.

'Is there a limit to the number of times I am permitted to call?' Tyler asked. 'It's the first I've heard of it.' So saying, he tapped smartly on the door, and Kimble answered it, welcoming Mr Tyler first and then Digby who trailed irritably in his relative's wake.

The gentlemen were shown into the saloon where Elfrida had received Rufus earlier in the day. It was a pleasant, cheerful room with an interesting view of the street and Tyler wandered over to the window to have a look outside whilst Digby stood fiddling miserably with the ornaments on the mantelpiece. If challenged, he would have been hard put to it to say why the presence of the other man annoyed him so much. Probably the reason was that knowing himself to be a poor actor at best, he did not relish the idea of playing any kind of role in front of a man who had known him from childhood.

A few moments later, Elfrida came in, to be followed by Prudence. Ater greeting one another formally, they all took their seats and Rufus said, 'I encountered Digby unexpectedly in St James's Street and some words of his reminded me of how very remiss I have been.'

'They did?' questioned Digby blankly.

'Most certainly. This morning, Miss Frobisher, when you told me that you were not sure how soon you would be leaving London, I did not assure you that you might depend upon my escort. I shall be going north myself, and it makes no difference to me when I go, so I can be entirely at your service.'

Digby made a strangled noise in his throat. 'But . . . but that's not fair,' he managed to gurgle. 'I was going to ask that.'

'Yes, he was,' Prudence agreed, then added quickly, 'I think . . . I mean . . . he just said so.'

'That is very kind of you, Mr Tyler,' Elfrida

said. 'We will be delighted to avail ourselves of your kind offer.' She turned to Digby. 'You are more than kind also, Lieutenant Collett, but as you see, Mr Tyler has already offered.' She looked at Rufus again. 'I have talked the matter over with my niece, Mr Tyler, and can now tell you that we are intending to leave on Saturday. We shall not be travelling on Sunday, naturally, but will resume our journey on Monday. My . . . my friend, the Revd Stanley Erskine, is to meet us in Grantham on Wednesday.'

'Then surely, you would allow yourselves plenty of time if you set out on Monday,' Rufus observed. In truth, he only had half his mind on the conversation. The rest of it was given to wondering why his offer to act as escort had been greeted by Digby with such consternation, and why Miss Winchcomb had appeared to know that Digby would offer the same service, before he had actually done so.

'Yes, perhaps,' Elfrida agreed in response to his words, 'but I wish to leave as soon as possible.' She was proud of herself for not allowing her colour to become heightened at these words.

'Then naturally I am at your disposal,' said Rufus politely, noting the way that she put up her chin, and guessing the reason for this. How soft her lips had felt, he thought.

'And so am I,' Digby put in swiftly, looking anxious. 'And I, too, can leave on Saturday.

Elfrida looked at her niece's face and felt her heart soften. She could not for the life of her see what Prudence saw in this rather ineffectual young man. She would have expected her to have been attracted by someone more manly — Captain Black, for instance — but surely it would do no harm to allow him to accompany them on the journey. There would be no social occasions providing opportunities for sneaking off into corners, and Mr Tyler would also be on hand to keep an eye on them. In a very few days they would be at Winchcomb Hall and her duties would be over. Surely Prudence would be more co-operative if she were given just a few chances to see the young man who, by virtue of close family acquaintance, could scarcely be shunned entirely, whatever Anthea's wishes might be? Furthermore, once they were back at Winchcomb Hall, if there were shunning to be done, Anthea would be the one to do it.

'Why not?' Elfrida said, smiling. 'If two gallant gentlemen are willing to escort us, who am I to object?' The two younger people immediately smiled with relief.

'With your permission then, ma'am, I will send word to the George in Huntingdon,

193

bespeaking rooms for us all. Do you wish to share with your niece, or to have separate rooms?'

'Share, I think, in a public inn,' Elfrida replied, thinking of the opportunities for dalliance that would no doubt present themselves to Prudence's ingenious mind.

'And what of your conveyance? Do you wish me to hire a chaise for you?'

'Yes, if you please; and another carriage for the servants and the luggage.'

Whilst Rufus was speaking to Elfrida, Digby found the chance to say to Prudence, 'What will you do now, with my kinsman hanging over our shoulders? Will that not ruin all your schemes?'

'Don't worry,' she replied, smiling a smile that he knew of old and over the years had come to dread. 'I've just thought of a really splendid plan that I think will do everybody some good.'

Digby, recalling one or two other splendid plans that Prudence had hatched over the years, felt his heart sinking down into his boots. If it actually did him any good, he would be very surprised.

He and Mr Tyler did not linger for long after the day and the time of departure had been set. Digby had dreaded another walk with his kinsman, but to his surprise, Tyler touched his hat and walked away, pleading an engagement in the opposite direction.

'Do me some good, indeed,' Digby muttered to himself. 'Fine chance!' By the time he reached his lodgings, however, he found that his sentiments had altered somewhat. If he were to give Prudence every assistance then, God willing, she would soon be married to Daniel Black. That done, the likelihood was that she would leave him in peace. This was such a beautiful thought that he quickened his step, already planning what he would need to take for these few days away from town. As he entered his lodgings and walked up the stairs, he realized that he was whistling.

12

The hired chaise set off promptly at ten o'clock on Saturday morning. A second carriage bearing the luggage, Prudence's abigail, and another maid, had gone on ahead. This conveyance had also taken up Mr Tyler's valet and most of his belongings. His groom, Alban, had also gone on ahead, driving his master's curricle.

To Elfrida's great relief, she and Prudence had had no further cross words. She could only assume that having won the privilege of having Digby escort them, the younger woman was satisfied. Furthermore, they had both been so busy performing the hundred and one little tasks that are necessary when a house is to be shut up that there had been no time for conversation other than comments like 'Are you certain the blue dressing case was put in the loft, because James cannot find it anywhere?' or, 'I'm sure that at least some of this linen is supposed to go back to Winchcomb Hall.'

After they had left Brook Street, they went first of all to Half Moon Street to collect Lieutenant Collett and his belongings, and then to Berkeley Square to take up Mr Tyler. The day was fine, everyone was in good spirits, and Elfrida was encouraged to think that she had been wise to grant Prudence this small indulgence. She would have to account for herself to her sister, but she resolved not to think about that until later. Her own conduct might mean that she would want to be less than completely frank. In the only conversation which had threatened to become less than cordial, her niece had suggested that each of them had something about which they would like the other to keep quiet.

'It would be a shocking thing if Mama were to hear about why you had felt the need to rush us away from London,' she had said thoughtfully, whilst they were sharing one of their last meals together in the Brook Street house.

'It would be just as shocking if she were to hear about that gown that you wore,' Elfrida replied, determined not to be bested.

'How dreadful that no one took responsibility for making sure I was properly dressed,' Prudence answered sweetly. Elfrida could not think of an answer to this, and after a moment or two, Prudence went on, 'Do you know, I hardly think it necessary to tell mama any of this. Do you?'

'She will probably find out anyway,' Elfrida

pointed out. 'Unless, of course, you persuade half of London to be quiet about it as well.'

'London will soon find something else to talk about,' Prudence replied, curiously echoing Mr Tyler's words on a previous occasion. 'No one need know. Unless you choose to mention it, of course.'

'Prudence, are you threatening me?' Elfrida asked, cautiously.

'Why should I do that?' her niece replied innocently. Immediately after this, she went on to talk about some different matter, and Elfrida, cursing herself for her lack of courage, allowed the business to be dropped.

But on the morning when they set out, all the bad feeling that there had been between them seemed to have vanished. Prudence was in buoyant mood and Elfrida felt unaccountably optimistic. This was partly because they were leaving London, she decided. It had never been a lucky place for her, although on this occasion, she had been happier than ever before, despite the problems that had occurred. Perhaps it had something to do with the fact that she would soon be seeing Revd Stanley Erskine again, she mused. She thought of the handsome rector and smiled, but her heart did not beat any faster; not even at the thought that he might well use the opportunity provided by the stay at Winchcomb Hall in order to propose. There must be some other reason for the feeling of excitement that was bubbling up inside her.

It was only when Mr Tyler ran athletically down the steps of his house, and after a brief parting word to his butler and a cheery word of greeting to his travelling companions sprang into the saddle that she suddenly realized what it might be. Colouring, she sat back in her place. Surely she was past the age of getting excited at the sight of a well-looking man! Prudence, noticing her heightened colour, eyed her with a sudden feeling of suspicion.

Somewhat to her surprise, both Mr Tyler and Lieutenant Collett had elected to ride, at least for the first part of the journey. She wondered whether Prudence would betray any disappointment, but if she was prey to such an emotion, she did not show it. No doubt she was looking forward to the chance of spending some time with Digby when they halted for meals and for overnight stays.

They took the Great North Road out of London, and at this time of year the thoroughfare was very busy. They continually seemed to be encountering other fine carriages, humbler conveyances, and riders on horseback. Occasionally, they would hear one of the gentlemen accompanying them — usually Mr Tyler — calling out a greeting.

They halted at Barnet to change the horses, and also to enjoy a light meal. The day was warm, and they all found that they were quite satisfied with some cold meat and bread and cheese. The gentlemen were glad to be offered a glass of ale, but Prudence and Elfrida were both very grateful for a cup of tea. Elfrida noticed that the atmosphere between Digby and Tyler appeared polite, rather than cordial. She fully expected the gentlemen to want to get into the carriage after Barnet, but Tyler explained that they would ride on horseback a little further.

'We'll wait until we've negotiated Barnet Hill and Pricklers Hill,' he said. 'One of those would be hard enough for a team of horses to cover, but with the two together I think we need to lighten the load.'

'Do we need to get out as well?' Elfrida asked.

'Spoken like a true countrywoman,' he answered with a smile. 'I think not today.'

It was late on Saturday afternoon when they arrived in Huntingdon, and it must be said that they were all very glad to reach the end of the journey.

After Pricklers Hill the gentlemen had indeed joined the ladies in the carriage, and the conversation, although lively at times, was not such as to make Elfrida feel either happy or relaxed. Lieutenant Collett was the least cheerful of them all, and seemed very much inclined to sulk. Prudence did her best to encourage him into a better humour, but although up to a point he attempted to respond to her attempts to flirt with him, his efforts very much conveyed a feeling of teeth gritted in order to perform an unpleasant duty.

It was Mr Tyler who saved the situation by talking lightly and easily on all kinds of topics. Elfrida, determined to avoid any awkward silences, responded at first out of desperation, but soon out of genuine interest, and she attempted to draw Prudence into the conversation whenever possible.

Tyler certainly seemed to have a very wide knowledge of the history of the Great North Road and the towns through which it passed. Without boring the company with tedious facts and figures, he was able to throw interesting light on the places through which they travelled.

'Baldock always looks to be an interesting place,' Elfrida remarked as they travelled. 'Such a curious name.'

'The story goes that it was called Baghdad at one time — named by the Knights Templar after their return from the crusades.'

'How extraordinary. But was there no settlement there before then?'

'I dare say there must have been some kind of Roman settlement. The Great North Road crosses one of the Roman roads thereabouts.'

'But Baghdad!' Elfrida exclaimed again. 'What a very odd notion. Is it anything like Baghdad? But no, I apologize. Why should I expect you to — ?'

'Yes, I have been to Baghdad,' Tyler replied, 'Although not for a good many years now. As far as I recall, Baldock isn't anything like it.'

'You will soon find, ma'am, that my kinsman has been everywhere,' Digby put in. He had intended to sound jocular, but only succeeded in sounding like someone with a mouthful of sour grapes.

Taking pity on him, Elfrida said, 'But you have been to different places too, surely, in the course of your soldiering career, and must have taken part in a number of battles.'

Digby reddened and looked away. 'Unfortunately not,' he said.

Elfrida waited for further enlightenment, but he said nothing more, and Prudence and Tyler both turned away to look out of the window. The atmosphere felt decidedly tense, so she reverted to the earlier topic, remarking, 'If indeed there was an earlier settlement at Baldock, it must have been called *something*.'

'I believe it was named something similar sounding to Baldock, and the Knights Templar simply made a play on words,' Tyler answered. He lounged very much at his ease, his legs crossed, one arm resting lightly on the window frame, the other hand beside him on the leather seat. He had shapely hands, Elfrida noted, both bare of rings save for a gold signet ring on the little finger of his right hand. His demeanour was in marked contrast to that of Digby, who looked tense and rather uncomfortable.

'How do you come to be so knowledgeable about these matters?' Elfrida asked the older man curiously. Baldock was not the only place about which he seemed to be well informed.

'During my soldiering career, I sustained rather a serious injury, and was obliged to convalesce for quite a long period,' he replied. 'I needed something to occupy my mind whilst I was confined to the house, and my youngest sister took pity on me. She entertained me by taking me on a long, imaginary journey along the Great North Road. We made a scrap book . . . '

'A scrap book!' Digby exclaimed, disbelievingly.

'Yes, a scrap book,' Tyler responded, completely unflustered by the almost sneering nature of Digby's tone. 'We put in drawings, maps, way bills and anything else that we could get hold of. I still have it at home somewhere.'

'How inventive,' remarked Elfrida. 'Do you not think so, Prudence?'

'Yes certainly,' Prudence responded, apparently unaffected by Digby's bad mood. 'How fascinated your family members will be to read it in a hundred years' time.'

'Indeed,' Elfrida agreed. 'When one thinks how travel has changed over the last century. Why, Mr Erskine' — and here she coloured a little — 'was remarking just before I came to London on how amazing it was that the journey from Grantham should take only sixteen hours.'

'I cannot wait to meet this famous Mr Erskine,' Prudence said, her demure tones in marked contrast to the mischievous expression on her face.

'Is he famous? *I* never heard of him,' commented Digby.

'You have not heard of everyone, dear boy,' murmured Mr Tyler, bringing a flush to the young lieutenant's cheek. 'Is Mr Erskine a student of different modes of travel, ma'am?' he asked Elfrida politely.

'No. That is to say, I do not think so,' Elfrida replied. 'I think his interests are more to do with ancient Greek and Hebrew.'

'Really?' murmured Mr Tyler with a wry smile. 'Poor Miss Frobisher.'

Elfrida glanced at him, and their eyes met, his still full of amusement. She would have liked to have asked for enlightenment with regard to his last speech, but was afraid that what he would say might not be strictly proper. Instead, she made some neutral comment about the passing scenery and hoped that everyone would take the hint and allow the subject of the Revd Stanley Erskine to drop. Knowing Prudence, however, she felt that she could not place any dependence upon her not bringing the subject up again out of sheer devilment.

Both Saturday and Sunday night were spent in Huntingdon at The George. Elfrida and Prudence shared one room and Digby and his kinsman shared another because the inn was busy. It had been Elfrida's choice to occupy the same room as her niece, but she could not imagine that Mr Tyler would ever choose to share a room with the younger man. When he murmured to her on their arrival in Huntingdon, 'I'll keep an eye on him for you,' she realized that he had chosen to do so in order to oblige her, and her heart gave a little unaccountable lift.

'You are very kind,' she murmured.

'I was brought up to care for the young and vulnerable,' he replied; which remark caused her heart to sink down into her boots. Obviously, he was concerned for his young kinsman, who was behaving very much like a man who, having been rejected by the lady of his choice, had decided to take it out on everybody else. She must not start behaving like some flustered elderly spinster, for ever imagining that the least little attention from a man was a compliment to her! And why should she be wanting compliments from Mr Tyler in any case?

★　★　★

They attended the parish church on the Sunday morning, where Prudence nearly proved to be her aunt's undoing by asking after the service in tones of deceptive innocence, 'The vicar is rather handsome, Aunt Elfrida. Is he as handsome as Mr Erskine, do you think?'

Elfrida hushed her down, but not before she had seen Mr Tyler eyeing her in a measuring way. Part of her did not want Mr Tyler to suppose that her connection with Mr Erskine was either definite or romantic. There

206

was, however, another part of her that wanted him to think that other men might find her desirable. Quite why this should be the case, she found it impossible to say.

As for Anthea's plans to marry Prudence off to Mr Tyler, Elfrida decided that only the most inveterate of optimists could now imagine that anything would come of them. If Prudence was not interested in Digby, she showed no signs of transferring her affections to Rufus Tyler. She did not even behave towards him in the *un*interested kind of way that seemed to pique some gentlemen. Tyler, for his part, showed no signs of being attracted to Prudence.

To her great relief, however, one thing seemed quite clear: the attraction between Digby and Prudence was on the wane. Digby could hardly bring himself to speak civilly to Prudence, and for her part, Prudence seemed supremely indifferent to his ill-humour. At least there would be one piece of good news to pass on to Anthea!

She would not have been nearly as sanguine if she could have heard the conversation that Prudence had with Digby on the Sunday afternoon when the four of them strolled around the town, the younger couple walking ahead by a few steps.

'I have decided that we will act tomorrow

night,' Prudence was saying. 'I was going to wait until Tuesday night, but frankly, I do not think that I can put up with your sulky face for another twenty-four hours.'

'Well I like that!' exclaimed Digby indignantly. 'Here I am, putting myself out for you and deceiving not just your aunt but my own kinsman — my rich and powerful kinsman — into the bargain! I would very much like to know what more I could be doing to support your cause!'

'You could put a smile on your face for a start,' Prudence retorted. 'Only the most demented person could possibly suppose that you were in love with me.'

'I can't help that,' Digby replied. 'I'm not an actor and I never thought I was supposed to be one.'

'Never mind all that,' Prudence said decisively. 'As I have already said, I have decided that the best thing that we can do is to make our move tomorrow night.'

'*Our* move?' Digby uttered cautiously.

'Yes, *our* move, for you know I cannot manage without you. But don't worry; there will not be a great deal for you to do. You will only have to keep Mr Tyler occupied whilst I deal with Aunt Elfrida.'

'Keep him occupied?' Digby exclaimed, in a voice that was rather close to being a squeak.

'Ssh!' Prudence responded. 'Do you want to arouse suspicion? Smile and look pleased to be with me.'

Digby did his best, but only the most uncritical person would have judged his expression to be anything other than rather sickly. 'How am I supposed to keep him occupied?' he asked, the fixed grin on his face giving his voice rather a constricted tone. 'I don't think he even likes me much above half.'

'I would have thought that that was perfectly obvious,' Prudence replied scornfully.

'Then you tell me if it is so obvious.'

'You know what men talk about,' Prudence answered. 'Gambling, horse-racing, wine; there must be any number of things. Just use your imagination.'

Digby tried to imagine himself entertaining Tyler, his distinguished relative, a man nearly twenty years his senior, and someone of whom he had always been somewhat in awe, to boot. 'I can't do that,' he protested, losing some of his colour.

'I don't see why not,' Prudence replied unsympathetically. 'I shall need to distract Aunt Elfrida and I am not complaining, and I have not met her nearly as often as you have met Mr Tyler. Why, you are almost neighbours.'

'But you don't understand,' Digby complained.

'No, I can't say that I do,' Prudence answered him in long-suffering tones. 'It seems to me that you are simply going out of your way to make difficulties. I am going to all this trouble to make arrangements, and all *you* can do is make piffling objections. I have to say that I am very disappointed in you, Digby. *Very disappointed.*'

This decisive remark coincided with their arrival back at The George, and Digby was left with the uncomfortable feeling that somehow, although this whole matter was nothing whatsoever to do with him, he was not pulling his weight. Of one thing he would be unreservedly glad, however: within a little more than a day and a half, Prudence's scheme would be put into action, with any luck she would be reunited with her captain, and her fate would no longer be any of his concern.

★ ★ ★

That night in their room, Elfrida ventured to speak to Prudence very gently on the subject of Digby. 'It seems to me, my dear, that you are not as close to him as once you were,' she suggested tactfully.

'Really, Aunt?' Prudence said warily, brushing her hair as she tried to work out which way this conversation was going to go.

'Do not think I blame you,' answered Elfrida, walking about the room as she sought to find the right way to express herself. 'I know that sometimes first romances can die a natural death when new scenes and new people come into view.'

'I suppose you are right,' Prudence agreed, still feeling her way. 'How did you come to the conclusion that we were . . . not so close?'

Elfrida smiled. 'Your demeanour towards one another is scarcely affectionate,' she replied. 'Have you had a sudden disagreement?'

'Why should you think that?' Prudence asked.

'Lieutenant Collett was very anxious to accompany us; indeed his manner towards Mr Tyler was almost aggressive. But now the pair of you look at times as if you can hardly bear to be in the same carriage,' Elfrida replied. 'Well, no doubt your mama will be pleased.'

Instantly, she wished the words unsaid. Prudence's reaction though was not as hasty as she had feared.

'I don't suppose you can wait to tell her,' was the girl's answer. 'Just don't expect me to turn from him to Rufus Tyler, because it won't happen.'

'I didn't think it would,' Elfrida replied. 'I have never thought that you were well suited.'

'I am sure you are right,' Prudence agreed. 'It is my belief that Mr Tyler is attracted to a very different kind of woman.'

Elfrida found herself colouring, and quickly introduced another topic of conversation. 'Why is it that Mr Collett is embarrassed about his military record?' she asked.

'It's rather unfortunate, and it isn't his fault,' Prudence replied. 'He joined up towards the end of the Peninsular War, but before he could see any action he caught the measles, and had to go home to recuperate. Then, just as he had recovered from that, he fell down the stairs and broke his ankle.'

'How dreadful,' Elfrida remarked.

'Yes, but that isn't all,' Prudence went on. 'He was nearly ready to join his regiment, when by the greatest ill fortune in the world he caught the mumps. By the time that he had recovered from that, the war was over. He only arrived at Waterloo in time to help clear up afterwards. He has hardly seen any active service at all.' She paused, then added, 'I think it very good-natured of Captain Graves and Captain Black to give him so much time.'

'Yes indeed,' Elfrida agreed. 'No wonder he is so sensitive about the matter.'

That night, after they had retired for the night, she remembered the earlier part of their conversation, and a new spectre arose in her mind. What if Prudence should tell Anthea that her aunt had sought to cut her out with Mr Tyler? The idea was too awful to contemplate. Unfortunately, the contemplation of it kept her awake long after her niece had gone to sleep.

13

The following day was the most overcast of the journey so far, but thankfully the weather kept fine, and to Elfrida's relief, the gentlemen rode. She had not been looking forward to a day with them all crammed together in the confined space of a closed carriage. The novelty of the proceedings having worn off, they had not proved to be a particularly congenial foursome. The atmosphere had not been improved by the slight disagreement that the gentlemen had had the previous evening.

It had been a trivial matter. The inn was quite busy, much of the accommodation was taken, and the company was quite mixed. After the meal was over, there was no suitable place to which the ladies might withdraw, so the party had remained together. Lieutenant Collett had consumed his wine rather rapidly and had become somewhat boisterous in his conversation. Mr Tyler, fearing that he might forget himself, had suggested in an undertone, which Elfrida had only just heard, that perhaps he had had enough.

'You needn't think you can order me

about, 'cause you can't,' Digby had replied in a louder voice. 'You ain't my commanding officer.'

'No, I'm not,' Tyler had agreed pleasantly. 'But there are ladies present.'

Digby had muttered to himself, but he had limited his consumption thereafter, and if he had sent one or two resentful looks in his kinsman's direction, he had not said anything more on the subject.

Following that incident, Elfrida had wondered whether the two gentlemen would want to be in one another's company when they set off the following morning, but although Digby had looked a little pale when he had come downstairs, he had consented to ride with Mr Tyler readily enough. In fact, Elfrida had Prudence to thank for this restraint on Digby's part. As they were preparing to take their places at table for breakfast, Digby whispered to Prudence, 'I shall be glad when I am no longer under my kinsman's eye. I am all out of patience with him.'

'Don't worry,' she replied. 'By this time tomorrow, you will have put him in his place in a perfectly splendid way.' After this conversation, Digby had taken to the saddle in a better mood.

On their arrival in Grantham, they stopped at the Mail Hotel, from where Elfrida had caught the London coach so very recently. In some ways, it seemed to her that it had only been five minutes since she had been there; in others, it seemed more like a lifetime.

Elfin, the landlord, greeted her with great pleasure and professed himself delighted to have the honour of serving her again. He also greeted her niece and other travelling companions with courtesy, announcing that he knew Mr Tyler very well, Lieutenant Collett less so. 'And how is the earl, if I may be so bold as to ask?' he enquired. 'I did hear that he was not so well recently.'

'That is correct, but my father is much better now, thank you,' Rufus replied.

'I'm pleased to hear it, sir. Miss Frobisher, there is a letter for you. It arrived this morning.'

Elfrida took the folded paper with a word of thanks, and opened it. 'It is from Mr Erskine,' she told her companions. 'He confirms that he will be meeting us here on Wednesday morning.' She turned to Digby and Tyler. 'I am known here, and Elfin will look after us very well. You must feel free to travel on tomorrow, or even this evening, if you wish. We shall be quite safe.'

'Thank you, ma'am, but we would not dream of deserting you,' Tyler replied. 'Would we, Digby?'

Digby flashed a resentful look at him before saying, 'I was going to say . . . that is, of course not! By no means!'

'You are very kind,' said Elfrida, feeling unaccountably relieved.

'For what hour would you like me to order dinner?' Rufus asked her.

While she was answering, Prudence looked at Digby in a very pointed way, then after Tyler had gone to speak to Elfin, she said, 'Do you mind, Aunt Elfrida, if Digby walks with me to a draper's shop? I should like to procure some ribbons which I forgot to get in London.'

'Very well,' Elfrida answered. 'Don't be too long.'

'What a relief,' she breathed, after the two had gone and Tyler had returned. Elfin had gone to make sure that the rooms were ready.

'Has she been such a trial to you?' Tyler asked sympathetically.

Elfrida sighed. 'I am sure I have made too much of it,' she confessed, 'but I never seem to be prepared, or at least, never prepared for the right thing. When I do try to exert my authority, I only make matters worse by setting her back up.'

'Trying to guide other people's children must always be a difficult task,' he replied. 'If you think you have done badly, remember how much Digby resents my interference. We shall both do much better with our own children, I'm sure.'

'I beg your pardon?' she asked, startled. Quite unexpectedly, a picture came into her mind of herself holding a baby with a head of copper-coloured hair, whilst Mr Tyler looked on, an expression of paternal pride on his face. Her eyes met his, her face flamed, but before she could think of a way of saying anything to make it clear that, of course, she understood that he was referring to any children that they might each have separately, Elfin came in to apologize for his muddle about the rooms and that they were ready.

Elfrida walked up the stairs, her mind a whirl. It had occurred to her that the notion of sharing an establishment and children with Mr Tyler was rather an appealing one.

In the meantime, Digby was accompanying Prudence along Grantham High Street. 'What was that about?' he asked her.

'Come on, there's a draper's shop over there. That will do,' Prudence said, not answering his question.

'You don't mean to say you really wanted to buy some blasted ribbon, do you?'

'Of course I don't,' Prudence replied scornfully. 'We have other things to do, and to discuss. But if we go back without any, Aunt

Elfrida will be suspicious.' Once inside the shop, she said to the assistant, 'I would like three yards of pink satin ribbon, two inches wide if you please.'

The shop assistant brought out a selection from under the counter for her inspection, but Prudence, ignoring his polite murmurings as to the suitability of different tones for different complexions, pointed to the first one and said 'That one, thank you.'

The purchase made, they left the shop and Prudence turned right, away from the inn. 'Now here's the plan,' she said. 'Tonight, after we retire, Aunt Elfrida will send for warm milk as she always does. I will slip some sleeping powder into it. You must do the same with Mr Tyler.'

'What?' exclaimed Digby, horrified. 'How on earth will I do that? He doesn't even drink warm milk.'

'Don't be silly,' Prudence answered, in the patient tones of someone trying to explain something very simple to a rather backward child. 'Suggest that you have some brandy before you retire. Put it in that.'

'But he is hardly likely to want to join me in a brandy,' Digby protested. 'Our relationship has not exactly been cordial on this journey, has it?'

'Whose fault is that?' Prudence asked

accusingly. 'You haven't been very friendly to him, have you?'

'If you recall, he went out of his way to make me drink less last night,' Digby pointed out. 'He will hardly want to drink more with me this evening.'

Prudence frowned for a moment, then her brow cleared. 'You must be more abstemious at dinner,' she said. 'Apologize for last night's over-indulgence. Say you were in a bad mood about something or other; maybe even because I seem to have lost interest in you. Then at bedtime, tell him that you particularly want to make up to him for your lack of cordiality and would he like to share a brandy with you? That should do the trick.'

'It might,' agreed Digby cautiously. 'What then?'

'Come and tap on our door when the deed is done. I shall certainly manage to do it before you do, as we always retire earlier.'

'And if you haven't?'

'Just pretend you're feeling sick. Aunt Elfrida will find you something, and while she's distracted, I will make sure she takes the drug. But in the meantime, there is another job for you to do.'

'What now?' sighed Digby.

'You must go to another hostelry that is near to The Mail and hire us a conveyance

— a gig will do — and do it under an assumed name. After we have drugged Aunt Elfrida and Mr Tyler, we will go and collect the gig and set off for Daniel's home. Once you have got me there, you may go wherever you please.'

'I shall be glad when this is all over,' uttered Digby, in tones of heartfelt sincerity.

'So shall I,' Prudence agreed, surprising him.

That evening, Digby made a real attempt to be more sociable, and the atmosphere at the table was markedly better, drawing a word of praise from Tyler after the ladies had gone upstairs.

'I'm sorry about last night, sir,' Digby replied, following Prudence's advice. 'The fact is, I was feeling a little blue-devilled, and made a bit of a fool myself.'

'Rejected you, has she?' Tyler asked. 'It does happen, you know. You have my sympathy, but I feel bound to tell you that I never thought you'd suit.'

'Neither do I think so now, sir,' Digby replied with perfect sincerity. 'I hope you'll allow me to order brandy for us; to drink to a better understanding, you know.'

For one heart-stopping moment Digby feared that his kinsman would refuse, but then the older man smiled. 'That's very kind of you. Come to my room and we can relax.'

To his room! It couldn't be better, Digby thought exultantly, touching in his pocket the screw of paper with the powder inside.

No two conspirators could ever have had an easier time of it. Neither victim queried the taste or colour of the drink offered to them, both drank as they were supposed to, and both fell deeply asleep, Elfrida sitting up in bed clad in her nightgown, and Mr Tyler slumped in a chair in his room, his coat, waistcoat and cravat discarded, his shirt unbuttoned at the neck.

As soon as he was quite certain that Rufus was sound asleep, Digby tiptoed to the opposite room, and knocked on the door. Prudence opened it so quickly that it seemed as if she must have been standing immediately behind it. She was dressed for travelling.

'Is he asleep?' she whispered. There were no sounds emerging from other rooms, and no sign that anyone was coming upstairs, but it did not do to be careless.

'Sound asleep,' replied Digby, in a similar tone. He was grinning now that the deed was done. 'He's sitting in a chair by the fireplace.'

'I'll come and help you put him in bed,' said Prudence, going with him into the other room. The sight of Mr Tyler sitting there gave even such a dauntless woman as Prudence

Winchcomb pause. However, she took a deep breath and said, 'Come on. Let's put him to bed. You take off his shoes and stockings whilst I turn the bed down.'

Digby did as he was bid, then Prudence came over to him and together, they lifted Rufus on to the bed, Digby taking his shoulders and Prudence his feet. 'Now I'll find his night shirt and you can get him undressed,' she said.

'What?' exclaimed Digby, his voice sounding very loud after all the whispering.

'Shh!' Prudence responded, horrified.

'I'm not going to undress him,' he said firmly, but once more in a low tone. 'It would feel like . . . like . . . well, it would feel wrong.'

A moment's thought was enough to convince Prudence of the justice of this. After all, she had not had to undress her aunt, for Elfrida had already been prepared for bed. 'Just take his shirt off, then,' she said eventually. 'Put it with the rest of his clothes in that bag, and bring them into our room.'

Digby still felt very awkward at removing Mr Tyler's shirt, and it seemed to him to take an eternity when the person being divested of his garment was not in a state to co-operate. Eventually he finished the task, then put the garments he had removed into the bag, together with the things that his kinsman had

223

already discarded. He then took the bag into the opposite room.

He found that Prudence had packed everything in the room, her aunt's things and her own, and had pulled the covers off Miss Frobisher's body. In her nightgown, she looked almost absurdly young.

'You take her shoulders and I'll take her feet, and we'll carry her through,' said Prudence.

'Into Tyler's room?' Digby asked, scandalized.

'Yes. I think it an excellent scheme,' replied Prudence. 'They are bound to pursue us, but they cannot very well do so until they have found their clothes and made their way out of a locked room. And besides, I have never thought that he was the man for me, but I have become convinced recently that he may be just the man for Aunt Elfrida. I am simply going to throw them together. Come on.'

Swept along by the authority in Prudence's voice, and by the feeling that things could hardly be worse, Digby did as he was told. They paused in the doorway, Prudence going first and glancing this way then that to make sure that they were not observed. She looked back at Digby in order to tell him that all was clear. Her eyes met his, the absurdity of what they were doing struck them both at the same time, and they began to giggle. For a few moments, they could do nothing but stand and shake, and the more they stood there, the motionless form of Miss Frobisher held between them quivering at the same time, the more they wanted to laugh.

Eventually, however, they gained enough control over themselves to hurry across the passage with their burden. 'Now what?' asked Digby.

'Just hold on to her for a moment while I put her feet down,' said Prudence, suiting her actions to her words.

'I say, be quick won't you?' said Digby in anxious tones, as he clasped Miss Frobisher to his manly bosom. 'This is feeling deuced improper.'

'I won't be a moment,' Prudence answered as she pulled down the bed clothes. 'Now, let's put her in.'

'In bed with my kinsman?' queried Digby, aghast.

'Do you want her to catch cold?' asked Prudence indignantly, bending to take hold of her aunt's feet. 'Come on. I don't know exactly how strong those sleeping powders are.'

The ideas that these words aroused were so horrific that Digby hurried to do as he was bid, and soon Elfrida and Rufus were tucked up together under the covers.

'Now you take their clothes down to the stables and hide them somewhere,' said Prudence. 'I'll lock the door. Then all we have to do is get our own things together and be away. Did you order the gig?' Digby nodded. 'Then let's hurry. Every minute saved is another stretch away from here.'

No hitch occurred to spoil their plans. Having hidden Miss Frobisher and Mr Tyler's bags, Digby returned to collect his own bag and Prudence's. Then together, they hurried a short distance down the road, collected the gig which Digby had bespoken the previous day, and in no time at all, they were on their way.

14

The following morning's awakening was like none that Elfrida had ever known. She gradually regained consciousness, aware that the pillow on which she was leaning was warmer, firmer and hairier than had been her experience heretofore. Finding the feeling of it not unpleasant, although rather unusual, she snuggled closer. It was only when an arm encircled her that she became fully awake. Thoroughly startled, she attempted to pull away, only to find herself drawn more firmly against what she now realized was a masculine chest.

'Too late to change your mind,' said a voice, that to her astonishment she recognized as Mr Tyler's. At the same moment, he sat up, and tipped her on to her back and looked down at her, his face shadowed by a night's growth of beard, and framed by a mop of tousled red hair. 'God, you're pretty,' he said, his eyes gleaming in the semi-darkness of the curtained room. 'I've always thought so.' Then his mouth descended on hers. She put out her hands to push him away, but when they met his bare shoulders, the same odd thing happened as when he had embraced her in the conservatory, for they seemed to linger quite of their own volition, absorbing the silken texture of his skin. Thankfully, before she could really disgrace herself by returning his embrace, she felt his hand working at the fastening of her nightgown; sanity returned, and she pushed against him with all her strength.

'No!' she exclaimed. 'No, this is wrong. What are you doing in my bed, sir?'

'It would seem to be more to the point to ask you what you are doing in mine,' he replied, making as if to take her in his arms again. 'Or can I hazard a guess?'

This time, she foiled him by getting out of the bed altogether. She looked round wildly. 'Good heavens, so I am!' she cried, her voice bewildered. 'How came this to be?' She turned to look accusingly at Rufus Tyler. 'You did this.'

'Did what?' he asked her, his voice honestly puzzled.

'You brought me in here; at dead of night.'

'I certainly didn't,' he answered. 'As far as I am aware, you arrived in my bed this morning like some delightful parcel — and it isn't even my birthday.'

'No, I did not,' she retorted, staring at him indignantly. Again she became aware of his naked chest, covered with a light dusting of hair, and she turned away, covering her confusion by saying crossly, 'I wish you would put something on.'

He sighed, murmured, 'What a missed opportunity,' and got off the bed, intending to oblige her. However, a few moments' search revealed to him that none of his clothes appeared to be in the room. 'This is beginning to look not just suspicious but sinister,' he said, his brow furrowed, as he closed the empty chest at the foot of the bed. 'Miss Frobisher, what is your last waking memory?'

Elfrida frowned. 'I was sitting up in bed, drinking my milk,' she replied. Feeling his ironic eye upon her, she looked straight at him and said defensively, 'There is nothing wrong in drinking warm milk at night! It helps me get to sleep.'

'We all have our own methods,' he replied, in deceptively innocent tones, as he made a more careful search of his room.

'I dare say,' she replied, her chin high. 'Anyway, I did go straight off to sleep, I believe, but that is not unusual for me. What of you?'

'Digby and I shared a brandy in this room, and before you ask, no, I did not over indulge; in fact, I was quite abstemious, partly to give my young relative a good example.' He looked thoughtful. 'The last thing I remember is sitting in that chair with a glass in my hand.'

'But surely, the brandy might have made you drowsy, might it not?' Rufus looked at her, one eyebrow raised. 'I was only asking,' she added defensively.

'Not in that quantity,' he assured her. 'Miss Frobisher, I believe we have been the victims of a plot.'

'You think they have eloped?' she exclaimed, aghast.

'I fear so. They must have drugged us, then made their escape.'

'Oh, the wicked girl!' Elfrida cried. 'And after all the sympathy I extended to her last night, as well.'

'It would appear that our sympathy was wasted,' he replied calmly.

'Indeed.' She began to pace about the room. 'She had me completely fooled. I was certain that the romance was at an end. She must have been laughing up her sleeve at me all the time.'

'That was no doubt what she intended you to think,' he agreed.

'We must get after them straight away!' she declared.

'Like this?' he asked her, his palms spread

open. She glanced again at his chest, then looked away. 'I've looked in all the cupboards, and my clothes have gone. I suppose I should count myself fortunate that they left me with my breeches.' He paused. 'I fear I misjudged the situation this morning; I'm sorry — on two counts.'

'Two?' Elfrida ventured.

'The first, that I subjected you to embarrassment; the second . . . ' He smiled, and she noticed for the first time what a very attractive smile he had. It crinkled up the corners of his eyes and softened his rather harsh features. 'Never mind that for now. Let's just get out of here.'

This was easier said than done. The door was locked; the key was gone, and was nowhere to be found. 'I could put my shoulder to it, but that would attract the kind of attention that we are most anxious to avoid,' said Rufus with a frown. 'There's nothing for it. We shall have to ring for help. Stay out of sight, behind the door. I'll pretend that I am alone in here, then when someone comes with a key, I'll distract him so that you can sneak across to your own room. Thank heaven our rooms are so close! My prayer is that your room will not be locked as well.'

'And if it is?'

He grinned. 'At least you're adequately covered.'

Elfrida glanced down at her nightgown-covered body. It was indeed a more modest garment than the evening gowns worn by many a society lady. If her door was locked, then she would just have to improvise some story.

Rufus rang the bell, and while they were waiting for someone to come in response, Elfrida said, 'I wonder what time it is?'

'I would guess quite late in the morning, from the sound of bustle outside,' he answered. 'Digby appears to have taken my watch along with my clothes, curse him. What I won't do to the little rat when I've caught him . . . '

'You must do as you see fit,' Elfrida responded, 'but I cannot help thinking that the little rat may have been acting under orders. What she sees in him — ' Suddenly realizing that she was addressing Digby's kinsman, she broke off, adding, 'I beg your pardon.'

'Not at all,' he reassured her. 'I've often thought the same. Your niece is, forgive the expression, ten times the man that Digby is. He has been woefully spoiled by his sisters, I fear.'

At that moment, they heard the sound of

footsteps in the passage and a servant knocked on the door. 'Can I help you, sir?' a man asked from the other side of the wood panel.

'I certainly hope so,' Rufus answered in an irascible tone. 'My kinsman has locked me in for a prank. Please find another key and let me out without delay.'

'Yes, sir, of course,' answered the servant. There was a moment's pause, then he went on, 'Are you alone in there, sir?'

'Of course I'm alone,' answered Mr Tyler, glancing at his companion.

'Only none of the rest of your party appears to be about.'

'Nonsense,' snapped Tyler irritably. 'Now fetch that damned key. If you think I want to bandy words with you through a locked door then you're very much mistaken.'

'Yes, sir.'

After he had gone, Tyler turned back to Elfrida. 'We will have to be very careful,' he said. Then he took in her appearance, her long hair hanging down her back, together with her nightdress, making her look very young, as Digby had noted the night before, and he felt suddenly protective. 'You *are* pretty,' he said. Their eyes met and held for a long moment, and neither of them heard the approaching steps of the landlord, so that his anxious voice came as a complete surprise.

'Mr Tyler, sir, I have a key here.'

Rufus gestured to Elfrida to stand behind the door. 'Thank heaven for that,' he answered. 'When I get hold of my young relative, I shall give him a good thrashing, I can tell you.'

They heard the sound of the key turning in the lock, and the door opened to reveal the landlord looking every bit as anxious as he had sounded. 'Mr Tyler, this is a dreadful thing, and no mistake,' he declared. 'Whatever made him do it, sir?'

'Sheer devilment, no doubt,' answered Rufus, holding the door and standing so that the landlord could not come past. 'The worst of it is that the young rascal has taken my clothes.'

'Your clothes, sir? What, all of them?'

'All of them that I had with me, apart from what you see before you. My servant has travelled ahead with most of my gear. My hope is that Digby will have hidden them somewhere in the inn. Send someone to shave me, and find me a shirt and some shoes, there's a good fellow, then I can go and look for them.'

'Of course, of course,' Elfin replied. 'I'll send a man up and I'll also set someone on to making a search of all possible places.'

As soon as Elfin had disappeared around the turn of the stairs, Tyler stepped back into the room. 'He's gone,' he said. 'Go back to your room and see if your things have gone too.'

She hurried to do as she was bid, but in her haste, caught the hem of her nightgown on a protruding nail near the bottom of the door. She turned to try and free herself and Tyler, perceiving her difficulty, came out to help her for speed's sake. He had just freed her garment and was rising to his feet, when they heard the sound of footsteps and, looking towards the staircase, they saw a gentleman emerge and look at them, an expression of horror and outrage upon his face.

'Mr Erskine!' Elfrida exclaimed. Then, since the reverend gentleman remained silent, she went on, 'Mr Tyler was ... was just freeing me from ... from ...'

'There is no need to explain yourself, my dear,' said Tyler, smiling at her kindly in a way which sought to convey reassurance. He then turned to Mr Erskine. 'Miss Frobisher and I have been the victims of an unkind practical joke, from which we were attempting to extricate ourselves. She had just come to tell me that she feared her niece had absconded with my kinsman. I already feared the worst, for my kinsman had locked me in my room and taken my clothes away. Miss Frobisher was just returning to her room to see whether her clothes, too, had been taken, when her nightgown became caught on that nail.'

'I see,' replied Mr Erskine, still looking disapproving. He was, Mr Tyler was irritated to discover, a very handsome man.

'Excuse me,' Elfrida murmured, and quickly crossed the corridor to her own room. So embarrassed was she by the scene that had just taken place, that she was inside the room with the door closed without even taking time to wonder whether the door would be locked or not. Why, she thought, as she looked at herself in the mirror. I must be utterly shameless! I have just confronted the rector dressed in my nightgown and I did not even blush!

She made a swift search of her room and discovered that her clothes had all been taken as well. How long would it take to find them, she wondered? The majority of her clothes, like those of Mr Tyler, had been sent on ahead, but she could always send to her home, which was quite nearby, and ask for some things to be brought to her from there. Whatever she did, she would have to find some solution to her problem quickly, for she would have to get after that mischievous pair as soon as possible. She must do her very best to prevent a marriage which Prudence's parents would deplore. In all this, she gave only a passing thought to the Revd Stanley Erskine and his suspicions. Amid the morass of confusion in which she found herself, that seemed to be the least of her worries.

Realizing that to give credence to Mr Tyler's story, she ought to act immediately, she rang the bell and, as soon as the maid had come, reported the loss of her clothes. 'Mr Tyler's things have been taken as well, apparently, so they may be together somewhere,' she added, without thinking how it would sound. She heard muffled giggling in the passage as she was closing the door. She decided that she would need to have her wits about her if she were not to become notorious in the Grantham area.

Fortunately, since Tuesday was the day when the head groom insisted on the stables being cleaned thoroughly, the things belonging to Mr Tyler and Miss Frobisher were soon found, and taken up to their rooms. This was more of a relief to Elfrida, for whilst Mr Tyler had been able to borrow some garments so that he could help with the search, there had been no one of Elfrida's size who had been able to lend her anything, so she had been obliged to stay upstairs in her nightgown.

Someone had brought her breakfast and a cup of tea, for which she had been grateful. She had found, however, that deciding to keep to one's room, and being obliged to do so, were two very different things, and she was heartily glad to be able to get dressed and go downstairs.

She was shown into the parlour which had been set on one side for their whole party's use, but was a little disconcerted to find the Revd Stanley Erskine waiting in there. Had she given the matter any thought, she would have guessed that he must have left the inn. She recalled how when she had last seen him, she had been in her night attire, and she blushed profusely.

Seeing this, his rather austere expression softened, and he stepped forward to take her hand. 'I am glad you have recovered your things,' he said. 'What an awkward time you have had.'

'Yes indeed, I — ' she began. Then she broke off as the door opened and Mr Tyler entered the room. It was the first time that she had seen him since he had put on a shirt and the memory of his unclad torso made her colour up even more. He was now dressed with propriety in a dark-green coat with buff breeches and exceedingly shiny top boots.

It was also the first time that Elfrida had

been able to compare the two men side by side at her leisure. Even after just a very short time in London, she now seemed to be able to detect that although Mr Tyler and Mr Erskine were wearing similar garments in number and nature, there was something about Rufus's apparel that said 'style'.

In looks, the clergyman was undoubtedly superior, being taller, and with classically handsome features. There was, however, something about Tyler, perhaps a mobility of feature, or a sense of repressed energy, that caught the eye after the gaze had passed on from the more overtly attractive man.

'Mr Erskine,' said Rufus, crossing the room and putting out his hand. 'Forgive my lack of manners at our first meeting. I was a little overset, due to my kinsman's unkind prank.'

'Not at all, sir,' Erskine replied, politely, but still with a degree of stiffness as, after a moment's hesitation, he took the hand offered to him. 'I believe that most people would have been similarly disconcerted.'

Rufus turned to Elfrida, taking care to stand between herself and the clergyman, so that her expression could not be seen. 'We must be very cautious under what circumstances we invite those two pranksters to our home when we are married, my dear,' he said in amused tones, but with a minatory glance and a warning squeeze of the hand.

'You are engaged?' exclaimed the rector. It was his turn to change colour, but unlike Elfrida he turned pale.

'Not formally, as yet,' answered Mr Tyler turning towards Erskine, but still keeping Elfrida slightly behind him. 'Of course Miss Frobisher is of age and need only consult her own preferences. But her family should be the first to know.'

'Of course,' echoed the rector in rather a hollow tone.

'I felt you should be told, lest you thought that there might be any impropriety in our staying here at this inn,' Rufus added. It was only now that he stepped to one side, and looked down at Elfrida, his gaze such a compelling one that she found herself unable to do anything other than return it. 'But I am sure that we may count upon your discretion, may we not, my dear?'

'Certainly,' she replied, realizing that some remark was called for from her, but not feeling able to come up with more than one word.

'I ... allow me to offer you my congratulations,' said the rector, his tone hesitant at first, but becoming almost embarrassingly hearty at the end. On his face was a rather artificial-looking smile. 'Is this not a little sudden, though?'

'Not at all,' answered Tyler, surprising them both. 'At least, not on my part. I met Miss Frobisher over ten years ago — in fact, my dear, I think it was nearer fifteen, was it not? — and fell head over heels instantly. However, I was rather a foolish young man — tricked out as a macaroni, would you believe? — and Elfrida very sensibly refused to have anything to do with me. But I never forgot her, and when I met her again in London, I was emboldened to press my suit. Luckily, Elfrida had not forgotten me either, had you, my dear? Apparently, she had always had a soft spot for me, and to my amazement, she accepted my proposal.'

'I had not realized that you had met before,' said Erskine, trying to sound interested, rather than forlorn.

There was a short silence and Elfrida, realizing that Tyler was expecting her to say something, said 'The meeting that my . . . my fiancé describes took place at a ball at Castle Clare.'

'Allow me to send for some refreshment so that you can drink our health,' said Rufus. 'It is not far short of noon, after all.'

'Thank you, no,' answered the rector disapprovingly. 'I never take strong drink in the middle of the day. I only called in briefly to see if there was any news of the travellers, then stayed on to see if I could be of service. But there are parish matters demanding my attention.' He swallowed. 'I presume, Miss Frobisher, that you will no longer be needing my escort tomorrow, if you have your . . . your promised husband to take care of you?'

'You are very kind,' replied Rufus. 'It will be my pleasure as well as my duty to escort Miss Frobisher to her family home. In any case, we are not at all sure whether we shall now be going there immediately. We must ascertain the whereabouts of our young relatives before we can attend to our own concerns, and Elfrida, I know, will not be happy until she is sure that Prudence is safe.'

Elfrida darted a look at him. She had not expected him to be so perceptive.

'Of course,' Erskine replied. He swallowed again. 'Should you . . . if you . . . that is, I would be honoured to conduct the ceremony if you wished. But I am sure you have other plans.'

Elfrida stepped forward then. 'You are very kind,' she said, her eyes full of sympathy. She was more than half inclined to tell him the truth, but Tyler laid a warning hand on her arm.

'Our plans are uncertain as yet,' he said

firmly. 'But thank you for your offer.'

'Then I will bid you good day,' said the rector, bowing stiffly, and leaving the room.

'Oh dear,' murmured Tyler. His words were sympathetic, but he did not sound particularly sorry.

His tone was not lost on Miss Frobisher, who answered accusingly, 'You needn't sound so pleased with yourself: you have just broken the poor man's heart.'

'I?' exclaimed Tyler, his brows soaring. 'I fear that was your doing, my sweet. After all, you have transferred your affections to another man.'

'I have done no such thing,' Elfrida retorted indignantly, 'and you know it. Why did you have to say that to him anyway?'

'Say what to him?'

'Why did you have to tell him that we are engaged?'

'To save your reputation, of course,' Tyler answered. 'Shall we ring for some coffee? I feel I could do with some.'

'My reputation would not have suffered,' Elfrida retorted. 'All we had to do was tell him the truth . . . ' Her voice faded away.

'Exactly,' Tyler replied, fixing her eyes with his. A servant came in answer to the bell and he ordered coffee for them. 'I told him as much of the truth as I thought he could bear.

Do you really think he would have been any happier if he had known that you and I had spent the night in bed together — in each other's arms?'

'Sshh!' Elfrida exclaimed, colouring all over again. 'Keep your voice down! It was not our fault.'

'And that makes it all right, does it?' said Tyler ironically. 'Don't forget the servants, either. Your staff or mine might hold their tongues, but inn servants aren't paid to be discreet. No one may know what happened last night for sure, but the tales of Miss Frobisher frolicking about in her nightwear with a semi-clad gentleman will be much too juicy to be kept secret.'

'Ooooh!' Elfrida exclaimed. Then, in her frustration she whirled round and said to him, 'It's all your fault!'

'Mine?' exclaimed Tyler. 'How should it be mine?'

'If you hadn't been wandering round with your chest — ' She halted abruptly.

'Exposed?' he suggested, grinning wickedly.

At that moment, fortunately for Elfrida's composure, the door opened and a servant came in with the coffee that Rufus had ordered. By the time the tray had been set down and the cups arranged, she had regained her poise. 'All this is getting us nowhere, sir,' she said. 'What we must do now is find out where those young people have gone and go after them.'

'Must we?' he murmured. He poured out some coffee, asking by gesture whether she wanted any cream, then brought her cup to her with the sugar bowl, from which she added a small spoonful. She could not help noticing how he carried out this traditionally female task with the same style that he brought to everything that he did.

'Of course we must,' she answered him indignantly. 'Prudence is my responsibility.'

He poured himself a cup of coffee, added neither cream nor sugar, and sat down, crossing his legs and looking very much at his ease. 'But Digby is not mine,' he reminded her. 'In fact, it is only my gallantry that has got me into this mess at all. Had I not offered to accompany you, then no doubt you would have accepted Digby's offer and Prudence would simply have drugged you, instead of both of us.'

'Exactly,' Elfrida agreed. 'In which case, no one would have seen us together, with you — ' Again she halted abruptly.

'With me half naked,' he agreed. 'My dear Miss Frobisher, how your mind does seem to keep going back to that moment, doesn't it?'

'It certainly does not,' she answered, her face aflame. 'I was not going to say that at all!'

He inclined his head. 'I beg your pardon,' he said. 'But to go back to Digby and Prudence, I think we probably put them out considerably, you and I.'

'What makes you say that?' Elfrida asked, her mind successfully diverted.

'I met Digby by chance as he was coming to your house on the day when we made the travelling arrangements. He was quite clearly a young man bent on an errand that gave him no pleasure at all, and was very displeased with me when I insisted on accompanying him inside the house.'

Elfrida nodded. 'Yes, I recall how disgruntled he was when you asked for permission to escort us before he could say anything,' she said thoughtfully. 'They must have been planning this for quite some time. No doubt they have now fled to the border.'

'Yes, but in what? The carriage is still in the stables.' Tyler got up and set his cup on the tray. 'If you will give orders for the carriage to be prepared and our belongings to be brought down, I will make investigations in the town,' he said. 'They must have hired another conveyance somewhere.'

'But I thought that you weren't going to help me?' she protested.

'Of course I'll help,' he answered, walking to the door. 'What self-respecting fiancé could do less?'

15

From Grantham, by the light of a clear moon, the runaway couple drove on to Lincoln, Digby handling the reins. Now that the deed had been accomplished, he had become almost euphoric, and was a much more cheerful travelling companion. He had harboured some anxieties as to what his kinsman might do to him when he caught up with him, but Prudence had managed to allay those.

'You need not worry,' she said. 'It is my belief that my aunt and Mr Tyler will make a match of it.'

'Really!' exclaimed Digby, so astounded at the novel idea of these rather elderly persons doing such a thing that he dropped his hands and was then obliged to pay some attention to his horses.

'Yes, of course,' Prudence answered impatiently. 'Did you not see how they were kissing in the conservatory? Mark my words, they will soon be so busy smelling of April and May themselves, they will have no time to worry about what we are doing.'

'They may even want to thank us for doing

them a favour,' suggested Digby.

Privately, Prudence thought that this was taking matters a little far, but she had no wish to spoil his more optimistic mood, and so instead, she began to speak of how they would get to Captain Black's home. 'When we get to Lincoln we will turn off for Gainsborough. Daniel's family live just a few miles from there.'

'And where are we to stay?' asked Digby. 'Or are we going to sleep overnight in a barn?'

Prudence smiled. 'I have organized things a little better than that,' she said smugly. 'I have a friend who lives in Lincoln. She knows all about Daniel and me and she will take us in.'

'And what will her family have to say about it?' Digby asked suspiciously.

'Susan is newly married and her husband is besotted with her — just like Daniel will be with me,' Prudence replied complacently. 'She will let us in and he will not have anything to say in the matter.'

'Does he know all about us then?'

Prudence shook her head. 'I have asked Susan to tell him that you are my brother,' she explained. 'We are hurrying north in order to claim an inheritance from an elderly relative who lives in Scunthorpe.'

'Why are we travelling so late?'

'Because our relative is like to die and we need to be there to be sure that the will is in our favour.'

'And your friend knows all about this scheme?'

'Oh yes. We corresponded about it. In fact, she contributed some of the detail.'

'Is she like you?' Digby asked suspiciously.

'A little — in some ways,' Prudence replied. Digby barely repressed a shudder.

He had to acknowledge that she was right in her assessment of matters, however. They arrived in Lincoln at an exceedingly late hour, and made their way to the home of Mr and Mrs Markham, a charming town house not very far from the cathedral. Late though it was, the young couple had stayed up to welcome them personally, and showed them to two comfortable rooms. Their horses were stabled just as comfortably, and on the morrow, after an excellent breakfast, they were on their way in good time, having said goodbye to their kindly and undemanding hosts.

'Next time I see you, you will be Mrs Daniel Black,' Susan whispered to her friend, as they climbed into the gig.

'Phew, that's a relief,' said Digby as they drove away. 'I nearly gave the whole thing away this morning. Your friend's husband

250

addressed me three times as Mr Winchcomb, before I remembered that I was supposed to be your brother.'

'What?' answered Prudence in a preoccupied tone. 'Oh . . . oh, yes, of course.'

The truth of the matter was that now that the adventure was nearly over, the moods of the two young people were almost exactly the reverse of what they had been at the start of things. Digby, who had been anxious, reluctant and preoccupied, was now bubbling over with good spirits. The part that he had been coerced into playing was almost at an end. Soon, he would willingly hand Prudence over to the man she loved. Then he would be able to please himself. He rather thought that an early encounter with Mr Tyler would not be a good idea, and certainly not until he was certain that a romance had indeed blossomed between Rufus and Prudence's aunt Elfrida. Of course, if this were the case, then that older pair of lovebirds might even see him as instrumental in bringing them together, and some form of largesse might be the result. If Prudence was mistaken, however, then playing least in sight might be a wise idea. Then, perhaps, he would be able to enjoy the blissful luxury of forgetting all about Prudence and her schemes.

Prudence's state of mind was quite different. Until that morning, the excitement of putting her scheme into action, and the planning which that had entailed had absorbed all her energies. Now, with all the work done, and just this final short journey to accomplish, amazed though Digby would have been to discover it, she was beginning to have second thoughts. It was not that she doubted her feelings for Daniel, or indeed, his for her. It was simply that she was trying to imagine what it would be like to walk up to the vicarage door and announce that she had come to elope with the son of the house. Whilst Digby was chattering merrily, picturing how amusing it would have been to witness their two relatives waking up in the same bed, and encouraging her to do the same, she was answering mechanically but at the same time trying to think of a better way of arranging a meeting with Daniel.

Eventually, she said, 'I know! When we get to the village where Daniel lives, we'll stop at the local inn. There is bound to be one. Then you can go to the vicarage and tell him that I am there.'

'Why can't you just go there yourself?' Digby asked. Prudence hesitated, and Digby, glancing at her, saw her face become suffused with colour. 'Aha!' he exclaimed.

'What do you mean, 'aha'?' Prudence asked defensively.

'You're afraid he'll turn you down,' Digby replied.

'No, I am not,' Prudence answered indignantly. 'It is simply that I cannot be sure of speaking privately to him at the vicarage.'

'You *are* afraid,' he insisted.

'Oh, hold your tongue,' she snapped.

Digby was not particularly perceptive, but this time, he detected the real note of panic in her voice. Although her controlling habits often irritated him, deep down he was very fond of her, so he said quickly, 'Only teasing! But I think you are very right to want to see him away from the vicarage. No doubt with Daniel home, all his little brothers and sisters'll be clamouring for his attention. You would find it very hard to speak to him alone.'

Prudence smiled gratefully. 'You've been a good friend, Digby,' she said. 'I've asked a lot of you and I haven't always been fair.'

'Nonsense,' he answered, but he was touched all the same.

The village of Horsfold was soon reached. It was not a large place, but in addition to the parish church, Prudence was pleased to see that it did boast an inn, and the landlord was able to settle miss in a private parlour, and find her some lemonade. 'I'll go and find Daniel straight away,' said Digby.

Once he had gone, Prudence was again assailed by doubts. What if Daniel should have left for America already? What would she do then? She had very thoroughly burned her boats by leaving her aunt in such an embarrassing situation. For the first time, she was overwhelmed by qualms of conscience. However could she have done such a thing? What would her mother say? How could she ever go home? She was still pacing the floor when the door opened to admit Daniel. He was no longer in his regimentals, but still looked exceedingly handsome in a coat of dark cloth with light breeches and shiny boots. On his face was a very anxious expression.

'Prudence! My darling!' he exclaimed. 'What has occurred?'

Prudence threw herself into his arms and, as much to her own astonishment as to his, burst into tears. He held her close, his heart beating fast, for he had steeled himself to never seeing her again. Then when her sobs had subsided, he guided her to the two-seater bench by the fireside, dried her tears, and took her hand.

'Now, sweetheart, you must tell me what is amiss. What brings you here? Are your parents ill? Has there been some mischance?'

'I have run away, Daniel,' she said in a small voice.

'Run away?' he said aghast. 'Has someone mistreated you? By God, he shall answer to me!' His firm, manly jaw hardened and his fine eyes sparkled. 'Was it Tyler?' he asked. 'Your mother told me that you were to marry him.'

'No one has mistreated me,' she answered, looking just as angry, 'but someone has certainly misrepresented me! How dare Mama say that I was to marry Mr Tyler?'

Had Prudence had any doubts about her captain's feelings for her, the glowing expression upon his face would instantly have put them to rest. 'You are not to marry him?' he exclaimed.

'No, never,' she answered. 'I shall never marry anyone but you.'

He stood up and walked away from her. 'My dearest, you tempt me with joys that can never be mine,' he said in a constrained tone. 'Your family will not permit you to marry a poor man, and whilst I hope to improve my prospects by my own exertions, I can make no promises.'

'Exactly,' she replied, standing up as well, 'which is why I have run away to be with you. My family will not permit our marriage, so we must elope.'

'Elope!' he exclaimed, turning towards her again, his face shocked.

She walked up to him and, turning her face downwards, played with the buttons on his waistcoat. 'I know you will say that it is dishonourable, but what else can we do?'

'I had steeled myself to say goodbye to you,' he answered, his tone uncertain.

'Yes, but *I* had not done so,' she replied. 'I am not strong like you, Daniel.'

He took a little step back and lifted her chin with one firm, brown hand. 'Prudence,' he said in an altered tone, 'you are the strongest woman I know.'

She looked straight into his eyes. 'In some ways,' she replied. 'I am strong enough to live with a man who has no money if I love him. I am strong enough to travel to America with him and work by his side. But I am not strong enough to live without him.' Her voice broke on her final words.

He pulled her into his arms and gave a deep sigh. 'In that case, there is only one thing to be done,' he said, 'and it is what we *will* do, no matter what you may say.'

'What is that, Daniel?' she asked him.

'We will go together to your father to ask for his consent.' She gave a tiny gasp, but anticipating that she might interrupt him, he said firmly, 'No, Prudence. I have decided. We will go to the vicarage to make some preparations, then we shall leave as soon as possible.'

In a meek tone which, if he had heard it, would have almost made Digby faint with shock, Prudence said, 'Very well, Daniel.'

★ ★ ★

It did not take Tyler very long to discover from which hostelry Prudence and Digby had hired a conveyance. The groom at the inn just down the road remembered Digby very clearly, and he was able to tell Tyler exactly what kind of vehicle the young man had hired.

'It was a gig, sir, pulled by two good chestnuts,' he said. 'One odd thing, though; he came to collect it very late at night. Why do you suppose that might be, sir?'

'Perhaps a tendency to suffer from sunstroke,' suggested Tyler blandly. 'Did the young man give any indication as to the direction that he was taking?'

Here the groom could not help him. 'He and his sister had to go on an urgent journey, that's all I can tell you, sir,' he said apologetically.

'What now?' Elfrida asked, when he reported his findings. While he had been gone, she had had their belongings brought downstairs as agreed, and they were now stowed on top of the carriage. That done, she had repaired to the little parlour in which they had drunk coffee in order to await his return.

'I could go to all the inns on all the possible roads out of Grantham and make enquiries,' he replied. 'Or alternatively, we could hazard a guess as to where we think they might have gone.'

'North?'

'I believe so. They would hardly have gone south; had they wanted to do that, they would not have travelled so far north in our company.'

Elfrida looked at him with a serious expression on her face. 'Oh Rufus, do you really think that they have gone to Gretna Green?' she asked him. 'Could she indeed be so dead to all propriety?' Then, suddenly realizing that she had called him by his Christian name, she blushed and added, 'Oh, I beg your pardon.'

'Not at all,' Rufus answered politely. 'I have already called you by your first name, have I not? As for Gretna, well, let us say that I am keeping an open mind. But I think that we should head for the Newark road, and ask there whether anyone has seen them.'

'And if not?'

'Then we try for Lincoln.'

'But what if we are too late, and they reach Gretna Green before we have caught them?' Elfrida asked anxiously.

'Then you will have to make the best of it, and encourage your family to do the same,' Rufus answered. 'He isn't the worst match in the world, after all.'

'That's not what Anthea thinks,' Elfrida retorted. 'And she will blame me for the whole — and quite rightly.' She began to pace agitatedly about the room, pulling her handkerchief between her hands.

'Quite wrongly,' Mr Tyler said firmly, taking hold of her shoulders so that she was forced to stop her anxious perambulation. 'Prudence is a young woman with a mind of her own. Believe me, if she was prepared to drug two people in order to run off with the young man of her choice, then no power on earth could have stopped her.'

She looked up into his face, and was at once reassured. She saw understanding there, but at the same time determination. He would catch up with the pair if it was at all possible. 'Yes. Thank you. You are very right.'

For a moment he stood holding her shoulders, and looking down at her. Then he released her saying in a changed tone, 'We must not linger. Time is of the essence.' He walked to the door and held it open for her. 'Recall, however, that we have more than one advantage. To start with, we do have money for the journey. Digby thought that he had taken all of mine, but in addition to what I kept in my coat, I have more concealed in the false bottom of my cloak bag, which he did not find. The other advantage we have is that we are driving a team whereas Digby is managing with a pair. We'll almost certainly out-pace him.'

If the runaway pair had met with good luck, fortune, in an even-handed manner that is not often seen, also favoured those pursuing them. Leaving the town by the Newark Road, they paused so that Tyler could make enquiries of a nearby hostelry. The groom in the yard could not help them, but the man he was talking to was able to give them some vital information. 'I see'd them yesterday, sir,' he volunteered. 'I was just leaving the Nag's Head, after a glass or two — '

' — Or three or four,' added his friend helpfully.

' — A glass or two,' the man went on with a virtuous expression, 'and this gig come past with a young man and young woman in it, like you said.'

'What did they look like?' asked Elfrida quickly.

'Couldn't rightly say, mum,' answered the man wrinkling his brow, 'it being dark 'n' all. They was quality, that's for sure.'

Tyler felt in his pocket for some coins. 'Which road did they take?'

'Why, didn't I say I was at the Nag's Head?' questioned the man, his eyes on the coins that Mr Tyler was drawing out.

'You did,' agreed Tyler, 'But as I don't know where the deuce it is, that don't help me much.'

'Well, sir, it's on the road out of town — the Lincoln road.'

Tyler threw both the men some coins with a word of thanks. 'That's saved us some time,' he remarked, whilst the coachman turned the carriage.

'Why Lincoln?' asked Elfrida.

'Well, that road will still take them north,' Tyler replied. 'Even so, I would have expected them to take the Newark Road. But perhaps Digby thought that I would be more likely to head for Newark, and he thinks to put me off the scent.'

'Yes, and I have thought of another reason,' said Elfrida, with dawning realization in her voice. 'Newark is where we would leave the main road to go to Prudence's home. She

261

probably thinks that they would be more likely to meet with people that they would recognize in Newark; perhaps even Anthea or Clive, if they should choose to go into town for some reason.'

'By Jove, yes,' Tyler agreed. 'That also answers another question. I'd been wondering why they did not make the most of the transport that they had already, and go with us as far as possible. But they would never have risked making the change in Newark.'

Elfrida imagined what would have happened had it been Anthea who had discovered herself and Mr Tyler upstairs and inadequately dressed, and she blushed at the thought. Tyler, glancing across at her, guessed correctly what was embarrassing her, and smiled to himself.

The journey was an uneventful one, no highwaymen appearing to cause them alarm, or any accident to the coach or to the horses occurring to discommode them. Elfrida, who had travelled this journey but seldom, had forgotten that Lincoln cathedral could be seen from a considerable distance, and she was grateful when Mr Tyler pointed it out to her. 'It is my favourite of all the cathedrals that I have seen, I think,' he said easily. Elfrida stared at him as if she had been struck. He burst out laughing. 'Oh dear, I have made a very bad impression upon you, haven't I?' he said. 'You did not believe that I would have the slightest interest in ecclesiastical architecture, did you? Go on, admit it!'

'It did surprise me, I confess,' Elfrida conceded. 'Although it did not surprise me as much as it would have done had I been told it after I first met you.'

'Good Lord, I should think it would have done,' he agreed. 'What a spectacle I made of myself to be sure.'

'What attracted you to the macaroni style?' Elfrida asked him curiously.

'Well, I was the youngest of the family by quite a few years, and I suppose I wanted to make my mark,' he said thoughtfully. 'Then, of course, I knew all my family would hate it. That acted as additional encouragement.'

'What made you abandon that particular mode?'

He smiled at her, an ironic expression on his face. 'Why, you did of course,' he replied.

'I?' she exclaimed in astonishment.

'Yes, you. Do you remember you threw my wig in the water? After I'd retrieved it, and I'd finished calling down curses upon your fair name, for which I trust you'll forgive me, I decided to retreat to my room by a back way, through the conservatory and out through the garden then up some back stairs so that I wouldn't be seen. But as I was leaving the conservatory itself, the light from a candle shone on the glass of one of the windows so that it acted almost like a mirror and I saw what a ridiculous figure I cut, with my fussy clothes, and my bald head and my wig in my hand. The next thing that I did was to tell my father that I wanted to join the army.'

'Was he agreeable to the idea?' she asked.

'My dear girl, he was so thankful that I had decided to abandon my macaroni phase that he kissed my hands and feet and sent me off with his blessing.'

'I am so very sorry,' Elfrida said remorsefully.

'Why?' he asked. 'You did me a good turn — more than one, in fact. You stopped me from making a worse fool of myself, and you spurred me into a profession that I very much enjoyed.'

'Did Major Fletcher also join the army as a consequence of that evening?' Elfrida asked curiously.

'He did,' Tyler replied. 'We met at Eton, went up to Cambridge, and have been good friends ever since, often doing things together. When Douglas decided to become a macaroni, I followed his lead, and then when I decided to join the army, Douglas came as well.' He paused. 'It's ironic really, when you think about it. I was the one who was all for joining up, but Douglas is the one who stayed, making it his profession.' He paused again. 'You apologized to me a few minutes ago. I think that I, in my turn, ought to apologize to you for that evening. I made you rather uncomfortable by my extravagant compliments, I fear. You were very young and you didn't deserve it.'

'You called me a 'tooththome wench',' she answered, trying to keep her voice solemn, but unable to keep it from breaking into a small giggle at the very end.

'I didn't, did I?' he answered with a chuckle. 'What an idiot! I'd forgotten about that lisp.'

Elfrida was touched at his ability to laugh at himself, but she merely said, 'You were very young, too.'

'Yes, I suppose I was,' he answered. Then, in quite a different tone, he said 'Why in heaven's name weren't you snapped up years ago?'

'I told you,' she replied calmly, but with a slightly heightened colour. 'I was the other Miss Frobisher. No one was ever interested in me once they'd seen Anthea.'

'I can't believe that,' he told her. 'Why even I, macaroni that I was and obsessed with my own appearance, could see that you were a

265

taking little thing.'

She smiled. 'The few who were interested didn't appeal to me,' she said.

'Well that's told me,' he murmured.

'I preferred to have my independence,' she added, her colour heightened.

'But are now considering exchanging it for a country vicarage, unless I miss my guess.'

'Mr Erskine would hardly be interested in me now that I have disgraced myself,' she reminded him.

'But you are not disgraced, you are engaged,' he pointed out. 'And engagements can be broken, you know. I promise to behave despicably, so that you will have cause to throw me over.'

'Thank you,' Elfrida replied, turning to look out of the window. The prospect of ending an engagement which had never really been an engagement at all should have caused her to feel relief if anything. To her dismay, the sinking sensation of which she was conscious at present did not seem anything like relief.

Tyler observed her, admiring the turn of her throat as she looked at the passing scenery. He had realized, as perhaps she had not, that their dash to the border would probably mean several nights spent in inns, for all of which they would be unchaperoned.

A broken engagement after a suitable time had passed with only one mild misdemeanour to be glossed over would just about be acceptable: after such a journey as they were to pass together, marriage would be the only possible outcome. He smiled briefly, then also turned his attention to the view outside the carriage.

16

The agreement between Digby and Prudence
had been that after he had made sure that the
meeting between Prudence and her captain
had taken place, he would take the gig back
to Grantham and return it to the inn whence
it had come. At first he had been a little
nervous about this idea, for a variety of
reasons.

'It would be just my luck to run slap into
your aunt and Tyler, and then I should really
be for it,' he had said frankly.

'No, you won't,' answered Prudence, 'and
in that lies the brilliance of my plan. Firstly,
they will be sure to think that we are flying
immediately for the border, so they will be
sure to go straight to Newark.'

'Why?' asked Digby.

'For two reasons. One is that that is the
most direct route; the other is that Aunt
Elfrida will not be able to reconcile it with
her conscience to know that I have absconded
and not tell Papa. So they will have to go to
Newark in order to visit my home and speak
to him.'

'But then he will be on your trail as well,'

Digby put in. 'How will that help?'

'No, he will not,' Prudence answered triumphantly. 'I had a letter from Mama just before we left London, telling me that Papa had gone away for at least a week to see to the affairs of an elderly cousin, so he will be from home. Aunt Elfrida and Mr Tyler will have a fruitless journey and will have to set out all over again, and I will have gained us some time.'

'Doesn't your aunt know that he is away?' Digby asked.

'Do you know, I think I forgot to mention it,' Prudence remarked airily.

He laughed but then said, 'There is still a risk that they may catch you on the way to the border. Tyler's carriage is pulled by a team, you know.'

'Yes, I do know, and that is why I think we should travel to Gretna by easy stages, and by lesser-known routes. Our relatives will dash there as fast as they can, but they will find no trail left by us. If they do proceed as far as Gretna under those circumstances, they will ask in vain — even if they did give the right description of the bridegroom, which they will not. Oh Digby, we can't fail!'

Digby could see that it was a good plan, but in all honesty, the part that concerned him most was not how Prudence and her captain would reach the border, but how he himself would escape retribution at the hands of his understandably wrathful kinsman. It occurred to him that to take his time would be his best bet, so that by the time he reached Grantham with the curricle, they would be long gone. When they had stayed the night in Lincoln, he had noticed a very snug-looking hostelry close to where Prudence's friends lived, and he decided to stay there for the night.

The welcome that he received there was every bit as good as he had hoped, and after having refreshed himself in the chamber allocated to him, he made his way downstairs to partake of dinner.

No sound of familiar voices warned him, no sixth sense prepared him for imminent disaster. He simply opened the door into the parlour set aside for guests of quality and found himself face to face with Rufus Tyler.

It was not his relative who spoke first however, but Miss Frobisher who instantly demanded, 'Mr Collett! Where is my niece?'

Digby's first instinct was to turn tail and run, but Tyler, anticipating this possibility, leaned behind him and closed the door, holding it shut with one firm hand.

'Well, my young friend, you have quite a lot of explaining to do, have you not? Where will you begin?'

'I know where I would like him to begin,' said Elfrida, before Digby could open his mouth. 'Mr Collett, where is my niece? Is she upstairs? I truly believe I would be able to forgive you everything else if only you have her here safely.'

It was on Mr Tyler's mind to say that Miss Frobisher might speak for herself in this matter, but that she certainly did not speak for him, but he held his peace. It suddenly occurred to him that he did not by any means want to put Digby on his guard.

The younger man hesitated until Elfrida said impatiently, 'I cannot wait. Mr Tyler, let me out if you please. I will find her even if I have to search every room in this place.'

'I see no reason for going to that trouble, my dear ma'am,' said Rufus in a silky voice. 'I will soon shake it out of him.'

'Take . . . take care,' said Digby, backing away from Tyler. 'I am a soldier.'

'So was I,' replied Tyler, bearing down upon him. 'Well? Have you anything to tell us before I disarrange that rather smart coat?'

'I . . . she is not here,' Digby admitted at last.

'Not here?' Elfrida echoed. Then her face took on a stern expression. 'By heaven, Mr Collett, if you have done anything to frighten her — '

Tyler gave a crack of laughter. 'Frighten her?' he exclaimed. 'My God, I should have thought that it was the other way round. Just look at him!'

'Oh stop it!' Elfrida snapped impatiently. 'While you are framing amusing remarks about your kinsman, Prudence may be out there somewhere, alone and friendless.'

Her expression was so anxious that Digby felt himself bound to say, 'She is not either of those things, I promise you, ma'am.'

'Do you indeed?' said Rufus. 'Then if she is not here, and not in your company, in whose company is she now, and where is she to be found?'

'She is perfectly safe,' Digby assured them, his tone confident this time, for he had certainly left her in Daniel's care.

'Is she?' asked Tyler, his tone deeply ironic. 'Forgive me, Digby, but your reputation for truth and honesty, not to mention fair play, has taken rather a battering over recent days. I think that Miss Frobisher might ask for more reliable credentials than your earnest expression.'

Elfrida laid a hand on Digby's arm. 'Please, Mr Collett, tell us what you know,' she said beseechingly. 'She is my responsibility and she is not of age.'

While Digby was still hesitating, Tyler

spoke again. 'She may be your responsibility for now, ma'am, but ultimately those who have dealings with her will find themselves obliged to answer to Clive Winchcomb.' He took his snuff box out, opened it and took a pinch. 'Don't underestimate Prudence's father, my dear fellow. I don't believe he's ever killed his man, but that wasn't because he couldn't aim straight.'

Digby had turned a little pale, but while he was still gnawing his lower lip, Elfrida said, 'Mr Collett, if you will not tell me where she is, will you not at least tell me who she is with?'

In face of her pleadings and Tyler's threats, Digby sighed resignedly. 'She cannot say I didn't try, can she?'

'By no means,' Elfrida replied encouragingly.

Digby was silent again for some time. Growing impatient, Tyler opened his mouth to speak, but Elfrida, sensing that the answer might be on the point of being revealed, quickly laid a hand on his arm. She was not to be disappointed. 'She is with Black,' he said at last.

'Black? Do you mean *Captain* Black?' Elfrida asked in astonishment.

Digby nodded. 'It was Black that she was in love with all along. She persuaded me to pretend that we wanted to marry, but it was only a ruse. She knew that her parents were very much against me. She decided that if they thought her heart was set on marrying me, then they would be so glad that she had turned to someone else that they would give their consent.'

'That being the case, why did she feel it necessary to elope?' Tyler asked curiously.

'Because her mother told Daniel that she would never be allowed to marry a penniless soldier, so Daniel resolved to be noble and renounce her,' Digby explained. 'He decided to seek his fortune in America, so Pru knew that she would have to go after him quickly if she wasn't to miss him altogether.' Now that he had realized that it was impossible to keep quiet about what he and Prudence had done, he could not seem to be able to stop talking about it.

'So young Prudence decided to take the matter into her own hands,' Tyler remarked. 'I see. I gather that Captain Black's family lives in this vicinity?'

Digby opened his mouth, then closed it again. Eventually he said 'I did not say that I would tell you where she was; just who she was with.'

Elfrida turned to Tyler. 'Where Captain Black lives is irrelevant, surely. After all, they will be well on their way to the border by now. We must set off straight away.'

'I think not,' Tyler replied.

'But we must! I have a duty — '

'Don't agitate yourself, my dear ma'am,' he said soothingly. 'I know Black, not well, but by reputation. He distinguished himself in the war, being mentioned more than once in despatches, and is the most transparently honourable man that you could ever hope to find. He will not elope with your niece.'

'Then what will he do?' asked Elfrida, only partially reassured.

'My guess is that he will spend a little time calming her down, then escort her to Winchcomb Hall, probably with his mother in tow, and ask her father for her hand in form.'

'Do you really think so?' she asked, hardly daring to hope.

'I would say almost certainly. But I doubt if he will do that tonight. She will be safe enough with his family, of that you may be quite sure.' He paused and looked around. 'This seems like a pleasant enough inn. What say we stay here for the night? Digby can chaperon us. After all that he has done to make our lives difficult, I would say that that is the least that he can do.'

Digby made haste to assure them that he

was more than ready to do all in his power to be helpful to them and Elfrida, since she was convinced of the justice of Tyler's argument, agreed that to stay would be the best scheme. Besides, she had not completely given up all hope of inducing Digby to disclose the whereabouts of Captain Black's family home.

Once the decision to stay had been made, rooms were booked and within a very short space of time, Elfrida had been shown into hers. As she busied herself attending to her appearance, her mind went back over the past days since she had arrived in London. Now that she knew that Prudence and Digby were not romantically attached to one another, she could only marvel that she had ever been foolish enough to believe that it was so. She had never had a brother of her own, but, even given that handicap, she could now see quite clearly that the relationship between Prudence and Digby was more like brother and sister than anything else.

Prudence had been very clever, she concluded. Even now, knowing that Daniel was the man of her choice, Elfrida could not think of a single occasion on which her niece had betrayed herself. The only thing that had given any possible indication of preference had been the visit by Captain Black to the family home. Anthea had concluded that he had come to plead his friend's cause. It was now clear that he had come to make an appeal on his own behalf. The trouble was that Anthea had been so sure that the attachment had been between Prudence and Digby, that her explanation of the situation had been accepted as fact.

Tyler was probably right, Elfrida concluded. Black had left London without making his proposal. He seemed to be too honourable a man to try to persuade a young woman into an elopement. If Digby would not disclose Black's whereabouts, then all she could do would be to trust in the young captain's innate sense of honour, which was clearly very strong. The fact remained, however, that they could not be sure that he would indeed do as Tyler had predicted. Whilst Elfrida knew that duty dictated that she should make her way to Winchcomb Hall as soon as possible to apprise them of recent events, her courage failed her at the idea of going to her sister and saying 'Your daughter has given me the slip and I don't know where she is.'

Then again, if Tyler *was* right and Prudence was safely with the Black family, and on the point of travelling to Winchcomb Hall, she would still have some explaining to do. Her sister would doubtless forgive her in time, but in the interests of short-term peace, it would probably be advisable for Elfrida to return to her own home and put a little distance between them. Then, as soon as possible, she would disabuse Mr Erskine of the idea that she was engaged, and perhaps eventually he would forgive her scandalous behaviour and make his long expected proposal.

It came as something of a shock to her that this idea, which had seemed perfectly acceptable and even desirable to her only a short time ago, now appeared quite impossible. She asked herself what had happened to her in the interim to cause this change of attitude. She pondered long and hard and looked at the situation from every possible way, but she could only come to one conclusion. The change had been brought about by Mr Tyler. Mr Tyler, who had at one time seemed destined for Prudence; Mr Tyler, who had given her not only her very first kiss, but also her most recent one — who had, in fact, been the only man ever to kiss her, Mr Erskine never having been so bold as to presume to attempt such a thing; Mr Tyler, whose bed she had unwittingly shared, but who had come to her aid despite the fact that her predicament had nothing whatsoever to do with him. He was the reason why marriage to Mr Erskine no longer had any appeal for her. He had come back into her life quite unexpectedly, but now she wondered how she was ever going to live without him.

This line of thought seemed to her to be quite dangerous, so before she could take it any further, she hurried to tidy herself and go downstairs to dinner.

Like herself, neither of the gentlemen present was in a position to don evening clothes, but both had made an effort to smarten themselves up, and they all greeted one another cordially. The dinner that was put before them was not elaborate, but it was well cooked and tasty, and Tyler was pleased to approve the wine that was served with it.

To Elfrida's surprise — and rather to her disappointment — Tyler did not mention his kinsman's part in their embarrassment earlier on that day. Nothing in Digby's demeanour indicated that Tyler had given him a dressing down either. He seemed to have shown more forbearance than she would have expected, or, in her opinion, than the occasion warranted. She was sorely tempted to say something herself, but for the fact that even to think about the matter conjured up an image of Mr Tyler's bare chest in her mind, making her blush profusely.

In keeping with her usual custom, she consumed only a small glass of wine, and then enjoyed the excellent lemonade made by the inn-keeper's wife. The gentlemen partook liberally of the wines that were brought out and Tyler, surely at his most genial, invited Digby's opinion on each.

Soon after the meal was over, Elfrida left them to their wine. As he held the door open for her, Tyler said, 'I think we should be up betimes in the morning if we are to make good progress towards Newark,' to which suggestion she nodded in agreement before going up to her room.

At first suspicious of his kinsman's amiable demeanour, Digby gradually unbent and before they retired, told Tyler in sentimental tones that he was his favourite relative in the whole world. 'That's very kind of you, young fellow,' Tyler said to Digby as he helped him out of the room and up the stairs. 'Now let me put you to bed.'

'You're very kind,' said Digby. 'So ver', ver' kind. I don't deserve such kindness.'

'No more you do,' agreed Tyler cheerfully. 'Come on up the stairs. One at a time.'

'They keep moving about,' Digby complained. But he allowed Tyler to help him upstairs and to assist him off with his boots. Before the task was finished, however, the younger man was out for the count, snoring loudly. Rufus stood for a time looking down at him and smiling, before leaving the room.

17

In compliance with Tyler's suggestion, Elfrida was awake and making ready to get up before the chambermaid knocked on the door, telling her that it was eight o'clock and asking her if she wanted her water for washing. She washed and dressed quickly, and arrived downstairs to find that Tyler was already partaking of breakfast. He stood at her entrance and pulled out a chair for her.

'Is Lieutenant Collett joining us?' she asked him.

'After last night's over indulgence?' questioned Tyler. 'He'll sleep that off for most of the morning.'

'You are not similarly affected, then.'

'I have a remarkably hard head,' he replied. 'Coffee?'

Their breakfast was soon consumed, and within a very short space of time they were off. 'Are we going straight to Newark?' asked Elfrida, as they drew out of the inn yard.

'No, with your permission we will go to Captain Black's home. It seemed to me that you would not rest easy whilst you were unsure of Prudence's whereabouts, so yesterday, after you had gone up to your room, I walked to the bishop's palace to find out if he could tell me the whereabouts of a clergyman named Black living locally whose son was a distinguished army officer with the rank of captain.'

Elfrida's face lit up. 'How clever you are,' she said admiringly. 'Did you succeed in your objective?'

So taken was he with how pretty she looked with that light in her eyes that he failed to catch what she was saying, and she was obliged to repeat herself. 'I did,' he replied. 'The bishop was not at home, but his chaplain was there and was able to help me. The family of Daniel Black lives in a small village not far from Gainsborough. We should be with them in a very short space of time.'

Elfrida was silent for a time, then said, 'Mr Tyler, do you really think that Captain Black will have conducted himself honourably?'

He leaned forward and swiftly grasped her hand. 'I'm convinced of it,' he said. 'He will not be persuaded into doing anything of a clandestine nature, you may be sure.' He released her hand, and leaned back in his place once more.

Elfrida coloured, then wrinkled her brow. 'You may say that, but recall that he did behave clandestinely in London. I have no doubt that Prudence initiated any secretive behaviour, but she could not have pulled the wool over my eyes without at least the tacit acquiescence of the captain.'

'You may be very sure that that was given against his better judgement,' Tyler replied. 'Love can turn the best of us into mush, you know.' Elfrida glanced at him quickly, then looked out of the window, her brow furrowed, though whether from anxiety about Prudence's fate or about her own, it would have been hard to say.

After a moment or two he said, 'Would you like to see something that will make you smile?' As she watched, he picked up a box which was on the seat next to him and opened it, showing her its contents. 'Digby Collett's boots,' he said. 'His clothes are in a trunk on the roof of this coach.'

'His clothes . . . ' breathed Elfrida. Her eyes met his, she covered her mouth with her hand and they both began to laugh. 'I fear I did you an injustice,' she said, as soon as she was able. 'I have to admit that I thought you had let him off rather lightly.'

'Digby has some good qualities, but I fear that he was spoiled by his older sisters,' he replied. 'Perhaps for this reason, he seems only to be able to understand the effect his behaviour has upon others if he is made to experience the same thing himself. His position is better than ours, in some respects. I have left him with his shirt, for example, I have paid his bill, and he does still have the gig at his disposal. But unless he finds some money from somewhere, he'll have to drive back to Grantham in his stockinged feet.'

This reflection caused them a good deal of merriment, so much so that Mr Tyler was still thinking how pretty she looked with the laughter dying out of her eyes when they reached Horsfold.

The village was a small place, consisting of very little more than a collection of houses, a small inn and a church gathered around a duck pond. The vicarage was easily found, being a rambling building next to the church, well kept but rather shabby, with a neat garden. On enquiring at the vicarage door, they were told that the vicar was in his study, and were politely invited to come in and sit in the parlour. As might have been predicted from the state of the garden, this room was scrupulously clean, but with shabby old furnishings. Daniel Black was clearly one of those poor soldiers from whom Prudence's aunt had been instructed to protect her niece. Elfrida sighed.

The door opened to admit a tall,

grey-haired, strikingly handsome man in clerical dress. His likeness to Daniel was so marked that there could be no doubt as to their relationship.

'Good morning,' he said. 'I am Frederick Black. In what way may I be of service to you?'

Tyler made his bow. 'I am Rufus Tyler,' he said, 'and this lady, whom I have the honour of escorting, is Miss Frobisher.' He made a gesture indicating that Elfrida should now speak.

'I am Prudence Winchcomb's aunt,' she said, 'and a few days ago, she left London in my company, in order to return to the home of her parents. Whilst we were staying at Grantham, she left my side, and set out on a journey of her own. Since then, I have been given reason to believe that she may have made arrangements to meet someone in your household. As you will understand, I am now very anxious, and would be most grateful if you would be able to tell me where she is.' Whilst she was speaking, the anxiety of not knowing Prudence's whereabouts suddenly overcame her. She finished her speech with a catch in her voice, and found that her eyes were filling with tears. Instantly, Mr Tyler took out a handkerchief and handed it to her.

'My dear Miss Frobisher, do not distress

yourself,' said Mr Black. 'I have already sent for tea so that you may refresh yourselves. Then I will tell you all about my part in the adventure of your niece who is, I assure you, quite safe.'

'Truly?' she asked.

'Truly,' answered the vicar gravely. Rufus stared at her unsmilingly for a moment, then walked to the window, his hands tightly clasped behind his back. Had he been told, he would never have believed how irritated he would feel at seeing her cry and being unable to hold her and comfort her.

Moments later, a neat-looking maid came into the parlour with a tray of tea and set it down on a little table. 'Now, Miss Frobisher, perhaps you will do the honours, whilst I explain to you the part that my family has played in this affair.'

Elfrida did as she was bid, whilst Mr Black invited Rufus to take a seat, then sat down himself. 'I should perhaps explain from the very beginning that I enjoy a very close relationship with my son,' he said. 'I have always encouraged him to confide in me, and he has continued to do so into adult life. I was well aware that he was deeply attached to your niece, but he always knew that his suit could not prosper because of his straitened means.'

The vicar's lips thinned a little, and Elfrida felt bound to say, 'I am sure that your son is a man of fine character, sir. That is wealth enough in itself.'

His expression lightened. 'Sadly the world does not see things in that light,' he said. 'And although I despise the desire of wealth for its own sake, even I can see that to support a wife and family, a man must have some means. Although he knew that the attachment was a mutual one, he decided that he must stand back and allow another man to court her.' He paused briefly, then glanced curiously at Tyler. 'He was under the impression, sir, that you were that man. Is it in this capacity that you have come in pursuit of her?'

Rufus shook his head. 'I did toy briefly with the idea of courting her, but realized very early on that we should not suit,' he said. 'Miss Winchcomb's mother was rather taken with the idea, however, and may have allowed her imagination to run away with her. I am here solely as an old friend of Miss Frobisher's family, in order to give her every assistance.'

'I see. However, I think that even if Daniel had known that you were not going to offer for Miss Winchcomb, his actions would have been the same. In worldly terms, she could do much better. Daniel left London at his mother's request in order to go to Dover and meet my brother-in-law off the packet. He came home after escorting his uncle to stay with some relatives. My wife was so anxious about his state of mind that she was relieved to have an excuse to draw him away from London. On his arrival here, he told us that he had made up his mind to sell out, and go to America to seek his fortune.

'Before he could carry his scheme any further forward, however, a young friend of his, Lieutenant Collett, appeared on our doorstep yesterday, and asked to see Daniel. The news that he brought made my son very agitated, and he hurried off to the inn. A little while later, he returned with a young lady.'

'Prudence!' Elfrida exclaimed. 'Oh, thank God.'

The vicar nodded gravely. 'Yes indeed,' he replied, though whether these words were in response to the identity of the young woman, or to Elfrida's pious utterance, she could not be sure. 'Your niece is clearly a strong-minded young woman of great resource,' he said. 'She told me about some of the stratagems that she had employed to throw others, and particularly your good self, off the scent, and I am convinced that there are other things that she left out of the telling that might earn my disapproval.' At this point, Elfrida very much wanted to look at Rufus but she resisted the temptation. 'She was very sorry for the distress that she had caused, but in her wish to be with Daniel no matter what his circumstances, she could not help but earn my admiration, even while I must deplore the boldness of her behaviour.' His expression softened. 'Forgive me; you are her aunt, and must be partial. I did not mean to offend you.'

'I am not offended,' Elfrida replied. 'She is a determined young woman, and not easily checked. What happened next?'

'I fear to shock you, Miss Frobisher,' said the vicar after some hesitation.

'You will not shock me,' she replied sincerely. 'You are going to tell me that she wanted to elope with your son, are you not?'

He looked relieved. 'That is so,' he agreed. 'She told him that was her plan, but he brought her here instead. He would never act in so dishonourable a way.'

'And is she here now?' asked Elfrida.

The vicar shook his head. 'She stayed here for the night. Daniel took a room at the inn and she slept here. This morning, accompanied by my wife, they set out in the only carriage that the inn has for hire. It is

Daniel's intention to speak to Mr Winch-comb, man to man, and ask for his daughter's hand. I only pray that he will see behind Daniel's circumstances to the solid worth that lies beneath.'

Tyler spoke for the first time. 'Of one thing I am sure, sir, and that is that Mr Winchcomb will be far more likely to give your son a hearing if he deals with him in this straightforward way, than if he went sneaking off to Gretna Green, and then tried to gain his approval afterwards.'

Mr Black invited them to stay with him for a simple lunch of bread and cheese, and after a little hesitation, they agreed.

'I have a great deal of explaining to do and many apologies to make when I meet my sister, but starving myself will not help,' Elfrida said ruefully.

The conversation around the table proved to be surprisingly lively. Mr Black's moral tone was very high, but he was not above appreciating a joke, and his interest in the things of the countryside and in his fellow man was very keen. Before they got up from the table, Tyler said, 'Do you have a particular attachment to this part of the country, sir, or would you consider moving?'

'I have never felt myself bound to a particular place,' the vicar replied. 'I seek to serve God where He has called me to be, but sometimes, He chooses to send us to other places.'

'In that case, I wonder whether you might consider moving to a parish on my estate in Hertfordshire where there is a vacancy. The living is considerably larger than this one, and might offer more scope for your undoubted abilities, as well as enabling you to support your family better. Unless, of course, you feel that my suggestion is not in keeping with your sense of call.'

'In this instance, you might well be God's instrument,' the vicar replied beaming.

'No one's ever called me that before,' Tyler answered frankly. 'But you seem to me to be just the kind of man we need. You must tell me how we go about arranging this with your bishop.'

Not long after this, the two travellers were once more on their way.

'That was kind of you,' Elfrida said, as they watched Mr Black waving goodbye from the vicarage gate.

'Not at all,' Rufus replied. 'He is clearly an excellent parish priest. I am simply looking after my own interests.'

'Perhaps; but a better living for the family will mean that Captain Black will not have to help them with any income of his own.'

'Possibly,' he answered in indifferent tones. Elfrida was not fooled and she smiled to herself as for a time they travelled along in silence.

'I wonder what kind of reception Captain Black will get?' she said eventually. 'Anthea is so very much against Prudence's marrying a man without wealth.'

'But the Winchcombs are not poor, are they?' answered Tyler.

'No, but they are not rich either. Now that Anthea is expecting another child they will have two to provide for instead of one.' She sighed. 'I will just have to tell them that I will settle my fortune on Prudence when I die.'

'She'll have a very long time to wait for it,' Tyler observed. 'And in any case, your husband might have something to say about that.'

'If I ever marry, which at my age is doubtful,' Elfrida replied. She was quite proud of how she did not colour up, but inside, her heart was beating rather faster than usual.

'I wouldn't say that,' he answered. 'I can think of one suitor, at any rate.' He was thinking of himself, and intending to tease her about their false engagement, but she misunderstood him.

'Yes, but I fear that Mr Erskine would not

have me now,' she said, desperate not to reveal that somehow over the last few days she had become convinced that if she could not marry Mr Tyler, she did not want to marry anyone at all. 'He thinks that I am a loose woman, and who is to blame him? And after all, that would never do for a clergyman's wife, would it?' She was talking too much and she knew it, but she did not seem to be able to stop. 'I expect you have noticed how handsome he is. He is quite the beau of our neighbourhood, you know. All the young ladies are mad for him.'

'I can imagine,' he replied expressionlessly. So it was Erskine that she wanted after all. Damn him and his good looks, and damn heredity that dictated that some should be saddled with the burden of red hair! They each lapsed into a depressed silence, which for some time they broke only occasionally with the odd remark.

The afternoon was far advanced by the time that they reached the midway point between Gainsborough and Newark. Elfrida was very anxious to reach Winchcomb Hall that night, but it was not to be. Just a mile or so from Newton on Trent, at a point where the road became narrow, they encountered a sporting curricle coming the other way at a reckless speed. Suddenly, without warning,

Mr Tyler's coachman found himself wrestling to control the horses, and in the confusion, the carriage was pulled over to the side and one wheel ended up in the ditch.

Mr Tyler, uttering one or two curses that Elfrida had never heard before, scrambled out and proceeded to upbraid the other driver heartily. The gentleman's curricle had come off worse from the encounter, having a broken wheel, and it took some time and patience to set the carriage to rights, and clear the way of obstruction for the sake of other road users. Consequently by the time they were ready to set off again, the hour was much further advanced than they had intended.

Annoyed though Mr Tyler might be, his common humanity did not permit him to leave the rather rash young gentleman to walk to the place to which he was going himself, so he invited him to climb into the carriage for the last mile or so. He was indeed a very young man, Elfrida noted, almost too young to be driving such a sporting vehicle.

'This is Mr Bentley, my dear,' Tyler said, as he climbed in, then made space for the curricle driver to sit down next to him. 'Bentley, this is Miss Frobisher, my promised wife.' At least I can say it, even if it isn't true, he thought to himself.

Elfrida, all too aware of the need to continue to guard her reputation, nodded politely. 'Do you have far to go, Mr Bentley?' she asked him.

'No, ma'am, not far,' he replied. 'I was only taking my father's curricle out for a short drive.' Then, recollecting his expensive mistake, he blushed profusely.

Tyler gave a crack of laughter. 'Your father's was it? Good grief!'

'Exactly, sir,' replied Bentley ruefully.

'He'll think twice before he lends it to you again,' the older man observed.

'Well . . . that is . . . he didn't exactly . . . ' said Bentley hesitantly.

'Oh dear,' murmured Tyler. 'You are in trouble, aren't you?'

Obviously something about Tyler's demeanour made the young man think that he was someone to confide in, for he said, 'What would you advise, sir?'

Tyler thought for a moment. 'My advice to you would be to stress first of all the fact that the horses are unharmed,' he said eventually. 'In my experience, a man can tolerate almost any damage to his property, as long as his horses are not hurt.'

Bentley brightened immediately. 'By Jove, you are right, sir,' he declared. 'I shall tell him about the accident, then assure him that the horses are well. What a stroke of luck that I ran into you!'

'No, would you say so indeed?' asked Tyler ironically. Elfrida was hard put to it to hide a smile.

There was a very respectable-looking inn at Newton on Trent, and it was there that they decided to stay, Miss Frobisher passing once again as Mr Tyler's betrothed. Mr Bentley declined Tyler's invitation to dine with them, pleading the need to speak to the wheelwright and then return home.

'Father will be mad as fire, but I would rather face him sooner than later.'

'Wise youth,' Tyler commented later. 'If there's unpleasant news to break, then the sooner it's done the better.'

Elfrida made no response. She was thinking of the scene awaiting her at Winchcomb Hall. Would that that were over and done with!

18

They were on the road in good time the following day, and much though Elfrida longed to have the interview with Anthea and Clive behind her, part of her wanted to be on the road with Rufus Tyler for ever. She looked across at him as he lounged in the backward-facing seat, his legs negligently crossed as he gazed out of the window. He was not as handsome as Mr Erskine, but his face was strong, with a slightly aquiline nose, high cheek bones, and strongly marked brows, and that remarkable red hair of his glinted in the sunshine. She had never thought that she would fall in love at her time of life, and for that reason, she had supposed that Erskine would do her very well. Now, however, she realized that marriage with the handsome rector would be quite impossible, for if she could not marry Rufus Tyler, she did not want to marry anyone, and whyever would Tyler want to marry a spinster who had been on the shelf for years, when as a noted matrimonial prize, he could have anyone he wanted? Just because a middle-aged spinster had fallen in love with him, it did not follow that he would ever return her feelings. This depressing thought kept her mind off the road for a good few miles, and it was with a feeling of surprise that she realized that they had arrived at their destination.

So convinced was she that a horrendous scene must have taken place as a consequence of the discovery of an attachment between Prudence and her soldier, that she was almost surprised to find that Winchcomb Hall was still standing. She had half expected it to have been razed to the ground.

As they drew up outside the front door, Elfrida turned to Rufus. 'If you prefer to travel on, I shall quite understand,' she said. 'I am only too grateful for all that you have done, and do not want to be presumptuous.'

'By no means,' he replied. 'In any case, I have been present for half the adventure; you cannot possibly be so cruel as to deny me the chance to be present at the denouement.'

'It might be helpful to have you here after all,' Elfrida remarked nervously. 'If Anthea throws me out on my ear, at least you will be able to escort me back to Newark so that I might catch the stage home.' She was only half joking.

Although it was mid-morning, and they had already been travelling since breakfast time, Elfrida was not really surprised to discover that Anthea had not yet emerged from her room. 'She will doubtless be down quite soon, ma'am,' said Pyle, the butler. 'Mrs Figgis has had the same room prepared for you as usual. Would you like to go up now?'

'Yes, thank you' said Elfrida, unable to think of a good reason for refusing. 'I can find my own way, Pyle. Would you be so good as to find some refreshment for Mr Tyler?'

She had completely forgotten about the fact that a room would have been prepared for her. No doubt her trunk, which had come on ahead of her, would have been unpacked, and all her things put away. How embarrassing it would be to have to ask for it all to be packed up again! It said much for her anxious state, that although she had stated half jokingly that Anthea might throw her out of the house, she was now considering this to be a likely outcome of the whole business. She would have liked to have asked Figgis if Miss Prudence was there, but such a request would reveal that she herself did not know for certain where her niece was. She would just have to wait and find out what Anthea would have to say to her.

These kinds of anxious thoughts meant that she lingered in her room for longer than she intended. Consequently, when she came downstairs, she could hear voices talking in the saloon and, surprisingly enough, she recognized the laughter of her sister. Could it be hysteria? What could be happening? She opened the door, to discover that Mr Tyler was the only other person present.

'Effie, my dear! How well you are looking! And how lovely that you have brought Mr Tyler with you!'

Elfrida smiled and embraced her sister. 'I think you are looking very well too, Anthea,' she replied. 'Country life is obviously agreeing with you.' This was what she said out loud. Inside, she was saying, I wish I knew whether Prudence was here or not. What am I to say next?

Thankfully, while she was still groping for words, Anthea spoke again. 'Mr Tyler has just been telling me that Prudence has been travelling here by a different route, so that she could spend the night with friends.'

'That's right, ma'am.'

'Is the family well known to you?' Anthea asked Rufus, her tone interested but not anxious. Elfrida reflected upon how much more weight one's words carried if one were a gentleman with a distinguished background.

'A very respectable family,' answered Rufus, without a blush. 'The father is a clergyman, who is shortly to take up an important appointment on my estate. Mrs

Black is to escort Miss Winchcomb here. They are to arrive today.'

'Black!' exclaimed Anthea. 'A young man by the name of Black called upon me in London. Would he be a connection of the family, Elfrida?'

'I . . . I believe so,' answered Elfrida.

At this moment, refreshments were brought in, and the conversation turned to other matters. Elfrida could not concentrate upon it. More than half her attention was given to any noises outside that might signal Prudence's arrival. Conscience dictated that she should disclose what she knew about Captain Black's aspirations, but her courage failed her. Eventually, the sound of footsteps was heard in the hall and as the door opened, Elfrida sat up, ready to face the worst. To her surprise, however, the arrivals were Mr Winchcomb and Mr Erskine.

'Clive, my dear, how lovely,' Anthea exclaimed, rising to greet her husband. 'I had not expected you to return just yet. And Mr Erskine!' Then her features took on a puzzled expression. 'I must have misunderstood, for surely the intention was that you should travel to us with my daughter and my sister. But my sister has arrived with Mr Tyler. Have you perhaps travelled with my daughter and Mrs Black?'

Mr Erskine had not had the advantage of being drilled in what he must or must not say. He did not have any talent for dissimulation either; nor did he have any idea that the name of Lieutenant Collett should not be mentioned. 'I am unacquainted with Mrs Black,' he answered, his handsome face rather flushed. 'I came alone. A chance encounter with Mr Collett persuaded me to do so.'

'Mr Collett!' Anthea exclaimed. 'You have seen him, then.'

'Yes, I met him, but not until after he had parted company with Miss Frobisher and Mr Tyler.' Belatedly, he glanced at Elfrida, who was unmistakably shaking her head at him. Unable to guess what it might be that he was to deny, he looked from Elfrida, to Mr Tyler, whose expression gave him no guidance at all, and then back to Elfrida again before stammering, 'That is, I met someone who . . . who was like him, but who was not . . . not in fact him . . . I think.'

Anthea turned white. 'Mr Collett was travelling in company with my sister and Mr Tyler,' she whispered, wisely ignoring the last part of the rector's speech. 'Has he also been in company with my daughter, then?'

Mr Erskine's instinctive leaning toward truthfulness warred with the feeling within him that whatever he might say upon this subject, he would be bound to cause trouble of some kind. Erring on the side of caution, he murmured that he could not say.

'Could not, or would not?' demanded Anthea. She rounded on her sister. 'Elfrida, I think you have some explaining to do. How could you have allowed Prudence to be in Mr Collett's company when I had expressly charged you to prevent that very thing?' She turned to Rufus. 'And you too, Mr Tyler. I do not hold you blameless either.'

'Anthea, my dear, you exercise yourself too much in this matter,' Clive Winchcomb drawled, strolling over to his wife's side, taking her hand and leading her to a chair. 'It is not at all good for you.' He turned his lazy blue gaze upon Tyler. 'If Mr Tyler tells us that Prudence is with a family named Black, then until he gives us good reason to doubt his word, I think that we should believe him.'

Anthea took a deep breath, her husband's calming tone having its usual effect upon her. 'Mr Tyler, do you indeed give me your word that Prudence is safe? Is she really with this Black family?'

Rufus walked over to her. 'I do indeed know the Black family, and I give you my word that Prudence is safe in their care,' he said seriously.

'There, you see?' said Clive Winchcomb.

'Now, allow me to order you a glass of red wine, which I think will do you good.' He walked to the bell pull and as he did so, his path crossed with that of Tyler, who had moved away from Anthea. As the two men met, Winchcomb said softly so that no one else could hear, 'If anything has happened to my daughter, you will answer to me.'

'Believe me, nothing has,' Tyler answered in the same low tone.

Elfrida was just trying to work out how to tell her sister that whilst Prudence might be safe from the clutches of one penniless soldier, she had in fact fallen into the hands of another when the door opened. 'Mrs Black and Captain Black with Miss Winchcomb,' the butler announced.

Anthea leaped to her feet. 'Prudence! My baby!' she exclaimed.

'Oh thank God,' Elfrida uttered devoutly.

At the same time Prudence said, 'Mama! Don't blame Aunt Elfrida, or anyone else, for it was my fault and all my own idea!'

It was Clive Winchcomb who came forward with his usual unshakeable calm and greeted Mrs Black and her son, inviting them to be seated.

'Thank you, sir,' replied the captain looking pale, resolute, and impossibly handsome, 'but I would be very grateful for a private interview with you, if you will be so good.'

'By all means,' replied Winchcomb, preparing to usher him out of the room.

'No, wait! I insist upon knowing what all this is about,' Anthea protested, getting to her feet.

'And so you shall, my dear, as soon as I have spoken to Captain Black,' replied her husband.

Anthea opened her mouth to speak again, but Prudence forestalled her. 'Mama,' she said imperatively, taking her mother's arm and leading her back to her chair. 'Pray be seated and I will tell you everything.'

Tyler came forward at this moment. 'Erskine, the day is fine. Let us take Mrs Black and Miss Frobisher into the gardens for a little airing.'

It was clearly politic to leave Prudence and her mother alone together, so the four visitors left the room by the French doors, which opened on to the terrace.

Mr Erskine looked as if he would very much have liked to walk with Elfrida but Mr Tyler, more adept in social behaviour, neatly out-manoeuvred him, so that the rector found himself discussing parish business with Mrs Black.

'Well, what do you think?' Rufus asked, as they strolled away from the house. 'Shall we find ourselves celebrating an engagement, or packing our bags?'

'Oh I don't know,' said Elfrida wretchedly, 'and I wish you would not joke about it. You may think it funny that I might be expelled from my sister's house, but I do not.'

'I beg your pardon,' he replied quietly. 'I had no wish to offend you.'

'No, I dare say you did not. Oh, how I wish I had never gone to London!' It seemed to Rufus as if the last sentence had been wrung out of her and, as he heard it, his heart sank. As they walked on in silence, his conscience pricked, reminding him that had she never gone to London, they would not have met again, and she would probably have been engaged to Mr Erskine by now. Well, at least he could make sure that she had every chance to find happiness, even if it were at cost of his own.

They reached the ha-ha which marked the end of the gardens, then turned to walk back to the house. This time, the two ladies went ahead, whilst the gentlemen walked behind.

'You must be Prudence's aunt,' said Mrs Black, as they walked. 'In all the confusion, no one was properly introduced, were they?' She was not astoundingly beautiful in the way that her son and her husband were handsome, but there was a gentle serenity about her expression that was very taking.

'No indeed,' Elfrida agreed. 'Everything was very confusing.' Then, because she was sure that Mrs Black could not be quite unaware of Prudence's character, and even if she was, she should not be, she added, 'I am afraid that my whole life has been confusing ever since I took charge of her.'

To her amazement, Mrs Black burst out laughing. 'I'm not surprised,' she replied. 'Prudence is a very resourceful young lady. She will make an admirable soldier's wife.'

'Did you know about the attachment between her and your son?' Elfrida asked.

'I only knew what he told me, which was that he was deeply in love, but that he knew that his suit would be unacceptable to the young lady's parents. I assure you, Miss Frobisher, that I had no idea of the plot that Prudence had hatched in order to reach my son and persuade him into an elopement. Had I known about it, I must have informed Mr and Mrs Winchcomb immediately.'

'So how did you find out about it?' Elfrida asked. They had by now descended from the terrace and were walking beneath the trees.

'The first I knew of it was when Daniel brought Prudence to our house. Eventually she confessed that she had slipped away from you by drugging you and locking you in your room, and persuading Mr Collett to do the same to Mr Tyler.'

'Yes, that is so,' Elfrida agreed, thinking of the moment when she had woken up with her cheek resting on Mr Tyler's hairy chest. At least it seemed as if Prudence had not told Mrs Black all the embarrassing details. 'I fear that I was very negligent in my care of her.'

'Nonsense,' replied Mrs Black briskly. 'You did the best you could. A young person will never pay as much attention to an aunt as to a parent, and especially when that young person is as strong-minded as Prudence.'

After a few moments' silence, Elfrida said cautiously, 'You said that you thought Prudence would make a good soldier's wife. Does that mean that you desire a match between her and your son?'

'To be frank with you, I'm not sure how I would have felt if I had heard about her adventures but not met her,' Mrs Black answered honestly. 'But her resourcefulness has to command respect, and her love for my son is as deep and as strong as is his for her. I hope with all my heart that her parents will agree for I think that they will be very good for one another. Daniel is not a wealthy man, but he is no fortune hunter, and he will make his way in the world, I have no doubt of that, whether he remains in the army or finds another profession.'

Elfrida, remembering the determined chin of the young army officer, could only concur.

Behind them, the two men talked desultorily of this and that. Eventually Tyler said, 'Did young Collett tell you the details of the trick that he and Miss Winchcomb played upon us?'

Mr Erskine, colouring, admitted that he had. 'It must have been very embarrassing for you,' he commented.

'Indeed it was,' agreed Tyler. 'It was more embarrassing for Miss Frobisher, of course. I should hate to think that anyone would judge her on the basis of that incident.'

'No one who knew her would do so, I am sure,' answered Erskine, his colour still high.

'I hope you are right. It would distress me more than I can say if I felt that she should have lost an opportunity for happiness because of my kinsman's thoughtless prank.'

They were silent for a short time, then Erskine said, 'Mr Tyler, pray be frank with me. Are you engaged to Miss Frobisher?'

Tyler took a deep breath, then answered, 'Mr Erskine I am not. The field is clear.'

'Thank you, sir,' the clergyman replied fervently.

On their return to the house, they found the Winchcomb family gathered together with

Captain Black, and they all seemed very happy. Elfrida was very touched when, on seeing her aunt, Prudence ran to throw her arms around her. 'Aunt Elfrida, wish me happy! Papa has consented to our engagement!'

'I am very happy for you,' Elfrida replied.

'But you are still angry with me,' Prudence put in.

'Not angry so much as disappointed. I just wish that you had seen fit to confide in me.'

'I dared not,' Prudence replied. 'You are Mama's sister, and I knew that you would be bound to carry out her wishes.'

'But did you have to make such a fool of me?' Elfrida whispered, blushing.

'It was wrong of me,' Prudence admitted, 'and indeed I am very sorry. But you must agree that it was all for the best!'

'How?' Elfrida asked. But with all the talk that was going on, there was neither the time nor the opportunity for Prudence to give her an answer. She would, she decided, have words with her niece later.

Amid all the congratulations, Elfrida found the opportunity to speak to her brother-in-law. 'I am surprised you gave your consent,' she said frankly. 'Anthea was so adamant that Prudence would not be permitted to marry a penniless man.'

'That depends very much on the man,' Clive replied. 'Naturally Anthea has her own views on the matter, but I've heard of Black. His courage and resource are bywords in Wellington's army, or so I'm told. And besides, I could show you half-a-dozen wealthy men who will almost certainly gamble away their substance within a few years. Black will use his gifts to rise rather than fall, any fool can see that. Prudence will be in safe hands.'

Glancing at her sister, Elfrida thought that she would soon become reconciled to the marriage. Anything that had her husband's approval would not be denied by her. In addition, Black was so very handsome and gallant, that she would not be able to resist him for long.

Now that everything had been happily resolved, her errors of judgement as a chaperon would no doubt conveniently be forgotten. This suited her very well, of course it did, but interwoven amongst those errors were her encounters with Mr Tyler, all of which were now burned into her memory. What would he do now? On two occasions he had announced that they were engaged, but on both of these occasions, his announcement had only been to save her reputation. He had never said anything to indicate that he wanted that engagement to become a reality. Well, she had already made enough of a fool of herself in his presence. She would not further embarrass herself by seeming to want to run after him. If he declared an intention of leaving, then she would not stop him. She would take it as a sign that he was keen to get away from the woman who had been nothing but trouble to him.

Suddenly she became aware that while she had been standing there abstracted, decisions had been made about the rest of the day, and the next few days. Mr Erskine had already been invited to stay, and his belongings had been taken up to his room. It seemed extraordinary to Elfrida that she had asked Anthea to invite the clergyman because she had thought that she might marry him. Now, she could only wonder how on earth she was to entertain him while they were in such close proximity.

Daniel and his mother were also invited to stay, and they agreed to do so for just one night. 'I cannot leave my husband for any longer, since there are children to attend to,' said Mrs Black. 'We have already spent one night on the road.' It was arranged that Daniel should escort his mother home, then come back to stay for a few days. Anthea soon realized that she would have an engagement party to organize, and this lifted her spirits hugely.

'Mr Tyler, you will stay as well, I hope,' said Anthea cordially. 'We have plenty of room.'

'You are very good, ma'am, but I think not,' he replied. 'I am happy to have been of service, and even happier to see such a satisfying resolution to our adventures, but I think I must go to Castle Clare, to visit my family.'

'Yes, of course,' Anthea replied. 'But perhaps when you have paid your respects, you will come to see us?'

'I do not think that that will be possible,' answered Tyler. 'The prince expects me at Brighton.'

'Surely not before luncheon,' murmured Mr Winchcomb.

Tyler smiled. 'You are very good,' he answered, with a bow.

So he was going. That settled it then. There was nothing left to hope for. Elfrida was determined not to give away anything of what she was feeling. She was not aware that anyone was watching her, but Prudence, whose gallant suitor had turned in order to speak to his mother, noticed her aunt's rigid stance, and watched her more keenly, her mind seething. She had been so sure that her aunt and Mr Tyler would make a good match.

She had been certain of it ever since she had seen them in each other's arms in the conservatory. But now Tyler was going, and Elfrida was looking miserable. Mr Tyler did not look very happy either, once the attention of the company had been diverted from him to something else. Mr Erskine, on the other hand, looked very pleased with himself. What could be the meaning of it all?

19

Mr Erskine proposed the following day. He waited until Captain Black and his mother had departed, waved off by Prudence and her father, and he then invited Elfrida to walk with him in the garden as he had something very particular that he wished to say to her. Elfrida had no desire to hear his proposal — for she felt sure that that was what it would be — but she knew that she could not avoid it for ever. Anthea, bless her, had no idea how she was feeling. She had been very gracious towards Mr Erskine, asking about his family, discreetly enquiring concerning his prospects, and assuring him of a welcome at Winchcomb Hall whenever he might choose to come. She never noticed her sister's lack of enthusiasm.

The clergyman himself did not detect that his suit might be less than welcome. He had always admired the way in which, unlike many ladies in his congregation, Miss Frobisher had made no attempt to throw herself at him. This modesty in her struck him as being very pleasing and appropriate for a clergyman's wife. Her present manner towards him, therefore, was everything that he could have wished for.

He was very much looking forward to being a married man. He had not liked seeing the lady of his choice going to London. He had found though that he could make the time pass quite agreeably by imagining how delightful his home would be with a wife installed. These agreeable thoughts had suffered a severe reverse when he had found Miss Frobisher frolicking upstairs with Mr Tyler at that inn in Grantham. The news that the two of them were engaged had been a shock. Although an attractive man, he was not vain, and could understand that Miss Frobisher might prefer someone else. It was undoubtedly true, however, that she was beyond the age when a single lady might expect to receive an offer of marriage, and therefore suitors would probably be thin on the ground. Furthermore, she had never given any indication that he might have a rival.

He had been obliged to accept the news, however, and had returned to his vicarage a deeply disappointed man. In order to take his mind off his troubles, he had undertaken a visit to Grantham on behalf of a parishioner, and whilst there, had felt himself unaccountably drawn towards the Mail Hotel. He had resisted the urge steadfastly until lunch time, but finding that his errand was taking him longer than expected, he had gone there for lunch. He had found a young man standing in the hall, arguing with the landlord. This, in itself, was not unusual. What was very strange, however, was the fact that the young man was standing in his shirt sleeves and stockinged feet.

He had never met Mr Collett before, but whilst the discussion between the two of them was taking place, the landlord had addressed the inadequately clad visitor by his name. 'I'm extremely sorry, Mr Collett, but I cannot see how I can lend you the gig without some form of surety,' he had said.

'But you can see how I'm placed,' the young man had protested. 'Damn it all, I don't even have any boots to wear.'

Elfin had strived ineffectively to hide a smile. 'Forgive me, sir, but is that not in some way your fault, after the trick you played upon Mr Tyler and Miss Frobisher?'

'Damn you for your insolence!' Digby had declared.

As if the mention of Elfrida's name had released him from some spell, Mr Erskine had stepped forward, asking, 'May I be of some assistance?'

Elfin had turned towards him with some

relief 'Mr Erskine, here is Mr Collett wanting me to lend him the gig without any payment, and that I fear I never do, nor ever will, however well I know my customers. It's my livelihood, sir.'

'But how the deuce am I to get home, with no boots on my feet?' Digby had asked indignantly.

'Pray allow me to lend you some money for footwear,' the rector had said. 'Should you be reluctant to accept money from a stranger, sir, let me assure you that I am acquainted with Miss Frobisher.' He had coloured a little.

'Of course!' Digby had declared, his brow clearing. 'You're the parson who was going to accompany her and Prudence — I mean, Miss Winchcomb — to Winchcomb Hall, and then stay for a few days.' Mr Erskine had agreed that this was so. There was an awkward silence, during which Erskine reflected upon the fact that he would not now be going to Winchcomb Hall, and Digby remembered that the failure of either of the two ladies to turn up at their family home could at least in part be laid at his door. Eventually, the rector had stated that he would go and request the local shoemaker to wait upon Lt. Collett, and had left the inn to make sure that this was done.

After he had fulfilled this errand, however, he had walked back in a thoughtful frame of mind. If he had been honest with himself, he would have owned that Mr Tyler's explanation of the embarrassing situation in which he had been found with Miss Frobisher had been rather unconvincing. Elfin's words to Digby, however, had assured him that Mr Tyler's account had been largely true. He decided, therefore, that it would be worth cultivating Mr Collett's acquaintance. What if the engagement had been arranged purely as a consequence of Collett's trick? It was true that Tyler had talked about knowing Miss Frobisher years before. What if he had only said this in order to make the engagement seem more authentic? In that case, such an engagement might easily be broken. Erskine's hopes had soared. He might be a man of the cloth, but he was a man first and foremost. He had decided to invite Mr Collett to have lunch with him at the inn, so that he could pump him for more information.

The results of his diligent questioning had been better than he could have hoped. Digby, having once spilled the beans to Mr Tyler and Miss Frobisher, had found it impossible to be discreet with Mr Erskine, especially since he had come to the conclusion that by now the young couple had either got far enough towards the border for there to be no risk of their being caught, or else their plans had been thwarted anyway.

'Then you are sure that Mr Tyler and Miss Frobisher were not engaged before they arrived at the inn?' Mr Erskine had pressed him eagerly.

Digby had shaken his head. 'Tyler wanted to marry Prudence at one time,' he assured him. 'In any case, Miss Frobisher will not marry now. She's been on the shelf for years.'

Stopping only to make sure that Mr Collett's boots had arrived, and to lend him the means to hire a horse to take him home, the rector had immediately returned to the vicarage and, lingering only to pack a small bag, in case he should be invited to stay, and to inform his curate that he would be absent after all, possibly for a few days, he had set off on horseback. He had stayed at Littleborough that night, and had arrived at Winchcomb Hall at about the same time as Miss Frobisher and Mr Tyler.

Watching the two of them carefully, it had seemed to him that there was very little that was lover-like between them, and this had given him cause for even more hope. Finally, Mr Tyler's words had convinced him that now was the time to put his fate to the test. He did not notice that as he was ushering

Elfrida out into the garden, Prudence, returning from waving to the Blacks, was watching them with narrowed eyes.

The rector escorted Elfrida to a secluded part of the garden and, in a modest, manly way made his proposal to her. Elfrida heard him out with a sinking heart. Had he but done this before she had gone to London, her whole life would have been different, she reflected. She would have gone to visit her sister an engaged woman, and would have been quite immune to the charms of Mr Tyler. In the gentlest way possible, she told the rector that she could not accept him.

His face fell. 'I watched you leave for London with great misgivings,' he said heavily. 'I fear that the excitement of town life has given you a distaste for country living.'

'By no means,' she exclaimed quickly, then coloured as she realized that had she agreed with him, this would have excused her from having to explain herself further.

'Then it is Mr Tyler after all,' he replied. 'And he assured me that there was nothing between you.'

'He spoke the truth,' Elfrida answered, feeling as if a cold weight were settling inside her in the region of her heart. 'There is indeed nothing between us. But pray believe me when I say that it is useless for you to persist in your suit. It is true that at one time I did believe that we might deal very well together, but if anything I said or did . . . '

He held up his hand. 'You have been all modesty and discretion,' he assured her. 'It is I alone who presumed too much. You will understand if I feel that I cannot remain here, under the circumstances. I shall tell your sister that I have recalled an urgent parish matter that must be dealt with. Pray accept my good wishes for your future happiness.'

Elfrida watched him walk away, her feelings very mixed. She felt sorry for his disappointment, and regret that he should have got his hopes up for nothing. She did not feel tempted to change her mind. Tyler had stolen her heart; if she were honest with herself, she would have to admit that whether she had gone to London engaged or not, the result would have been the same.

Prudence, observing their parting from an unseen vantage point, stood with a thoughtful expression upon her face. Clearly, the rector had proposed and, by the demeanour of the two of them, been rejected. She had never believed that they would make a match of it. She had always thought that her aunt and Mr Tyler made a far more suitable couple, but Mr Tyler had left, courteously, but looking more serious than usual; now her aunt was pacing up and down restlessly.

Impulsively, she walked over to meet her aunt. Because of all the comings and goings, it was the first time that they had had a chance of private conversation since their arrival at the house. 'Aunt Elfrida . . . ' she began, then, for all her assurance, her voice faded away before the stony expression upon her aunt's face which looked more like resigned depression than anything else.

'Well?' Elfrida replied. Her tone was no more encouraging than her expression. 'Is there anything else you have in mind in order to make my life more difficult and unpleasant, or have you gone your length?'

'Aunt Elfrida,' Prudence began again.

'I only came to London in order to help,' Elfrida broke in, not allowing her to finish her sentence. 'What did I get from you? Lies, unkindness, mockery, embarrassment. Most of all embarrassment! I don't suppose you have told your Mama about all the tricks you played, have you?' The younger woman coloured and turned away, confirming the truth of Elfrida's words. 'How could you do it, Prudence? How could you expose me so, in front of him?'

'Mr Erskine?' Prudence ventured.

Elfrida stared at her, then quickly looked away. 'Of course Mr Erskine,' she replied, her voice sounding hesitant for the first time during the whole exchange. 'I left my home in order to look after you. How can I go back now? Thanks to your wickedness, you have made me the talk of Grantham.' Her voice broke, and she turned away, hurrying towards the house.

Prudence stared after her, her own eyes filling with tears. Aunt Elfrida had always been kind to her, and her own behaviour had been a very poor return for that. It was time that she tried to do her aunt some good instead. She took out her handkerchief and vigorously dried her eyes. Tears would not help now. It was time to take action. She walked purposefully to the stables in order to seek out one of the stable lads whose sister worked for the Colletts. He would be able to find out which members of the family were at home at present. She might require Digby's help one last time.

* * *

A few days later, Elfrida received a letter that shocked her very much indeed. It was delivered by hand, and no one seemed to have any idea where it might have come from. It did not address her by name, nor was it signed.

325

If the lady who stayed so improperly with Mr R. T., at the Mail Inn wishes to keep the matter private, she will come to the Nag's Head Inn at five o'clock tomorrow evening. On arrival, she must say that she is to meet her husband in room 9. She must bring £100 with her. Failure to comply will mean an increase in the sum, or disgrace to her whole family.

What could she do? Her first instinct was to contact Mr Tyler, but she hesitated. It was through her that he had become embroiled in this mess. It would be very wrong of her to mix him up in it even further. What if he thought that she expected him to find the £100? That could not be borne. Furthermore, he had told them that he was going to Brighton. Perhaps he had already left.

It did occur to her that a resourceful young woman like Prudence would have plenty of ideas about how to approach a blackmailer, but she shrank from employing her niece in that way. Anthea already believed that she had been somewhat negligent in her chaperonage of the younger woman. She could not imagine what her sister would say if she were to embroil Prudence in such a scheme. She had made her peace with Prudence, apologizing for her intemperate language, and her apology had been unreservedly accepted. If she were to bring this problem to Prudence now, her niece would start to think that her aunt never had any normal dealings with the rest of the human race. She would just have to deal with this matter by herself.

She would make some excuse to be away from home the following day, and she would take the money out of the bank. Fortunately, in the past she had found it convenient to arrange for funds to be available to her when she was staying with Anthea near Newark. Then she would go to the Nag's Head and confront her blackmailer. After that, she decided, she would return to her home, and hide away until any scandal about her conduct had been overtaken by some other matter.

As far as the next day's arrangements were concerned, luck favoured her. For one thing, Captain Black arrived for a visit, and this naturally drew attention away from her and on to the engaged couple. For another, the whole family was invited to visit friends unknown to her in the afternoon, and to stay for dinner. It was not difficult for Elfrida to plead a headache and excuse herself. Anthea, most commendably, had said very little about Mr Erskine's proposal. She had merely remarked that at her age she must be mad to throw away such an opportunity and that a period of quiet reflection in order to consider her good fortune in attracting such a suitor would do her good. Sadly, the more time that Elfrida spent in quiet reflection, the more she found herself only able to think about Mr Tyler, but naturally this was something that she could not tell her sister.

After she had waved the others off, Elfrida gave orders for the gig to be brought round and hurried to get her bonnet. No doubt the head groom would find it strange when she refused the company of one of his lads, but it could not be helped. The less people who knew about where she was going the better.

The Nag's Head was a mean establishment of a type that she would never normally have patronized, and the innkeeper, she was pleased to note, was not known to her at all. He greeted her with a smirk, and seemed quite unsurprised when she said, with a blush, that she was to meet her husband in room 9. 'Everything is ready for you, ma'am — if you know what I mean,' he said.

Elfrida, already flustered by the nature of her errand and thinking him a little insolent, thanked him frostily, and followed him upstairs. 'Here we are, ma'am,' he said, opening the door. She walked inside, and as he closed the door behind her, she saw that a man was standing in front of the window with his back to the room. The colour of his hair gave him away immediately. It was Mr Tyler. 'Good gracious!' she exclaimed. 'What on earth are you doing here?'

He turned round then, clearly just astonished as was she. 'I might ask you the same question,' he said.

'I received a note,' she began; then recollected that she had resolved not to tell him about the attempt to blackmail her.

'As did I,' he replied, taking a folded sheet of paper from inside his coat. As he opened it, Elfrida could see that the handwriting appeared to be the same as that in the letter which she had received. Slowly, she opened her reticule, and after a moment handed her note over to him. 'It would appear that we have been duped,' he said after reading it. He passed his own letter to her and she saw that essentially it was the same as hers. He was threatened with exposure; he was to come to the Nag's Head and ask for his wife who would be in room 9; he was to bring £100.

'But what can this mean?' Elfrida asked. 'Surely the landlord must know something.' She walked to the door and turned the handle, but to no effect. 'We have been locked in,' she said.

'Again?' murmured Rufus, walking to the

door. 'Perhaps it is just stiff.' But after turning the knob and pushing and pulling at the door, he came to the same conclusion. After directing a long glance at her, he walked to the mantelpiece and pulled the bell. 'At least we have all our clothes on this time,' he remarked. She coloured and turned away, walking to the window.

There was a long silence which neither of them broke for some time. Eventually, however, it dawned upon them that no one was going to come in response to their summons. 'What now?' said Elfrida 'Is that bell broken, do you suppose? Why does no one come? Do you think we ought to shout?' She was conscious that she was gabbling, but she did not seem to be able to think about anything properly whilst he was so near to her.

'I think, perhaps, that rather than shout, or do anything else, we ought to think about why we have been locked in here together,' said Mr Tyler. She had started to pace about the room. He took hold of her fluttering hands and led her to sit down on the bed, the only piece of furniture which was available to them, apart from one straight-backed chair and a rather rickety looking stool. He then sat down next to her, taking possession of her hands.

'Well, isn't it obvious?' said Elfrida, unconsciously returning the clasp of his hands, before realizing what she was doing and snatching them away. 'Someone wishes to blackmail us.'

'Really? And who might that be?' he asked.

'I have been wondering whether it might not be Lieutenant Collett,' she replied. 'After all, he is always short of money.'

'He might be short of money, but he don't have a death wish,' replied Rufus frankly. 'He knows that in playing that trick on us before, he went his length. He would never dare try blackmail. And there *is* no one else — unless, of course, you suspect Elfin, or your betrothed.'

'My betrothed?' asked Elfrida.

'Your friend Erskine. He did propose, didn't he?'

'Yes he did.' Suddenly Elfrida recollected something. 'By the way, what did you mean by telling him that he might propose to me? You had no right to do so.'

'I didn't say that,' he replied, his expression unreadable. 'I told him that I had no claim upon you.'

She stood up abruptly. 'I cannot see why the two of you should have been discussing me at all.'

He stood up himself. 'We weren't discussing you,' he said. 'But I knew that you were on the point of marrying this parson before you came to London. He asked me point blank if you and I were engaged and I told him the truth. You know that I only told him that we were engaged to get us out of the embarrassing situation that Digby and Prudence had put us in.' He paused, then said in altered tones, 'My God, that's what it is! Prudence and Digby again.'

'Prudence and Digby! But why?' She exclaimed. 'Prudence has obtained her father's consent to her marriage with Captain Black, so why . . . ?' She looked up into his face and saw that he was smiling down at her. 'Oh no,' she breathed. 'No, she couldn't have.' She turned away from him again.

'Elfrida,' he said, standing behind her and taking hold of her by the shoulders. 'I think you know why she did it as well as I do.'

'Then she was very wrong to do it,' Elfrida replied, in a voice that was not quite steady. 'It was quite unfair to you, to put you in this kind of position.'

'Unfair to me?' he queried, leaning round her in an effort to look at her face. 'Why not unfair to you as well?'

'Because . . . because . . . Oh, I don't know,' she finished breathlessly.

'Well if you don't, I think I do,' he answered, turning her round to face him.

'Perhaps it was a little unfair of her, but I forgive her everything if only because it has given me the chance to be alone with you, and to say what is in my heart. Elfrida, my dear . . . '

At that inopportune moment, before he could complete what surely must have been a declaration, there was a commotion outside, the door opened and Anthea Winchcomb stood on the threshold, her husband behind her.

'Elfrida!' she declared in shocked tones. 'Had I not seen and heard for myself, I would never have believed it! To think that you would deliberately avoid an engagement with your own family in order to keep an illicit rendezvous! Never would I have permitted you to chaperon Prudence had I known it! Never!'

Clive Winchcomb took a pinch of snuff. 'Forgive me, my dear, for seeming trivial, but you could not have known about it could you, these events taking place *after* your sister's visit to London.'

'That is nonsense, Clive, and you know it,' Anthea snapped. 'It is my sister's moral tone that concerns me.'

'There is nothing wrong with my moral tone,' replied Elfrida. 'On the other hand — '

Sensing that Elfrida might be on the point

of making some remark about Prudence that could not easily be forgiven, Rufus interrupted her. 'Forgive me, ma'am, but how did you know about our . . . er . . . rendezvous?' he asked Anthea.

Anthea took a note from her reticule. 'This letter was delivered to me at the Stokeses this afternoon. As you will see, it tells me that my sister will be meeting a man today at this inn, and that to prevent scandal they will be going under the names of Mr and Mrs Smith. Naturally we made some excuse to leave and I insisted that we should come to investigate. I did hope that it might prove to be nothing but a prank, and that would be bad enough, but this!'

Rufus took the note, glanced at it and handed it back. 'Clearly, some prankster has been at work,' he remarked. 'How regrettable that you should be dragged out so unnecessarily, simply because of a misunderstanding.'

'A misunderstanding?' uttered Anthea, every inch the outraged matron. 'Explain yourself, sir.'

'Certainly,' replied Rufus, taking Elfrida's hand in his.

Yet again, however, he was destined not to finish his speech, for the door opened once again to admit Prudence and Digby, ushered in by the formidable figure of Captain Black, his chiselled features bearing a stern expression. 'If an explanation is called for, ma'am, I fear it is not Mr Tyler or Miss Frobisher who should be called upon to give it,' he said firmly.

'Prudence!' Elfrida exclaimed. 'Not again!' Her niece had the grace to blush.

'Digby Collett!' Anthea cried. 'I might have guessed you would be at the bottom of this!'

'I say!' Digby responded. 'If that ain't the richest thing . . . '

'One moment,' said Clive Winchcomb, raising his hand. 'This room, surely not the most commodious of inn chambers, is becoming remarkably crowded. Might it not be possible for us to adjourn to Winchcomb Hall in order to continue this conversation in comfort and assured privacy?'

This was clearly such a sensible suggestion, that all of them concurred. The problem then arose as to who was to travel with whom. Captain Black, Prudence and Digby had all come in the same carriage, and could easily travel back together. But Anthea declared that although her sister might have arrived alone in the gig she was not by any means to travel back in the same way. Rufus's suggestion that he should ride alongside the gig was utterly rejected by Anthea.

At this point, Elfrida lost her temper. 'I am

thirty-four years old,' she declared. 'I can surely be trusted to drive a gig in a gentleman's company.'

'When I consider the way in which you have behaved, I do not think that you can expect to be trusted to do *anything* in a gentleman's company,' Anthea retorted.

'Mama,' Prudence began.

'Enough,' Mr Winchcomb stated. 'The gig may remain here, and not because Elfrida cannot be trusted, but because Colman, my stockman, told me earlier that there is rain in the air, and Colman is always right in matters concerning the weather. Mr Tyler may accompany us in the carriage for the same reason. Now, let us go.'

There was not very much conversation in either carriage. In fact, Digby, Prudence and Captain Black said nothing at all, whilst in the other carriage all the talk was between the gentlemen, who confined their remarks to the merits of boots made by Hoby, and who had last been seen shooting at Manton's gallery. The ladies stared venomously at one another, then looked out of the window.

When they arrived at the house, there was still no sign of rain. Anthea ushered her sister out of the carriage and swept into the hall. Rufus glanced upwards, held his hand out, and glanced quizzically at his host. 'He didn't say when,' Winchcomb murmured, as they followed the ladies inside.

'Now, Elfrida,' said Anthea, as soon as they were all inside the saloon with the door closed. 'I insist upon knowing the meaning of your appalling conduct.'

'One moment,' said Captain Black, raising his hand. 'Before any more is said, I think that Prudence has something to tell you. Prudence, my dear?'

His tone was gentle but firm, and to Elfrida's astonishment, she heard her niece begin her tale of how she had fooled everyone concerning her false romance with Digby. Anthea attempted to interrupt on several occasions, but was prevented by her husband. Prudence was frank about all her misbehaviour, her only omissions being those matters which directly affected her aunt's reputation.

'Prudence, how could you?' Anthea exclaimed, shocked. 'Elfrida, my dear, I have completely misjudged you.'

'And now, perhaps, you'll believe that all of this isn't my fault,' Digby put in, addressing the whole company. 'In fact, *none* of it is my fault. I've only ever done what *she* wanted me to do.'

Elfrida, perceiving that her own misdemeanours were about to be conveniently forgotten, was on the point of breathing a sigh of relief, when Rufus Tyler turned to Prudence and remarked, 'You forgot to say how I kissed your aunt in the conservatory.'

'What?' Anthea cried.

'I kissed Elfrida in the conservatory,' Rufus replied. 'It was not the first time, either. Nor, I hope, will it be the last. I intend to kiss her in every possible conservatory that I can find.'

'You . . . ' Anthea began.

Completely ignoring her and everyone else, he crossed the room to where Elfrida stood, colouring furiously. 'Elfrida, my darling, it seems that I am destined not to have any privacy to propose to you, so I had better do it here and now.' He took hold of her hands in his.

There was much here that Anthea did not understand, but she knew what a proposal was and where her duty lay. Without ceremony, she took steps to usher the rest of the party out of the room as swiftly as possible, but Prudence, seeing her intention, darted round her and caught her aunt in a convulsive hug. 'I'm sorry, truly I am,' she said sincerely. 'But at least part of what I did was because I wanted you to be happy.'

'She will be,' Rufus answered firmly, 'if only I can have the opportunity to arrange it.'

To Anthea's shocked exclamation, Prudence quickly kissed Mr Tyler as well. 'I do like you,' she said. 'But I'm glad that *I'm* not going to marry you.'

'So am I,' Tyler answered cordially, escorting her firmly to the door. 'It would be hell.' Her laughter echoed from behind the closed door.

'But you do not want to marry me,' Elfrida protested, as he came towards her.

'And what makes you think that?' he asked her, smiling down at her and squeezing her hands.

'You want to be free to pursue women like Mrs Fossey,' she told him.

'Oh, do I?' he said. 'Then tell me, why is it that she and I ended our association at about the same time that I met you?'

'*Because* of me?' she ventured hopefully.

He smiled ruefully. 'Not entirely,' he answered. 'You see what a good effect you have upon me; I have to tell the truth. And the truth is that I had begun to realize that the kind of life that I had been enjoying in London was no longer satisfying me. I wanted something more, but I didn't know what that was, until I met you again. By the way, my dear, I hope that you are prepared for the fact that you may be a countess one day? My brother's children are all girls.'

She struggled to disengage her hands from his. 'Then you should not be marrying me,' she told him resolutely. 'You ought to be marrying a young woman like Prudence who will . . . ' she gulped ' . . . provide you with an heir.'

He allowed her hands to escape from his but only so that he could pull her into his arms. 'The only children I want are the ones that you will give me,' he replied. 'As for a wife like Prudence, perish the thought! I could kiss her hands and feet for what she has done for us today, the little baggage, but if I married her, she would drive me demented in a week. No, I want to marry a woman who, in the midst of all my youthful stupidity, I had the great good sense to recognize as a toothsome wench right from the start.'

'But I did not like you at all — at least, not then,' she corrected scrupulously.

'But you do like me now,' he hazarded.

'Oh, so very much,' she sighed. He pulled her closer and lowered his mouth to meet hers. On other occasions when he had kissed her, she had felt drawn to him, but had fought against her inclinations. This time, she gave in to her feelings, put her arms around his neck, and joyfully returned his embrace. 'I did not think you liked me,' she confessed, as soon as she was able. 'You seemed to be all too anxious to thrust me at Mr Erskine.'

340

'That was my conscience at work,' he answered.

'Oh, do you have one?' she asked him innocently.

'Yes I do, you minx,' he answered, tapping her gently on the rear. 'And although it told me that I ought to pretend to be engaged to you in order to protect your reputation, it also told me that if you really loved Erskine, I ought not to stand in your way. You didn't love him, did you?' He led her to a sofa where they sat down, very close together, his arm about her shoulders.

She shook her head. 'There was a time when I thought that he would do very well, and I did like him, but I did not love him.'

'And, by inference,' he replied, 'you do love me.'

'Yes, I do,' she confessed. He tilted her chin with one hand, and kissed her, gently and lingeringly.

'I'm glad you haven't said that I will do very well,' he said, when at last their lips parted. 'I should take that very much amiss.'

All at once, Elfrida remembered something that had been hovering in the back of her mind. 'After we had stayed in the inn at Grantham — you know, that time — ' she blushed.

He kissed her on the nose. 'You know, that

time, *Rufus*,' he corrected her.

'Rufus,' she said obediently. 'You said that you were sorry for two things, but you only told me what one of them was.'

He wrinkled his brow for a moment. 'Ah yes, I apologized for the embarrassment that you had suffered,' he replied. 'Very gentlemanlike of me too, I think.'

'Yes, but what was the other?' she asked him.

'Ah. That. You will think me so very wicked that I hardly dare tell you, my sweet.'

'Have courage, Rufus,' she murmured, smoothing his lapels.

'I was simply sorry on my own account — that I hadn't taken advantage of you when I had the opportunity.'

She raised her face to his, trying very hard to look shocked. 'Rufus! I had no idea you were so unprincipled.'

'Hadn't you guessed?' he said, as he pulled her closer. 'A man who can call you a toothsome wench is capable of anything.'

Elfrida looked around. 'Good heavens, you are right,' she exclaimed. 'We are alone and I am ruined.'

'Splendid,' he replied, preparing to kiss her again. 'You need ruining. And I'm just the man to do it.'

We do hope that you have enjoyed reading this large print book.

Did you know that all of our titles are available for purchase?

We publish a wide range of high quality large print books including:
Romances, Mysteries, Classics
General Fiction
Non Fiction and Westerns

Special interest titles available in large print are:
The Little Oxford Dictionary
Music Book
Song Book
Hymn Book
Service Book

Also available from us courtesy of Oxford University Press:
Young Readers' Dictionary
(large print edition)
Young Readers' Thesaurus
(large print edition)

For further information or a free brochure, please contact us at:
Ulverscroft Large Print Books Ltd.,
The Green, Bradgate Road, Anstey,
Leicester, LE7 7FU, England.
Tel: (00 44) **0116 236 4325**
Fax: (00 44) **0116 234 0205**

THE ADVENTURESS

Ann Barker

Florence Browne lives in poverty with her miserly father, but seeking adventure, she goes to Bath under the assumed name Lady Firenza Le Grey. But there, she meets a man calling himself Sir Vittorio Le Grey, who accuses her of being an adventuress. When her previous suitor, Gilbert Stapleton, visits Bath, Florence is plagued by doubts. Is Sir Vittorio the wicked Italian he appears to be? Are Mr Stapleton's professions of love sincere? And how can she accept an offer of marriage from anyone while she is still living a lie?